Lake Shore SANCTUARY

A REDEMPTION SHORES NOVEL

JENNIFER RODEWALD

Rooted Publishing

Lake Shore Sanctuary

ISBN: 979-8-9874510-7-6

Front-cover images shutterstock.com. Design by Jennifer Rodewald.

First printing edition 2025.

Rooted Publishing

McCook, NE 69001

Email: jen@authorjenrodewald.com

https://authorjenrodewald.com/

Contents

One

Isa froze with the bear claw in her hand. Her heart stopped beating while her lungs squeezed the breath from her body.

Maybe it was her imagination. Her lingering fear . . .

She held her gaze on the man outside the window, across the street from Janie's Café. He began to turn, slowly allowing her the same profile view she'd just glimpsed. Same nose. Same hard mouth, which could be charming if he wished it. Same chiseled jawline.

But younger. By twenty years, at least.

That was no comfort. In fact, it was worse. Terrifyingly worse.

Her pulse kicked into a sprint, and her body quivered. Before the man could look into the café, Isa dropped to the wood planks and tucked herself tight against the shelves beneath the island counter.

"Isa?" Grady Briggs had been the only customer in the café—which happened regularly on his day off. He wasn't part of the old-man coffee club, and he preferred to come in before the lunch rush. Just one of many tells of his rather unsociable personality. His low voice held its usual sharpness when he deigned to speak with her—which wasn't often, because that would be beneath him—but with it was a hint of concern.

She heard the scuffle of Grady's boots on the other side of the counter, then the creak of the floorboards as he rounded the counter to her side.

"Isa, are you okay?" he asked, in a gentle tone foreign to what Isa typically heard from him.

Isa wrapped her arms around her legs and squeezed her eyes shut. Heat and moisture stung behind her lids, while terror buzzed in her mind. "Please," she whispered as the bell chimed a warning.

Junior cometh.

He'd found her. How had he found her? Only her family knew where she'd gone. And she hadn't given Francisco her real name—first or last. Her one smart choice among a million other really, really bad ones.

Oh God, help!

The floorboard groaned under the weight of Junior's entry. "You work here?" His question to Grady wasn't friendly.

Grady moved closer to Isa, as though the proximity of his muscular legs near her huddled-up body should help ease her fears. "Can I help you?" His question to Junior rang clear.

"I'm looking for a girl." Francisco Junior's demanding response gave Isa shivers.

Grady's quiet laugh startled her. "Aren't we all, brother."

No response. Just a weighted silence that preceded the sound of the man's palm against the counter. "*This* girl."

Isa peeked up as Grady reached across the counter. He pulled back a cell phone. Stared at the image on the screen.

"Her name is Victoria."

"Never heard of a Victoria."

"Have you *seen* that girl?"

Grady jammed a hand into his jeans pocket, passed the phone back to the man on the other side, and shook his head. "Nope. Like I said, I've never met a Victoria, and I'd definitely remember meeting a woman like that. She your girlfriend?"

A snort sufficed for an answer. Then, "You work here?"

Grady shrugged.

"Seems like a woman would be behind the counter."

"That's fairly toxic male of you."

"Do you own this place?"

"Maybe. Maybe not." Grady crossed his arms.

Wow. He had some muscles under those Game and Parks uniforms. Not that Isa hadn't noticed before that Grady was a well-built man. But . . . was he flexing right now?

"I don't like this interrogation. Makes me wonder why you're looking for a woman who clearly left you. Makes me think maybe I need to contact the law."

"You don't want on my list."

Isa swallowed hard at the ice in that threat. *Grady, trust me—you don't want on the Lopez's list.* With a quivering hand, she silently reached to wrap her hand around his ankle.

Grady lowered his hands, and once they were below countertop level, he wiggled his fingers at her. "What list is that?"

Isa held her breath. Clearly he hadn't understood her warning.

After a stiff pause, Junior chuckled. "Right. Look, buddy, I'm just uptight right now. Victoria . . . I need to find her. It's important, and having her missing is making me crazy, you know?"

And there was the deceptive charm. A family trait, passed from father to son, no doubt.

"I see. A man obsessed."

"Right. Love. It makes you crazy."

"I wouldn't know."

"Well, like you said, a woman who looks like this . . . she can steal your sanity. That's why I need to find her."

"Got it." Grady braced his palms against the countertop. "And like I said, I haven't seen her. What's more, this is a really small town, and everyone comes into this café. If she hasn't been here, she isn't in Luna."

"If you're sure, I'll be on my way." A pause froze the air, with implied warning. "You're sure?"

Grady crossed his arms, tilted his head, and lifted his eyebrows. This version of Mr. Games and Parks Isa was familiar with. Chilled. Disapproving. Intimidating.

All the things that frustrated Isa. And drove her to both ignore him and secretly hope that he'd warm up to her at the same time. In the months that she'd been in Luna, working for Janie Wallace at the café, Isa had been mostly successful at the first and a spectacular failure at the second.

Why did she always want what she couldn't have?

Junior laughed again. "Think I'll just check around town, just to make sure. Don't you worry. I'll find her." The last line was more than a promise. It was a threat.

Footfalls thumped against the floor. "You enjoy your day, café man."

After a few breaths, the bell over the door chimed again. Grady held his place, even grabbing the dishcloth from a small bucket of sanitizing water Isa kept beneath the counter, and wiped down the polished pine top as if he did work there.

Though minutes passed before Grady knelt beside Isa, she still shook. At the feel of his hand on her shoulder, she startled.

He eased back, lifting his hand slowly, as if she were a wounded animal he'd found on the trail. "Easy there, Isa. He's gone."

His gentle whisper caused a surge of overwhelming emotion. Now he was warm and caring toward her?

Isa couldn't stop her lips from trembling or the tears from leaking. "Thank you," she stuttered.

Grady peeked over the counter, then reached for her again. Slowly. His fingers wrapped around hers. "I'm just going to help you up, okay?"

Nodding, Isa wished she could tell him she was fine. She dug around in her wrecked heart for the fiery girl she usually was. Where was the resilient, sassy smile? The flirty laugh? The defiance that had propelled her before?

Fear had buried it. All of it.

Grady pulled her to her feet and guided her to the door that led to the kitchen, shielding her from the view outside of the front windows. Once safely tucked in the back, he grabbed a clean dish towel and handed it to her. "I take it you're Victoria."

Isa couldn't look at him. She nodded. "That's what he thinks my name is."

"And he's the reason you suddenly ended up in Luna, working for Janie."

She swallowed. Shame filled her like lava, mixing toxically with the lingering terror.

"How about you tell me what's going on?"

Now she forced herself to meet his eyes. They were intense—not smiling, but not unkind either. Deeply concerned—without the disapproval she usually read in them when Grady looked at her.

That was about to come back, she was certain. Isa had never once gained Grady Briggs's approval, and now she would prove his censure right. She was not a woman who deserved his warm smile—the kind that she'd witnessed and envied when Grady had been dating Janie last fall.

"I got involved with a man I shouldn't have. I didn't know who he was—that he was . . . dangerous."

Grady dipped one nod. "The man who was here."

She shook her head. "No. That was . . . that's his . . ." Isa released a shuddering breath. ". . . his son."

Grady's brow lifted. "I see."

As she lowered her head—not wanting to see that condemnation creep back into Grady's eyes—Isa felt the cold terror wrap around her body all over again. "I didn't know who he was . . ." she whispered. She wrapped both arms around herself as another wave of shivers rolled through her body.

"Who is he?"

"The man? Francisco Lopez." She gulped. "And that was his son, Francisco Lopez Junior. Junior, or Cisco, depending on who you ask."

His face was stone. Was it contempt that caused him to look so severe? It shouldn't matter. Grady already looked down on her. Called her a flirt. Kept her at a frozen arm's length. She shouldn't care that he now thought even less of her.

Even so, she writhed—as she always did—at Grady's scorn. He was a kind man—to everyone else. Her being the obvious exception felt like . . . like God's displeasure.

God's condemnation.

"Francisco Lopez," Grady repeated.

She nodded.

"And he thinks your name is Victoria?"

"Yes. Victoria Molina."

"Why?"

"Because I didn't want my family to know what I was doing—who I was with." A fresh set of tears—this time of shame—ran down her face. "And I didn't want to drag their good name into my . . . rebellion."

Grady nodded. "Why is Junior searching for you?"

Isa's chin shook violently. She did *not* want to say it out loud. Not to anyone. Not to this man who already thought so badly of her. But she was stripped down to nothing but the truth. The frightening, shameful truth. "I'm pregnant, and I told Francisco before I left Bozeman. I thought . . . I thought he'd help me with expenses." Her lips quivered violently as she ended her confession.

Grady winced, then looked down at the floor. "He wouldn't?"

"I didn't hear from him. But two days after I told him, I was rear-ended. It was a hit and run—and was intentional."

"Cisco?"

Isa nodded. As the full force of every emotion that had been building inside for the past three months burst forth, she covered her face with her hands and sobbed.

Silence gripped the kitchen. Only the sounds of her soft whimpers and sniffs. And then . . .

Then a pair of strong hands enclosed her shoulders. Before she could look up, she was engulfed in Grady's arms.

Two

Isa was in trouble. A whole lot of trouble. Did she really understand how much danger she was truly in?

Grady balled his fist and laid it on the windowsill as he looked over Main Street. Cisco Lopez wasn't in sight, but Grady didn't even hope the man had left town yet.

As he turned to look at the closed door to Isa's bedroom, Grady doubted the woman fully comprehended the situation. She couldn't possibly know all the things Grady knew.

Isabel Romero had a beautiful face. An unmistakable—and unforgettable—loveliness. Grady had thought so from the first time they'd met the previous fall. At the time, he'd silently acknowledged her attractiveness and turned his attention back to Janie. Because he'd been dating Janie. As the evening wore on, he'd become annoyed with Isabel though.

The beautiful young woman was an unrepentant flirt. That evening Isa's target had been Hunter, which shouldn't have bothered Grady in the slightest.

But it had.

He'd told himself it was because Isa's flirting with Hunter had obviously bothered Janie, and that was what had bothered him. But now?

Grady had been batting against the truth for months, but now he had to admit it. Isabel Romero was an unforgettably beautiful woman *he* had been attracted to from the first night they'd met. Which was why he was so annoyed with her. Cold toward her.

He hadn't wanted to like her. And this was why.

She was trouble.

No—she was *in* trouble. Grady drew a long breath and sorted his thoughts from his emotions. He needed only clear thinking right now.

The phone in his right hand buzzed, and a sense of dread flooded him as he raised the screen to read the incoming text. A response to the one he'd sent to the special agent in charge back at the Denver office.

Grady: POI found. situation not good.

Agent Malcom: Confirm POI identity required.

The hairs on Grady's arms and neck spiked as he recalled what he'd seen less than twenty minutes before. Again, he glanced back at the closed door. Isa had gone to change, and then they would talk.

First, about the fact that she needed to stay out of sight for a few days. And then . . .

Then Grady needed her to confirm what he was 99 percent sure he'd seen. Seemed like a superfluous detail. Cisco Lopez was a name he knew well enough—and he was a little blindsided by the brazen arrogance of the guy, who just went around out in the open using it. But the Denver office required confirmation—Lopez being the common name that it was.

The door hinges creaked behind him, and Grady turned from the window. Isa had washed her face, but it was still splotchy, and her eyes were red rimmed. His heart clenched looking at her, and hot adrenaline raced through his veins, along with the urge to pull her into his arms again.

That was normal though. The instinct to protect, which was why Grady had gone down the career path he had.

"You're still here." Isa fiddled with her fingers.

"You didn't think I would be?"

She shrugged, not looking at him.

Grady could feel her humiliation, and it made him ache. So odd. In the months he'd known her up until today, he'd wanted her to quit with the haughtiness. The incessant flirting. The over-the-top confidence. To save her charm and sweet smiles for someone worth giving them to, rather than dousing them on anyone with XY chromosomes.

Now . . . now he would do almost anything to see that bright, carefree smile. To hear the spirited, sassy laugh that grated his nerves and made him jealous at the same time.

Turned out, that smile hadn't been so carefree. It had been a mask, hiding a girl in a desperate situation. One shielding her humiliation.

"Isa . . ." Grady drew in a steadying breath. "The man who came looking for you—Cisco. He had a tattoo on the inside of his bicep."

She lifted her eyes. "Did he?"

"Does his father have one?"

Her brows folded inward. "Yes."

"A double-headed snake?"

She drew back. "Yes. Why?"

Grady rubbed his jawline, weighing how much he should tell her. "That tat is a calling card. A mark of membership." And a show of arrogance that the man would go around, knowing he was wanted by the FBI, and flash it without a care. Clearly the Lopez clan felt pretty cozy in their Montana hideout.

"Of what?"

Grady held Isa in his gaze. She was already scared. If she knew the full scope . . .

Isa drew up straight—a hint of the independent woman he was familiar with surfacing as she posted a hand on her hip. "How do you know whatever it is that you're not telling me?"

Pressing his lips tight, Grady stared at her. She'd had her secrets—and now he knew them. Did he dare tell her his?

He could be in a lot of trouble if he did. And put her in danger. But she already was in danger—more than she imagined. Whether he told her the truth or not, she was involved.

Man, this got complicated fast.

Grady raked his fingers through his hair and gripped his neck. "Look. Right now I think you need to lay low. Stay up here."

"In my apartment?"

He nodded.

"Who's going to run the café? Janie is—"

"I will."

"You?" Her brow shot up with a mocking measure of incredulity. Then she snorted. "That seems quite a bit beneath you, GP."

"GP?"

"Game and Parks."

That had been Hunter's nickname for him—and not one of respect. At least, not at the beginning. When had Isa adopted it?

Skip it. Didn't matter. The tasks for the moment were to confirm Cisco Lopez's identity so the field agents in Denver would take action, and to keep Isa out of danger's reach. In reverse order.

Grady shrugged, hoping to deescalate this conversation. His side of it in particular. "I can run a café for a few days."

"A few days?" Isa shook her head. "Junior will move on by sunset. He's scary, but he's sloppy—drove his father crazy with how careless he is. It became a wedge between them."

Sloppy, or brazen?

Isa didn't give him a chance to sort that one out. "More than likely, he just meant to warn me off. Maybe he's trying to work his way back into his father's good graces. By a conversation I overheard, Cisco was getting cut off."

That just showed how much Isa underestimated this situation. The Lopez clan was not known for issuing *warnings*. They threatened. Then they followed through.

"And anyway," Isa continued, confidence building in her voice, "I'm not hiding up here for a few days. Janie will fire me, and I can't afford to lose what I've got here."

Grady gripped his shoulder as he returned to the window. The street below was still normal. He could see Mama Bulldog on the boardwalk across Main, old T-shirt wadded up in one hand as she washed the windows. Bennett Crofton parked his Jeep in front of Tara Crofton's clinic—likely to help with the finishing touches before his mom opened her new establishment next week. Grady noted Bennett's drawn expression. Likely as not, the long expression had something to do with having recently put his two younger siblings on a plane headed back to their dad's place in Chicago.

"Are you ignoring me now?" Isa huffed. "That didn't take long . . ."

His shoulders folded inward as the jab of that comment hit like a center punch. Grady sighed, then turned to look at the fiery, frustrating, captivating woman. "I'm processing."

That Isa was grateful for the chance Janie had given her hit Grady with a measure of unexpected humility on Isa's part. Janie hadn't been a big fan of Isa's, which had a lot to do with Isa's penchant for flirting. Continually. Grady hadn't seen any measure of Isa being anything other than . . . happy slappy about where she was and what she was doing in Luna, which was irritating, because he was fairly certain that Janie's offer of not only a job but a place to live came with a measure of will bending before God—and perhaps her husband.

Humility was a trait that Grady held in high honor. Entitlement, however, was not.

But maybe Grady didn't see everything as it really was. Maybe *he* needed to start excavating some humility in his own heart.

"GP, believe me. I was just shocked to see him. What you saw downstairs was just . . . just a knee-jerk reaction."

No, it was pure terror. And it was justified.

Isa tossed her dark hair and gathered it over one shoulder. "But don't worry about me. I can hold my own. I don't need a babysitter."

Grady frowned. This GP nickname irked him. And this slide back toward sassy, carefree-girl persona also irked him. How was it that this beautiful little thing knew exactly how to rub him the wrong way every single time? "This is the kind of foolish streak of independence that gets girls like you into a lot of trouble."

"Girls like *me*? What is that supposed to mean?" And there it was on full display. Sassy, independent, and imprudent.

"It means that you're in a lot of trouble, Isa." Grady reached for her shoulder. "The kind that you can't grin and flirt your way out of."

With a hard scowl, Isa pulled away. "I want to know why you think you know anything about it."

He pressed his lips together.

"Just because you witnessed my little panic attack doesn't mean you know—"

"I know things." All thoughts of humility vanished. This woman really, really got under his skin, and she could do it faster than a rattlesnake could strike. "That's all I'm going to tell you right now, until I sort through some other stuff."

Crossing his arms, Grady stepped into her space, as if he were in the middle of a heated interrogation. "For this moment, you're just going to have to take my word on this. I *know* Cisco Lopez. I know what he does and what he's capable of. And I know that you are in a dangerous situation. So for now, you stay put. Camp up here out of sight. If people ask, you're sick." He shifted enough to point to the door behind him. "If someone other than me, Janie, or Hunter knocks on that door, you're not here."

"I'm sick? With what?"

"The flu. Chicken pox. Malaria." Malaria? See, this was how maddening this woman could be. He couldn't even think straight. "Whatever. Sick enough that you can't be seen."

"And you're going to run the café?" Her doubtful, mocking tone aggravated his already fired-up nerves.

"Right."

"And you're going to make that okay with Janie?"

"I'll figure it out."

She stepped back, shooting a look of disapproval and skepticism. "When did you decide you wanted to be my hero?"

"What?"

"You've had nothing but disapproval and contempt for me since the day we met. Why all the sudden are you looking out for me?"

"I didn't hold you in contempt."

She lifted a single, challenging brow at him. "Like you're not right now?"

That was a shot of ice water against his smoldering frustration. "Fine." Grady shook his head, silently trying to dispel the sinking sense of guilt. Yeah, he'd been less than kind to Isa. Because he didn't like her fake flirting. He didn't like the desperate need for attention she seemed to unashamedly display.

She irritated him.

And he couldn't help being caught by her loveliness.

That last part was on him though. His own weakness making itself known. He was a man who appreciated substance, yet he had been captivated by nothing more than her pretty face and form. More than once he'd been jealous that her sassy smile hadn't been aimed at him. What exactly did that say about him at his core?

He irritated himself.

With a long exhale, Grady looked toward his boots and stepped back, leaving a more respectful, less intimidating gap between himself and Isa.

Silence stamped tension into the small space of her apartment. Beyond the window at his back came the sounds of Bennett calling something and then a car door smacking shut.

A soft sniffle broke through the stillness in the room. Isa stood with her face tipped toward the coffee table at her side, her face averted. But he could see the gleam of a trickling tear against the profile of her nose.

His chest clenched. That was his doing. Not Cisco's. His.

He rolled his fists tight and then slowly released his fingers into a wide stretch. "Isa."

She lifted her chin but didn't turn her eyes to meet his.

"I don't hold you in contempt." He shouldn't. After all, he didn't truly know her at all. Hadn't given her a chance. Didn't know her story, her heart.

He wouldn't hold her in contempt. Not anymore.

A soft, hard laugh moved from her chest. "Sure. And I don't flirt my way into trouble." She did look at him then, letting those big dark-brown eyes meet his gaze in full. No mask. Just honest, raw emotion.

And what he saw split his heart and made him ache.

Three

Nathan: I'll make him change his mind. And if he doesn't, he'll regret it.

BLOWING OUT A LONG sigh, Bennett scrolled through the text conversation between himself and Nate as he pushed through the door into Janie's Café. Isa made a near perfect replica of his favorite spoiled-city-boy coffee (Hazel's tag for the drink)—a dark-chocolate hazelnut decaf cold brew with almond cold foam. Yeah, Hazel was probably dead on with that moniker. Be that as it may, Bennett was in the mood for a treat. Especially as he sorted through the discouragement he could hear in Nate's texts. It had only been three weeks since the kids had gone back to Chicago, but they'd been long, hard weeks for all of them.

Bennett: Don't do anything that will make things worse.

Bennett hit Send as the bell behind him finished chiming its cheerful welcome. "I sure could use a cup of your magic coffee, Isa." Lowering his phone, he looked up.

Not Isa.

"Grady?" Bennett could count on one hand the number of times he'd seen the Game and Parks guy not dressed in his uniform, and none of those times ever had the man standing behind the counter at Janie's Café—and that counted the few months when Grady had been dating the owner.

"Good afternoon, Bennett."

"Sure." Bennett stopped next to a barstool and set his phone on the blue-stained pine counter. "What are you doing?"

"Making you a coffee, apparently." Grady reached for a mug. "What are you drinking?"

"Do you know how to make a coffee?"

"Magic coffee? That's doubtful. I can do coffee black, coffee with sugar, coffee with cream, coffee with milk. Except in any of the last three options, you'll need to put in your own additives." Grady raised a judgmental brow. "I don't make magic coffee."

Grady's dry humor bordered on captious, but Bennett knew him well enough to know he was a decent man who didn't mean offense. He was just . . . serious. About everything. "I'll take a black coffee then. And again, what are you doing?"

Grady shrugged and turned to fill the mug with a nearly empty glass carafe.

That was it? A shrug? Grady wasn't the oversharing type, but he was usually friendly enough.

"Where's Isa?"

"She's not feeling well." Grady set the mug on the counter.

"That's not good." Bennett took a sip. Then spat it back into the mug. Acrid. Burnt. Nasty. "When was the last time you made a fresh brew?"

"I haven't."

"Might want to give that a try." Bennett passed the mug back. "Why are you filling in for Isa?"

"I told you—she's sick."

Bennett lifted one brow. "And she asked *you* to fill in for her?" Isa had been the one exception to that *friendly enough* observation. Grady kept a solid, unmistakable glacier between himself and Isa, and *captious* was a nice word for his thinly veiled attitude toward José's little sister.

Although, when Grady thought no one noticed, the man could sure fall into a spell . . .

"Sure." Grady took the mug of stale coffee and dumped it into the small sink behind the counter. "Why not?"

"Because you've made it plain that you don't like her?" Except when he sat transfixed by her.

Grady's back was to Bennett, but he could see his shoulders stiffen. His head lifted. For a long breath, the man stood still. Then he rinsed out the mug and went to work making a fresh pot. All without a response.

"Maybe I'll just go check in with Isa." Bennett stepped back from the counter and moved like he would go back into the kitchen. From there, he'd go up the stairs to the apartment Janie leased to her hired help.

"Think you should let her rest." Grady's tone shifted to iron. When he turned to meet Bennett's stare, his expression was also hard. "She doesn't feel well."

Something was off here, and Bennett would put money on whatever it was having to do with the stranger in town earlier that day.

"There was a guy going around looking for a woman."

Grady's stone expression didn't change, but his Adam's apple bobbed when he swallowed. "Yeah. He was here. Looking for a girl named Victoria."

"Right." Bennett tipped his head, trying to read the indiscernible. What was going on here? And how was Grady involved? "Seemed like a guy up to no good."

Grady kept his mouth shut.

"He showed me a picture. She kind of looked like Isa."

"A little." Grady crossed his arms. "I've never met a Victoria. Isa said she hasn't either."

"Did she?"

Grady turned back to the coffeepot. "Yep."

"So she saw the guy?"

"Yep."

"Before she got sick?"

"Yep."

The coffeepot gurgled loudly. Grady rolled his head one direction, then the other, producing a loud pop from his neck. Then he turned back to Bennett. "Coffee will be done in just a minute. Did you want anything else?"

"No." Bennett tapped the counter with his phone. "No, come to think of it, I don't need anything right now. Janie invited Hazel and me to supper tonight." He pocketed his phone and bumped the counter with his fist one last time. "I'll be sure to mention to Hunter and Janie that Isa isn't feeling well. Doubt you filling in here is a good long-term plan for Janie's Café."

Grady nodded, and that was it.

Something wasn't right. But Bennett couldn't imagine that Grady was up to no good. Everyone knew that he was cold to Isa—but almost everyone also guessed that was because the man had a crush on her and didn't know what to do with it.

Grady was just a good guy with a thing for a firecracker of a woman—the kind that could intimidate a fellow at the same time she entirely captivated him. Bennett knew from experience—sometimes liking that sort of woman made you crazy. Who was he to hold it against Grady?

"Something is wrong at the café." Bennett squared his gaze on Hunter, though his comment was about Janie's establishment.

As a group, they all knew the situation with Isa—that she'd come to Luna to escape the youthful missteps she'd made back home. What those were, exactly, none of them were sure, but José had been confident his sister would land on her feet if given a fresh chance.

Hunter frowned as he exchanged a glance with his wife.

Janie sighed. "What's going on?"

"Not sure." Bennett lifted his glass of iced lemon water, the cold perspiration of the glass wetting his palm. "But Grady was working for Isa."

He set the water back on the table and rubbed his damp hand against his jeans. Janie had prepared an amazing meal—tender grilled chicken with a savory mushroom gravy, freshly snapped green beans, and a side of creamy mashed potatoes. Back in Chicago, he'd have paid a healthy chunk of cash for such a delicious meal—and it would have been worth it.

"Grady?" Janie's brow folded into lines.

"Did she call you about not feeling well?" Bennett asked.

"No." Janie looked at Hunter again. "Why would she have *Grady* fill in for her?"

Hunter shrugged, taking the story in with less concern than his wife. "Don't know. But she had it covered, sounds like."

"He said he was there when she got sick." Bennett lifted his fork and dipped it into the potatoes, causing the gravy that had been pooled in the middle to seep in a delicious river onto his plate.

With a nod, Hunter nudged his wife. "See. There you go."

"She doesn't like him." Janie met Hunter's gaze. "And more to the point, *he* doesn't like her."

Hazel snorted. "At least not when she's flirting with high school boys."

Huh. Hazel noticed these things? She was getting better and better at reading people. "How about when she's not flirting with high school boys?" Bennett couldn't resist teasing her.

"Then she's flirting with old men." Janie sighed again, and this time the sound ended with a little growl. "I've talked with her about it before. It didn't seem to sink in."

"Maybe Isa is just one of those people who doesn't know the difference between flirting and being friendly."

Hunter was living dangerously, defending the lovely young woman whom Janie hadn't liked at the beginning. Particularly since that lovely young woman had set her flirtatious aim on Hunter for a time.

"Think that's a real thing?" Janie asked. "Not knowing that you're being a flirt?"

"Hazel doesn't always know when she's being a bear, so . . ." Hunter grinned wide and winked at his sister.

Hazel raised her hand and curved her fingers into a claw. "I know what I'm doing."

Bennett chuckled. "That's not true." He covered her hand and brought it to rest on his leg. "Not always. And sometimes you do it because you don't know how else to handle a situation. It's your fight-or-flight response."

"Like when a man shows up for an elk hunt with a twenty-two?"

Bennett leaned down until his nose nearly touched hers. "When a handsome, irresistible man walks into your world and makes you blush."

"I didn't blush."

"You lit up like a bonfire."

"Okay, you two." Hunter clinked his fork against his plate, like a father about to reprimand his children. "We're all glad you've finally figured out you're in love. But we're at the table."

Bennett didn't shift his gaze from Hazel's beautiful hazel eyes. He leaned down farther and whispered near her ear. "I love it when you blush."

With a firm palm against his shoulder, she pushed him out of her space. And yes, she was blushing—while trying, ineffectively, to pin down a grin.

"Talk about flirting . . ." Janie made an *ew* face, then winked at Hazel. "Think Grady doesn't like Isa only because she *never* flirts with him?"

"I think Grady and Isa are polar opposites who simply can't tolerate being together. Like a blizzard on the Fourth of July. The pair just don't go together."

"Huh." Hunter pointed his fork at Hazel, then Bennett. "So you two would be . . ."

"A miracle," Bennett said.

The quartet around the table laughed.

Hazel slipped her hand into his. "A whole constellation of miracles."

"And we sing a hallelujah." Bennett meant that with every inch of his heart.

He'd never stop praising the God who set the stars in the sky, raised the mountains up and sank the valleys low, and told the waters where to gather. That same God had turned his life around, had reached the mountain lioness at his side, and had blessed them with a love neither of them had believed possible.

Life ahead looked pretty spectacular, and Bennett was thrilled. He just needed to seal the deal—and he had a plan for that.

However, Bennett also had some issues elsewhere he needed to address. One, whatever was going on at the café—and there was *something* going on there. But he'd told Hunter and Janie, and now that situation was in their hands. The second warning, though, wasn't one he could hand off.

"Nathan texted me today."

Hazel's head lifted, her eyes darting to Bennett. "Is he better now?"

"No."

The fact that Hazel's eyes darkened made him both sad and grateful. Hazel had really—and shockingly—connected with his difficult younger brother, and she genuinely cared about not only his well-being but Nathan's heart. In a way that probably no one else could, Hazel understood Nathan. And she missed him.

Bennett sighed. "He keeps saying he's not going to stay there."

"Think he means it?" Hazel asked.

"You know Nathan."

"Yeah." Hazel's brow creased. "Yeah, I do. And I think he's giving you an honest warning. Has he talked with your dad?"

"No one *talks* with Chip." The man, whom Bennett still resented and still had a hard time calling *Dad*, did all the talking and none of the listening.

Concern laced Hazel's demeanor. "I'll call Nate."

"Yeah?" Bennett exhaled a mix of relief, surprise, and gratitude. Hazel making a phone call was like a snowstorm in August—it happened there in the Montana mountains, but not on the regular.

"Look at my baby sister." Hunter reached across the table and shook Hazel's arm. "Being all grown up and caring. Love brings out the best in you, Zel."

At Hazel's dagger-glare—feigned, Bennett was pretty sure—Janie leaned into Hunter. "You, as usual, bring out the spite in her."

"What do I bring out of you, wife?"

Being the newlywed she was, Janie blushed. Furiously. Hunter grinned. Triumphantly. And Bennett looked away, catching Hazel squirming. He caught her eye and grinned.

Their turn was coming, and Bennett could hardly wait.

Four

Grady stared into the darkness, his arm draped over his head. Just outside his window, the scritch-scratch of the pine tree brushing up against the peeling siding of his tiny house amplified the coiled tension that hadn't left him. With an aggravated growl, he rolled his left wrist in front of his face to check the time: 2:00 a.m.

It'd been hours since he'd dropped onto his bed. Not for one minute had he relaxed enough to sleep. One moment he'd replay the image of Isa huddled behind the counter and trembling. The next he remembered the feel of her small frame tucked tight against his chest. Then he'd hear the devastating sound of her whimpering sobs and the crack of her voice as she told him she was pregnant.

And there, he would breathe against the throb in his chest. What was Isa going to do? Lots of women were single moms. They managed. Many of them, like his own mom had for a while, did dang well at it. But it was still sad, and Isa's situation was beyond sad.

He was truly scared for her.

Don't you worry. I will find her. Cisco's threat made Grady's heart pound.

Francisco Lopez was known for his taste for pretty young women, but not usually for harming them. But there was also the well-told rumor of his wife's manic jealousy. It had been reported that Anitra Lopez had once taken a mushroom knife to one of her husband's mistresses, carving the woman's face into ribbons. A separate story had Mrs. Lopez scalding one of Francisco's young lovers with acid.

Not a woman to anger, for sure.

Had Anitra sent her son to do her vindictive dirty work?

Grady's stomach churned as again those chilling words rolled through his mind. He had no reason to think Cisco wouldn't follow through. No reason to believe that the only son of the crime boss would do exactly as he intended.

The worst of it was that the FBI, for whom Grady conspicuously scouted under the cover of his working title of forest ranger, was only after the senior Franscico Lopez. The phone conversation he'd had that evening had made that frustratingly clear. After he'd closed Janie's Café, checked on Isa one last time to reemphasize that she needed to remain out of sight, and then made it to his lonely one-bedroom alley rental on the west side of Luna, he'd called Agent Malcom to confirm the identity.

"You saw Cisco Lopez. As in Junior?" Malcom had clarified.

"Yes, that's correct."

"We're looking for Francisco." The dry statement came off like a reprimand.

"I realize that. But my source has the father and son connected. We track Cisco, we'll get the father."

"Your source? I thought you saw him yourself."

"I did."

"Who is this source?"

"That's not something I'm going to divulge."

"I beg your pardon?"

"I'm not going to give you a name. But the source is reliable."

"That's not good enough, Briggs, and you know it. You're not an agent, and I can't move resources on a hunch you're not going to give me details about."

Grady had jammed his hand into his hair and gripped with furious frustration. He knew protocol. He'd also known before he made this phone call that he would never, under any circumstances, share the reason he'd come across Cisco Lopez. He would never betray Isa, never tell a soul why she was connected with the Lopez family, and never, ever breathe a word about her pregnancy. Even if all of that was important and actionable information for the FBI.

"It's not a hunch. Cisco came here specifically looking for my source because of the connection they have with his father." He swallowed, silently begging God to bend Malcom's will to Grady's desperation. "I promise you the information is good. I promise you I saw Cisco Lopez here in Montana. I promise you I have a reliable source placing Junior with his father in Montana. And I promise you that the situation is precarious. People are in danger. I need you to trust me."

In the background, the sound of a chair creaking and then the legs smacking a wood floor filled the void of Malcom's lack of response. Then, "Look, kid, I barely know you. You're not part of my team, and I wasn't keen on your being pulled into this case. I don't have a reason to trust your list of promises. My best guess, you've come across one of Cisco's women, and she's scared. That's a problem, I'll give you that, but not one I'm chasing down. I can't. Francisco is the target, not his son."

"Sir—"

"And as for you working this case, as far as I'm concerned, you're a forest ranger with a limited background in criminal investigation.

If you want to tell me about the spotted skunk, I'll believe every word you say. But when it comes to hunting FBI most wanted crime families, I think you're out of your depth, even if you have the title of undercover asset."

That had been hours ago, but Grady's head still throbbed. Partly with angry frustration—why the heck had he been looped in on this case if the agent in charge didn't want him? It wasn't like he'd been itching to track a criminal. Switching tracks to forest ranger had been an intentional career move. Grady had despised seeing the worst of humanity, and two years as a criminal investigator had been two years too many. This job was supposed to put him outside, largely alone, and away from metropolitan areas, where crime was particularly awful.

And the other part of the pounding in his head? The fact that Malcom had nearly center punched the reason Cisco had shown up in Luna. Only part he'd not gotten right was that Isa wasn't Cisco's woman—she'd been with the father.

Burning nausea rolled hard in his gut, and Grady sat up. With fist rolled tight, he pressed the heel of his hand to his head and willed his supper to stay where it was supposed to. The thought of Isa with a man as vile as Lopez, though . . .

Grady went to the bathroom and rinsed his face with cool water. Palm pressed against the cool Formica of the bathroom counter, Grady wiped his skin dry with a towel, then squeezed his eyes shut. In the darkness, he found the haunting memories of his stepdad. Drunk, wildly out of control, and both hands wrapped around his mother's neck.

Bile burned the back of his throat.

He had to banish those thoughts. What was done was done, and there was only figuring out what to do now. Isa wasn't safe, and she wasn't going to be safe while Cisco Lopez had free rein. Agent Malcom wasn't going to be helpful.

That left Grady on his own.

Isa sat at the window overlooking Main, alternating between searching the shadows below for anything that would hint that a villainous man was lurking, looking, hunting . . . and the other part staring at the moon. That great white orb in the sky had been nearly full, sending down glowing-white light to the dark earth below.

Was that meant as a beacon of hope for Isa, or was it shedding a lit path for the Lopezes' retribution?

She thought the second option didn't seem like the God her family had served and loved for her whole life. They clung to a God of grace and mercy, One of second, third, and fourth chances. But maybe Isa had worn out all her chances. After all, what kind of woman got herself into this deep of a mess?

But as hope sank into the chilled pit dug out by shame, Isa covered her still-flat stomach, her hand shielding the scrap of a babe, secret in her womb. There in the light of the moon, she shut her eyes, a tear slipping past her lashes, and hung her head.

"God, please don't turn your back on me."

There, in the midst of her fear and loneliness, she heard the distant memory of her mama reading Psalm 71 out loud. *Sé para mí una roca de refugio, adonde recurra yo continuamente.*

Would God be her rock of refuge, even if it was she who had caused the storm in her life? Could she still go to Him, though she'd given Him her back?

Porque tú eres mi roca y mi fortaleza.

"I'm scared," she whispered, her breath a fog against the windowpane. "Please, still be my fortress."

The moon continued to shine into the night, and Isa wandered her way back to her bed. Somewhere between that infant morning hour and this breaking of day, she must have drifted to sleep. Now, waking with a mild headache, her thoughts drifted back to that psalm and to her prayer.

Feet on the chilled floor, Isa rolled her neck, trying to stretch out some of the knotted tension, and then pushed off the mattress. She padded across the shaggy gray area rug and out of the bedroom. In the small living space of her apartment, she continued until she came to a narrow bookshelf. There, she found the Bible José had gifted her on her sixteenth birthday. Dark-brown leather bound, with *Isabelle Esperanza Romero* embossed in gold at the bottom of the front cover.

It still looked brand new, though Isa was now twenty-two years old.

Isa winced. The shelves before her were loaded with books—mostly novels, and many of which her mama would blush and then burn if she ever read them. Several of those books were well worn.

But not her Bible.

Her eyes fell shut, chin sank toward her chest. Would God still be her rock and refuge? Why should He be?

The soft, cool leather between her hands drew her attention again. Though she'd been raised in a home that read God's Word regularly, Isa had no idea where to start. Was the Bible like a prescription drug, where there were certain passages for specific scenarios? That seemed . . . well, not the way Mami and Papi and José approached it. At least, she didn't think so. But then again, she didn't exactly know what they did other than they read the Bible.

It was a big book though.

On impulse, and before she could overthink it, Isa scurried to her room to retrieve her phone and wrote a hurried text to her brother.

What should I read in the Bible?

It was random and maybe a little desperate. But José would answer her, she felt sure. For the past year, he'd been trying hard to connect with her. He'd told her often that he was worried for her. That she was recklessly charging down a dangerous path.

For most of the past year, she'd blown him off. Honestly, she didn't even know why.

Most people had a reason for rebellion, didn't they? Some kind of trauma or a home life that was too restrictive or not attentive, or whatever.

Isa?

Isa didn't have any excuse. She'd just wanted what she wanted. Adventure. Freedom. Her own way.

She laid the book on the coffee table and snatched the blanket she'd tossed onto the chair last night when she'd finally wandered back to bed. Wrapping it around her tank top, sinking into the soft warmth, Isa paced to her Keurig and inserted a pod of half caff.

She'd read caffeine was bad for developing babies. At the time she'd been in denial—she couldn't be pregnant. She wasn't *that* kind of girl. She was the sort of girl who had *fun*. Not the sort who ended up as a single mom.

Why did people think things would never happen to them, when that was the natural consequence of an action?

Isa didn't know. All she knew was she didn't think it would happen to her. Even when she'd missed a period. Even when the test stick floated a positive sign. Even when she'd experienced mild queasiness in the morning.

It just couldn't happen. God wouldn't let *that* happen.

Had it sunk in now? She'd not told a soul until yesterday morning. How was it that Grady Briggs had become her confidant?

In that moment, his arms a sturdy fortress around her, he'd become more than that. In that moment, for that moment, he'd been her rock and shield.

The machine spit out the last drops of her brew. Wrapping both hands around the warmth of the mug, Isa inhaled, willing the pungent aroma to sweep away the exhausted fog in her brain.

A soft knock on the door pulled her away from that small window of reprieve.

"Isa." Grady's low voice. "It's just me. Can I see you?"

He sounded so . . . humble. Kind. And tired. None of those things she'd ever associated with Grady Briggs. Fisting the blanket so that it would remain securely around her body, she crossed to the door, released the folds of the fabric just long enough to unlock and open it, and then stepped back. "You can come in."

By the dark shadows around his eyes, Isa guessed Grady had slept about as much as she had. He studied her, taking her in head to toe, as if looking for something amiss.

"Nothing out of the ordinary happened last night, right?"

"There was nearly a full moon and a clear sky." She tipped her head to that sassy angle that usually won her a smirk of interest. Except, it never had with this man.

Grady scowled. Then he gently grasped her shoulder. "I think you're not letting this situation sink in."

The one about the baby? No. She'd still not fully absorbed that one. The one about Junior showing up in her new town? That had stuck. Enough to keep her up, scared, most of the night, despite her brushing it off yesterday, and to have disruptive dreams when she'd finally drifted off to sleep.

"I need you to take this seriously." Grady shook his head, as if to clear it. "*You* need you to take this seriously."

"You're pretty worked up for a man who would rather I disappear from his life."

He held an unreadable look on her.

Why did she wish she could hear his thoughts? Likely they weren't charitable. Likely they'd hurt her already smashed pride.

"I don't want you to disappear." His hold on her arm tightened. Not in a menacing way. In a . . .

Isa sighed, irritated with her imagination. She read way too many romance novels. Way. Too. Many.

Grady lowered his hand and shoved it into his pocket. "I just wanted to check on you and let you know I've got the café covered again."

"How long do you think I need to play the mouse?" She shouldn't jut her chin up like that—like a stubborn, foolish woman who didn't appreciate that this man was looking out for her even though he didn't even like her. But she hated feeling this way—like she *needed* him to look out for her.

Grady's shoulders stiffened, but his expression hardened back to impassiveness as his attention drifted toward the window that faced Main Street. "Give it a couple more days."

"Then you'll feel safe?" The sass! Why did she have to be this way? "You can feel okay about going back to looking down on me while simultaneously ignoring me?"

"I'm trying to help you, Isa. Why are you so bitter about that?"

"I'm not bitter about it."

"You're acting like a rabid animal."

"You've made it clear you don't like it when I'm nice to you."

He frowned and crossed his arms over his chest. "Flirt, Isa. You flirt. With everyone."

She raised a brow. Nope. She didn't flirt with Grady. Hadn't for months—since he'd returned her first few attempts with pure disdain.

Was that why she was so bitter at him?

I'm not bitter!

For not being bitter, she sure was spiny and defensive.

A low growl of frustration slipped from Grady's throat. He gave her his back, striding toward the window while he raked a hand through his hair.

Sheesh. She hadn't even responded. How was it possible that she could get under his skin while simply breathing?

"Look, Isa . . ." He turned, arms doubled over his chest again. "I've been up most of the night trying to work my way through this mess."

"Why?" She set her mug on the coffee table. It clunked with a sound that mirrored her frustration. The blanket slipped off her shoulders, draping against her back, allowing the chilly morning air to kiss her bare shoulders. Gooseflesh rippled along her skin. "It's not actually your mess."

Grady stared at her. Then he blinked and shifted his gaze toward the coffee mug on the table. "I have connections with the FBI."

What was with the pink touching his cheeks above his dark beard?

"Like you have a buddy who works there?"

"No. Like I have a *connection*." He made eye contact with her again, and this time he didn't allow his gaze to wander from her face. "Look, I still don't think I can tell you everything. But I am willing to tell you that my contact was less than helpful last night."

"You *told* someone about this?" Isa stepped forward as indignation flared. "What'd you do, post it on your socials? Broadcast it that I'm stupid, pregnant, and alone?"

Grady flinched. "I don't think you're stupid."

Dang it, but a heated glaze blurred her vision. "How could you? I mean, I know that you don't like me, but I didn't think you were cruel. Definitely didn't figure you for a gossip."

"Isa, I didn't tell anyone here—and I didn't tell my contact that you're pregnant. I'm not going to."

Pregnant. It was starting to sink in. Isa stepped back, lowering her chin until she saw only the sunflower pattern on the soft blanket at her waist.

A long stretch of uncomfortable silence spanned between them. Then Grady moved toward her. Slowly, like he was approaching one of his rarely seen animals out in the woods. He stood only a foot away before his low whisper feathered against the screaming silence.

"Isa."

She bit her lip and forced herself to look up.

"I swear to you—I'm not going to betray what you've entrusted to me."

Feeling small and foolish, Isa nodded and lowered her face again. Of all the men in the world, why did it have to be this one to witness her deeply humiliating failure?

She sucked in a sharp breath when the side of his knuckle trailed one of her arms. Gently he pinched the blanket at her elbows and lifted, replacing the soft warmth to her shoulders.

Isa fought against the urge to lean forward and press her forehead to his chest. Instead, she cleared her throat. "Who is this contact? Why did you think you should reach out to him?"

"I need you to keep my secrets, okay?" He lifted her chin so that she met his eyes again. "Promise me."

"I promise," she whispered.

"Before I worked for Game and Parks, I was a criminal investigator."

"With the FBI?"

"No, but I worked with them a few times. One of the senior agents noticed my work and recommended me for Basic Field Training Course. He thought I'd be a good candidate for SASS—to become a special agent."

"Why didn't you?"

His Adam's apple bobbed. "I . . . couldn't stomach what I was doing as a criminal investigator. I didn't want deeper in that life. It was . . . disturbing."

"Why did you become one in the first place?"

Emotion tore through his expression—something fiery and painful and fierce. "That's a long, separate story. Look, here's the thing—I had the wildlife biology background and the law enforcement background to switch to forest ranger. It was a better fit for me. But when this senior agent found out I'd gone that route, he pulled me into an investigation as an undercover asset."

"I don't know what that means."

"It means that I don't work for the FBI per se, but my assignment with Game and Parks put me in a position that was convenient for the FBI to pull me in on their search. Sort of like an informant—but I'm not a criminal insider. I just have the right location and background training."

"Search . . ." Ah. It was coming together. "For Junior?"

Grady shook his head. "Not Cisco. His father."

Isa felt the heat drain from her body. She must have looked like she'd go down, because Grady grasped her by both elbows.

Wanted by the FBI? Who was this man she'd gotten mixed up with? How could she have been that . . . *stupid*!

"The Lopezes are part of one of the largest cartels working in the western US. Francisco is evasive—partly because he doesn't come off as dangerous. He's . . . charming. And he generally keeps his hands clean. He's also slippery. A little over a year ago, the California agency lost track of him. They got a tip that he'd gone to some remote part of Montana, which happened to be in the area I'd been assigned. I'm supposed to keep eyes and ears out for . . ."

She nodded. As the call of a mountain bird trilled into the dusty light of morning, Isa felt a fresh wave of shame wash away all hope of moving on. This town was supposed to be her fresh start. Not just a place of refuge, but one of redefinement. Who had she been kidding?

"Can they help me?" she whispered, fully aware of how helpless and pathetic she sounded.

Grady slipped a hand beneath Isa's jaw.

Jarred by the intimacy of such a touch, Isa sucked in a breath and looked up at him. The intensity of his stare burned into her heart.

"I won't let them hurt you." His hand fell away. "I promise."

Five

While the warm sun soaked into her shoulders, Hazel lifted her face to the breeze swishing through the forest along the trail. It smelled of cold river, damp earth, and sweet spruce. Shutting her eyes and lifting a grin, she tipped her face up to the golden light dancing through the rustling aspen leaves.

"I think the trees sing too," she said.

Bennett's arms eased around her shoulders from behind, and he pulled her against his chest. "What do they sing?"

"Since there are no words, I can only guess. But I hear the melody. Don't you?"

A soft growl of satisfaction rumbled from his chest, and then he chuckled. "I hear the breeze and the trees and the rolling water. If that's a song of praise, then, yes, I hear the melody too."

Hazel twisted her neck to look back at him. "Are you making fun of me?"

Bennett kissed her nose. "No. I am still in wonder. I love that you hear the praise of creation."

Satisfied with his answer, Hazel gripped his hand, kissed the back of it, then untangled herself from his arms. Bennett regripped that hand she'd used to free herself, and they started on the trail beside Elk Creek again. Fingers laced, their conversation gave way to the music of the forest.

Hazel loved that they were as comfortable without words as they were in conversation. Too many words made her exhausted. But she loved having this man beside her.

The sound of shale clanking against shale caused their feet to halt simultaneously. Scanning the thick green of the forest undergrowth, Hazel spotted the source of disruption. She elbowed Bennett gently, then pointed across the width of the river. Above a stand of bushes sat a majestic rack of antlers. The elk—an aged bull by the size of that eight-point rack—turned his regal face, giving them a perfect profile view.

Bennett raised the Nikon Coolpix from the strap around his neck and aimed the lens at the animal. Hazel grinned, recalling his eye roll and smirk when she'd given him the camera for his birthday and declared that "now you can be honest about what you're doing here—and have something you can shoot."

He'd been good humored about her ribbing him. And grateful for the camera. Hazel had to admit, he was a natural with it. His photos got better and better with each shot, and it wouldn't be long before he'd outgrow the beginner equipment.

As if he could hear the clicking of Bennett's camera, the elk turned to look directly at them, then huffed and turned toward the slope that climbed away from the river. With an impressive show of athleticism and balance, that great beast galloped up the shale, through the patches of trees, and out of view.

Bennett scanned through the images he'd captured, then showed a few to Hazel.

She smiled at his success. "You should order a few large prints, frame them, and take them to Mama Bulldog. She could sell them to the tourists, I'll bet."

Nodding, Bennett wore an expression of pleasure. "I'll see if Hunter wants one for the lodge." Lowering the camera back to his chest, he gave Hazel his full attention. "What would a guy that size be called?"

"A monarch."

"King of the mountain, huh? That seems fitting. He was impressive." He caught her hand again, and they resumed the hike. After several paces, he spoke again. "Speaking of Hunter and the lodge, how's Janie doing, juggling the café and the lodge while Isa's sick?"

Hazel shrugged. "I think she's fine—seems like the timing is good. Their first full week booking at the lodge is in late August. Janie has a little while before she needs to figure out how to really juggle. So right now, while Isa's down, she goes in to do the cooking. Grady insists on working the front." She looked up at Bennett. "That's kind of strange, don't you think?"

"The whole thing is a little off." Bennett shrugged. "Thought so from the day I found Grady serving bad coffee. But I figure maybe he thinks this is his shot."

Hazel snorted. "You really think he *likes* her?"

Bennett bobbed his head side to side and shrugged again. "Wouldn't be the first time a man fell for a woman who drove him a little nuts."

"They're nothing alike."

"Huh. Who do we know that are like that?"

"Okay, okay." Hazel chuckled. "So sometimes opposites work. But seriously, Grady could barely stand to look at Isa. What gives with that?"

"Jealousy."

"What?"

"Isa is always smiling and talking and being friendly with everyone who isn't named Grady. Maybe *that's* the real rub."

"Hmm." Hazel nudged him with her shoulder. "You're such a romantic."

With an arm around her shoulder, Bennett pinned her at his side. "Aren't you glad?"

As Hazel tipped her grin up to meet his kiss, a flash of white appeared on the trail. She leaned into him to peer around the bend in the path. That spot of white became a girl dressed in an easy-fitting tank top and a pair of dark bootcut jeans. Her twin boxer braids helped Hazel remember exactly who this cute high school kid was.

"Ella." Bennett beat Hazel to the greeting.

The girl's head lifted with a jolt. Clearly she'd been lost in thought. Or something else, given that she pulled an earbud from her right ear. "Mr. Crofton." She looked relieved.

Hazel bit her lip, refraining from a comment about listening to the movement of the forest if one didn't want to be startled on a hike. Maybe she should say it though, as it was a safety concern.

"How are you, Ella?" Bennett spoke with friendly ease, and there went the opportunity to issue the warning. Likely just as well. Hazel knew she could be a curmudgeon.

Ella shrugged. "Pretty good."

"Summer going well?"

"I guess." She bit her lip and eyed the river. Then she sighed and looked back at Bennett. "Have you heard from Nathan lately?"

Bennett's arm slipped away from Hazel, and he adjusted the ball cap on his head. "Yeah. Here and there. He's . . . settling in."

She looked like she debated what and how much to say. Finally, she shook her head. "He's not happy, Mr. Crofton. He says he hates it there, that he hates his dad, and . . . and that he might do something drastic." She winced, looked toward the dark earth of the dirt path and then back up again. Now there was a sheen in her eyes. "I don't know what that means, but it makes me so worried about him."

Hazel could feel Bennett stiffen at her side. She reached for his hand and threaded her fingers with his. For an intense moment, the river's song became the only sound between them. Then Bennett cleared his throat. "Thank you for telling me, Ella. I'll talk to him."

"Please don't tell him I told you. He'll be mad—and he won't trust me anymore."

"I'll say that you're worried about him, and that's all." Bennett reached out to lay a hand on the girl's slim shoulder. "I think it will matter to him that you care enough to tell me that you're worried."

After three days spent in her apartment, Isa was done with confinement. Janie had stopped to check on her, and Isa had played the part of a sick employee. After all the lying she'd done to her family, one would think that playing a charade to her boss wouldn't have fazed Isa in the slightest.

She felt awful about it.

Actually, she felt awful about all her deceitful actions. She'd already lost the trust and the respect of her family. Apparently lying was a slippery slope—one harder than expected to step away from.

Grady had shown up twice a day to check in with her. Once in the early hours of morning, and once at night. Only the first morning had he touched her. Now he'd gone back to the old gruff Grady—cold, impersonal, and ever disapproving. It was foolish of Isa to wish back the warmth of that rough hand against her skin.

She was collapsing in on herself.

This wasn't acceptable. This wasn't who she was. Isabel Romero was a spitfire. A woman with a spine and boldness that set others aback. Hiding was suffocating her, snuffing out that boldness. That wouldn't do—not when she'd need every scrap of it when she finally told her family about the baby.

Decision made, Isa waited for Grady's appearance. Nine thirty, predictably. That was Grady Briggs—Mr. Predictable. Mr. Serious and Responsible. Shirt pressed and buttoned. Beard neat and trimmed. Eyes searching for flaws, and certainly discerning them.

Isa's shoulders tensed. By the time his knock sounded, she'd worked up all that resentment into a blistering shot of false courage.

The door leapt open by the force of her pull.

Grady's eyebrows lifted. Yet another moment of him judging her every action.

"I'm done with this." Isa turned and strode back to her kitchen.

"What's that?" The door clicked softly shut behind her.

His controlled response was a shot of heat to her boiling temper. Couldn't this man just be . . . ugh! Something other than this?

Ignoring the smell of turkey pot pie that had wafted into her space along with Grady, as well as the filled plate in his hands, Isa turned back to him and planted her hands on her hips. "I said I'm done with this. I'm not hiding anymore."

Grady simply watched her, his gaze chilling with disapproval. "The agent in charge is still refusing to investigate."

"Then he clearly thinks this isn't a big deal." Inside, Isa shivered. It was a big deal, and she knew it. Cisco Lopez terrified her, and the fact that he'd tracked her to Luna still kept her from a decent night's sleep.

Grady scowled as he walked to her small table and set the plate down.

His lack of response made Isa angrier. Couldn't this man do more than scowl and silently judge and scowl some more?

"Look, Junior has moved on—just like I told you he would. He doesn't even know my real name." Isa pushed back the thick mess of dark hair that had fallen over the side of her face. "And anyway, I'm nothing to Francisco. Just a fling he had—one among many."

"You're pregnant."

She lifted one eyebrow, as if that were a minor detail. "He doesn't care."

Grady mirrored that single brow arch. What did that mean? A challenge to her proclamation that her former lover didn't care about his procreation? Or was he questioning if *she* cared about the baby?

Anger tapped a staccato rhythm in her veins. "Look, you've done your duty. Actually, it wasn't even your duty. I'm sorry that I pulled you into this. But the truth is, I'm fine. I'll be just fine. Junior has moved on, Francisco has no interest in me or my baby, and I'll figure out how to be a single mom. None of this is your problem, so I'm officially releasing you of whatever responsibility it is you think you have here."

"I made you a promise."

"What?"

"The other morning, when you asked if the FBI could help you. I gave you my word."

Isa wrapped her arms around her shoulders, as if that could shield her heart from him. She willed away the memory of his fingers against her skin. She steeled her emotions against the soft resolve that had been in his voice. *That* Grady had been tender beneath his stern determination. And that version of Grady could do so much more damage to Isa's heart than the cold and detached one ever could.

But *that* Grady would never want *this* Isa—the one he already didn't approve of and was now carrying a crime boss's baby.

Why had she gone down the path of wild impulse? Why hadn't she stayed on the straight and narrow, like her family had taught her?

Grady closed the gap of wood flooring between them. He waited until she tipped her chin up and met his gaze.

"I keep my word."

This time he didn't touch her. But she felt the impact of that statement all the way to her soul.

Six

Grady flung the three-foot-long branch he'd snapped off a tree, grunting with the energy he put into it. The bent thing whirled around like a boomerang, soaring over the top of the river until it crashed into the shale field on the opposite side. The stick snapped in two as the clatter of impact bounced across the water. The sticky pine sap gummed his thumb and palm, and the rough bark left a small scrape on his pinky.

All in all, his little outburst had done nothing to make things better. Man, it was a good thing he'd been assigned to check a trail that wasn't in high use. He wasn't in any form to encounter people that day.

With his sticky hand, he dug his phone out of his back pocket and scrolled through the string of texts he and Malcom had exchanged. The man was exceptionally arrogant and equally unhelpful. Why did he dislike Grady this much anyway? The man had zero respect for him, and in more than one text had plainly told him to stick to things he knew—like tree names and animal scat.

What a jerk.

Blowing out a harsh breath of frustration, Grady tapped his contacts and scrolled for Mitchel—the FBI agent in California who had originally suggested that Grady consider Quantico. Even when Grady had given a firm no, Mitchel had insisted Grady was FBI material and then passed his contact information along to the Denver office and basically demanded Grady be brought in as an undercover asset. Basically, a tracker—a man hunter under the cover of forest ranger.

Grady had wanted none of that. He hadn't declined the suggestion that he train as an agent because he was afraid he wouldn't be good at it. He'd declined because he didn't want to be involved in the sort of cases that continued to give him an up-close showcase of humanity's most despicable acts. And he certainly didn't want to go looking for the world's most debauched men.

Somehow, here he was though.

A few days ago, it seemed like the reason why had been made known. Sort of like that moment in the book of Esther when her cousin tells her that this was the reason she had been made queen. To save her people. Grady had been connected to the Lopez case to help Isa.

Only Isa didn't want saving or even help—or at least she didn't think she needed it. Not now, after her initial panic had subsided. In fact, she seemed to resent Grady's efforts.

As to his connection to the FBI? Fruitless. He might as well be some random guy off the street telling Malcom he'd spotted one of the most searched for bad guys in the men's restroom.

Malcom didn't believe him, and he didn't care enough to look into it.

Before another bout of temper overtook him, Grady scrolled to Mitchel's number, opened a new text, and started typing.

> Don't know what you can do, if anything, but I'm at a brick wall. I've had a run-in with Cisco Lopez, and I have a believable source who verifies that his father is up here with him. Malcom doesn't seem to think it's credible.

Send.

Pocketing his phone, Grady turned from the river to walk the narrow trail back to the Black Gulch trailhead. His shoulders sagged, eyes cast down on the dirt path. Man, it'd been years since he'd felt like this—helpless and trapped. It was . . . suffocating.

"What do I do?" Grady muttered his prayer out loud, wondering if the only ears his query reached belonged to birds and squirrels. Lately it had sure felt like anyone beyond the canopy of the forest had become deaf to his requests.

A scroll of examples rolled through his mind.

Will You show me a path away from the things that haunt my heart and dreams? That, Grady had prayed for when he'd decided that not only was he not interested in Quantico, but he really didn't want to be a criminal investigator at all. For a minute, the forest ranger gig had seemed like the right course. But then he'd landed a floating position, which had left him with a distinct sense of detachment—like he was being punished for abandoning his post. But when he'd asked, *Are You upset that I stopped investigating crimes?* There had been only silence.

So he'd moved to Luna, Montana, and accepted the undercover asset-man-hunter role as a not-really FBI agent. It was like a compromise between both worlds, because he really didn't want God to be disappointed in him.

Is she the reason I'm in Luna, Montana, of all places? That had been his prayer last fall, when he'd met Janie. He'd had high hopes there . . . God had been silent, allowing him to pursue a woman who had never been over her first love. It sure would have been nice to have had a warning on that. At least he hadn't made a fool of himself—at least not entirely.

Now here he was again. Asking for direction from the God who had seemed to tune him out.

At his vehicle, Grady opened the driver's-side door, reached in for the waterproof-cased clipboard, and filled out the paperwork. No visitors: date, sign. No trail damage: date, sign. Two possible widow-makers: location, date, sign.

Standard operational procedures. He'd go back to the trees he'd noted and mark them with a red dot, and later that fall he'd likely be the one-man maintenance crew who would be tasked with their removal. The glamorous life of a forest ranger. It was way better than removing dead bodies though.

Done with the paperwork, Grady shut the door, leaned his back against it, and tapped his head against the window.

"Please don't shut me out forever." He squeezed his eyes closed.

A distantly familiar sense of being abandoned and scared seeped into the warm summer breeze that filled his lungs. While squirrels chitter-chatted from one bough to another and birds chirped their conversations, Grady felt the keen ache of isolation.

He hated it. Had since he'd been a scared little boy digging into his soul for the courage he would need to stand up for his mom.

The phone vibrated in his back pocket—a welcome distraction from the past he wished would fade into nothing. There were days he'd envied the stories of Bennett's temporary amnesia—only Grady would have liked to keep the blank spaces of lost memories, whereas Bennett's had returned.

He focused his thoughts on the message rather than trekking down wishes-and-buts lane.

Mitchel: Retirement doesn't give me much authority anymore.

Malcom is full of himself and not much else. I'll see what I can do. Is there trouble?

At least Mitchel wasn't abandoning him.

Maybe, yeah. My contact is a woman. One who got mixed up with the Lopezes. I have a pressing feeling that she's not safe. The Lopezes have a reason to come for her.

Grady considered carefully before he pressed Send. Revealing Isa's gender was by itself a risk. But he trusted Mitchel—more than most men. Which perhaps wasn't saying much, because he didn't trust people in general. Men in authority least of all.

"God?"

The gurgle of the river, the ongoing calls of the forest fauna, pines, and spruce swishing as a breeze played in their boughs. But no answer from heaven.

Grady was backed against a wall. He'd have to trust Mitchel.

"Have you tried reaching Nathan?" Bennett barely waited for Hazel to step outside her front door and onto the deck before he asked.

Hazel shielded her eyes from the late-morning sunshine. She'd already thought it odd that Bennett had come up to the cabin at 11:00 a.m. on a Tuesday. He was diligent about keeping work hours, even though he ran his business from the renovated house in Luna.

"Sloppy doesn't get success," he'd told Hazel when she'd teased him about it.

He would know. Bennett was a perennial success in whatever he did. One of those irritating people who really couldn't fail.

Well, that wasn't *exactly* true. Hazel knew that if she told him she thought such of him, his expression would fall, he'd cast his gaze toward his feet, and he'd shake his head. He'd tell her he'd been an epic failure in things that matter a whole lot more than business. And then he'd say something like, "Thank God that He's a redeeming God."

Hazel was learning daily how right Bennett was—not that he was an epic failure but that God was and is working to redeem broken people who wrestle in their broken lives. And the work was not done yet.

The latest worries with Nathan the present proof. Hazel rubbed Bennett's back, noting the knotted tension that balled his muscles tight. "I tried Nate last night. I can try again now."

"I think he blocked me, but I can't figure out why." Bennett turned his worried gaze to meet hers. "Maybe I shouldn't have given in so easily to Chip."

"What else could you have done? He *is* their dad."

Chip. *Their* dad. The distance Bennett kept between himself and his father was notable—and sad, even to Hazel. She'd watched the way Bennett was with his mom. Their relationship was genuine and warm and full of trust—something that Bennett had told Hazel was a miracle because he'd been pretty awful to his mom for a long time. If Hazel had not met the man Bennett had been before his accident nearly two years before, she wasn't likely to believe that he could be awful.

But he could. Bennett had the capacity to be a monumental jerk. Just like Hazel had the capacity to be a stubborn idiot.

Thank You, God, that You're a redeeming God.

She slipped her hand down his arm and laced her fingers with his. "Bennett?"

As he drank in a long breath of mountain air, he turned from the view of the lake to look down at her. "I'm scared, Zel. Nate and I—we're not much different. I mean, we don't see eye to eye, and we've had a rough go at things between us when they were here, but I *know* what he's thinking. What he's feeling—especially when it comes to our dad."

"What is he feeling?"

"Resentment." Bennett winced. "Rage."

"Do you still feel that way about him?"

His gaze lowered farther, and his mouth twisted. A slow nod preceded the sagging of his shoulders. "Yeah. Most of the time, yeah, I do. I can't seem to get past it. I think I'm moving forward, and then Chip does stuff like—" A ragged huff blew from his lips.

"Like shove his kids on you, only to demand them back the minute things smooth out?"

Agony and frustration filled his expression. "Yeah. Like that."

With a half step forward, Hazel was in his arms, twining hers around his waist.

He rested his chin on the top of her head and sighed. "How can I help Nathan when I still can't wrestle this down for myself?"

"You're here, and Nathan knows that you're *for* him, and for Gemma. That matters."

"Doesn't look like it does—probably because to Nathan, it doesn't look like I'm in his corner. I just . . . let them go. Let Chip win."

Laying a palm to his chest, Hazel stepped back. "You didn't."

"I'm going to call my lawyer. There's got to be a way."

Hazel nodded. Bennett's determined jaw set in the way that declared that he wouldn't quit until he got what he wanted. At one time that sheer determination infuriated her. Now she hoped it wouldn't bend. She moved her hand from his chest to cup his jaw. "You're a good one, Benji."

That won her a small grin and a gentle kiss.

"You'll text Nathan?" he asked.

"Yeah." She stepped back and then paused. "Actually, no. I'll call him."

"He won't answer."

"I have as much stubbornness in me as you have."

"That is an understatement."

She smirked, then chuckled. "Good thing I met my match."

Seven

Isa wove her way around the tables in the dining room, wiping off crumbs from the wooden tops and straightening chairs.

"You're sure you're feeling better?" Janie's question was the third of that variety that morning. "I don't mind taking the whole day for the rest of the week. I used to do it by myself all day, every day, you know."

"I know." Isa flashed her best sunshine smile. "I'm all better now though."

"Must have been some kind of fierce cold. Sure hit you hard and fast." Janie finished layering her freshly baked cherry chocolate scones in the pastry counter near the checkout, then straightened to look at Isa. "Good thing Grady was around to help you out." And there, the woman winked.

Winked.

Isa's chest constricted as something cruel gripped her heart. "Sure. Grady was just the right person for the job." Sarcasm dripped from her tongue.

Janie frowned. "He wasn't helpful?"

"He was helpful."

"Then . . ."

"Grady is overbearing. And he thinks he's better than everyone."

"I don't think that's true. He was always nice to me—even after I ditched him to come home."

"To come back to Hunter?" Isa wanted to clap her hand over her mouth. Why was she bringing out the claws? Wasn't like Janie deserved her disdain. More like Isa probably deserved Janie's disapproval—at least a little bit. And she'd sure have it, if Janie knew all the facts about Isa's wayward choices in the recent past.

Wouldn't be long before *everyone* knew. Then what was Isa going to do?

"Yes, actually." Janie used a tone that sounded very . . . big sister-ish. Laced with mild rebuke and a call back to reality. "He was kind. Didn't make a fuss. Came to the wedding, shook Hunter's hand, gave us a gift, and wished us well."

Fire crawled up Isa's neck. "I'm sorry," she whispered. "I had no reason to say that."

"I think maybe you do have a reason—but it doesn't really have anything to do with me." Janie spread both hands against the polished blue-streaked pine. "What's the deal between you and Grady Briggs?"

Swallowing, Isa wished she'd never bumbled her way into this conversation. She shrugged and turned to wipe down a table by the front window.

"No, I don't think I'm going to accept that," Janie pushed. "You two have been silent enemies since the day you started at the café. What's the deal?"

Isa looked out the window. The summer morning couldn't have been more perfect if she'd scripted it herself. Bright sunshine crawled over the peaks to the east, rose and apricot streaking across the wakening sky. Birds chirped and sang from the swaying branches of aspen and spruce. And Luna's Main Street held still with quiet expectation.

A new day was born. Shouldn't she whisper *aleluya*, like her mother often did?

As emotion swelled upward, Isa suddenly wished she was like her mother. Calm, quiet, dignified. Peaceful. Faithful. A woman who would never have found the crisis Isa had blundered her way into. A woman Grady Briggs would like.

"Isa?"

"He doesn't like me." She rolled her fingers into the rag and squeezed hard as she fought back the tide of regret and the gaping sense of insufficiency.

"What?" Janie asked, likely because she hadn't been able to discern Isa's hoarsely whispered confession.

Isa cleared her throat. "He doesn't like me." That time she let the statement fall like it was a weight she didn't need in her life. Firmly. Then she whipped around to face Janie. "And frankly, I'm not a fan of his."

"Do you have a reason?"

"Does he?"

"I don't know—does he?"

"He thinks I'm a reckless flirt and am therefore beneath him." She walked toward the counter, then around to where Janie stood listening. She bent to retrieve the cleaning bucket from below the counter as the front bell jingled. "I think he's a sour-faced fun-hater. We are two clashes of nature, and that's all there is to it." She stood back up and caught the flashes of green and khaki near the front windows out of the corner of her eye.

Her heart sank even before she slid her attention from Janie's pained expression to the man who just entered the café.

"Sour-faced *and* a fun-hater?" Grady raised his eyebrows.

Isa swallowed. Then she replanted her stance, as if ready for a fight, and crossed her arms. "I have yet to see anything else from you."

His mouth remained firmly seamed.

Janie cleared her throat. "Coffee, Grady?"

"Thanks."

"And a scone? Huckleberry this morning."

"Have any of those pear turnovers left?"

Janie nodded. "In the kitchen. Be back in just a sec." She skedaddled from the tension swallowing the dining room, leaving Isa stuck with Grady.

After moments of heart-throbbing strain passed, Isa peeked back at him. "Is pear your favorite?" she squeaked.

He shrugged. "I like apple too." His boots clopped against the wooden floor as he strode toward the counter. "I prefer turnovers to scones."

Good to know—though there was no reason Isa should care. "You're early this morning. We haven't even officially opened yet."

"Wanted to check on you."

She glanced at the kitchen door, then leaned toward Grady to whisper. "I wasn't actually sick, you know. I don't need you to check on me."

"I know." He held her with such an intense look.

Isa couldn't decide if he was angry or . . . No. He was angry. At least irritated. When it came to her, he was always irritated.

"Denver still won't look into—"

"Leave it." Isa pushed back from the counter and strode to the coffeepot. Just as she topped a mug, Janie came through the door with a plated turnover.

"Warmed it a touch for you, Grady." Janie set the plate in front of the man.

"Thanks."

Isa passed the mug of coffee to Janie and then spun away. She pushed through the door to the kitchen without an explanation, unsure if her hands shook because of anger or something else.

Anger. It needed to be anger. Fear, or anything else, wouldn't do her any good. She had to be strong. Self-sufficient. For herself and for the baby. And most of all, so that Grady could see the truth.

She didn't need him.

EIGHT

LUNA WAS WAKING UP. Mama Bulldog had opened the front door to the Pantry and was sweeping the section of boardwalk that spanned the front of her store. Tara Crofton walked out the front door of the soon-to-open clinic, waving to MB as she moved to cross the dirt road toward Janie's. Marvin and Hiram, two of the five men Janie referred to as the "old-man coffee club," ambled side by side from the west side of town, no doubt making their way to the café.

It was time to get on with the day.

Coffee in his to-go insulated mug, Grady slid into his government-issued vehicle and aimed the truck north from Main Street. He had work to do, and he should get after it. Isa could just . . . be Isa. Janie was there, so at least someone would have eyes on the woman—and he wouldn't be forced to play spectator to Isa's insatiable flirting.

Grady winced at that.

He'd never been called sour faced. Serious, yes. Even a fun-hater—on one occasion in college that involved a date who drank way too much and his aversion to joining her in her inebriation. That hadn't hurt his feelings one bit.

But never sour faced.

Isa did tend to draw out his frown though. Maybe she had him there, from her perspective.

He wanted to shake that off. Not care. Isa was a flirt. She was a flighty, silly woman. He shouldn't care that she thought he was . . . not likable.

The nagging of it, however, was not shaking loose. Rather, he kept hearing that line running on repeat in his mind. *I think he's a sour-faced fun-hater.*

The truck bounced along the dirt road, the washboard condition indicating this section was in need of grading. Likely that wouldn't happen until fall—this section wasn't traveled much by the summer tourists. The few souls who made a home back in this section of the forest simply had to deal with bumpy roads.

He passed the turnoff that would have taken him toward Elk Lake and the Splendor. With a glance in that direction, Grady briefly wondered how married life was for Hunter and Janie. By the fresh vibe of energy and the peaceful joy that made Janie glow, Grady would wager domestic life was good.

A small pang of jealousy pinched his middle. Not for Janie specifically. Just for the obvious happiness and love that she and Hunter shared.

A hollow yearning yawned—same as it had for much of his life when he'd realized other kids had homes that were happy and full of love. Homes they actually wanted to go back to from school. Grady had ached for that since the first time he'd hidden under his bed when his stepdad had come home roaring drunk and wildly violent. Had he been five then, or six? Grady wasn't sure—but old enough not to wet his pants.

In his defense, he'd been too terrified to leave his hiding spot to use the toilet. Mom hadn't scolded him. Just whispered that she'd wash his pants and underwear and to take a quick shower before he got ready to go to school. That morning they'd crept around the house like mice around a feral cat, careful not to wake his passed-out stepdad. It became SOP for them for several years.

Way too many years.

Grady shoved back those memories and refocused on the road. Up ahead, at the small pullout near a stand of fir trees, he'd park the government vehicle, strap on his daypack, and walk the game trail he'd followed for the past six months, to check the cameras he'd set up. Hopefully, this time there would be more than a passing deer or the occasional moose on the footage. best-case scenario, he'd find a spotted skunk on a frame.

That would confirm the critters were still in the area. The BLM would be satisfied, and he could take on a permanent assignment inside one of the national parks, like he'd hoped to in the first place. He could walk away from Luna and never have to think about why Isa Romero crawled under his skin and kept his thoughts spinning like a dust devil.

He guided the truck into the narrow pullout and shifted into Park.

Was that really what he hoped?

I think he's a sour-faced fun-hater.

Enough.

He thought she was a ridiculous flirt looking for trouble, so that made them even.

She's in so much trouble.

The thought turned his gut so powerfully Grady had to grip the steering wheel to abate the sharp pain.

Snatching his daypack from the passenger seat, he ignored the turmoil of his distracting thoughts, jumped from the truck, and smacked the door shut. As he slipped his arms through the straps of the backpack, his phone chimed. He snapped the buckle at his chest together before he reached into his pocket for the cell.

This your contact?

Mitchel's text was followed by another—a picture of a small-town newspaper headline: "Woman Found Dead in Forest. Cartel Boss Suspected."

Beneath that, a black-and-white picture of a young woman—obviously the image had been taken some time before, because that pretty blonde was looking at whoever snapped that photo, smiling.

Grady's heart seized as he stared at the image, then reread the headline. *Woman Found Dead . . .* His throat closed in a thick swell of terrified panic as he gripped his phone hard. He scanned the picture of the newspaper to find a location. Lander, Wyoming.

That was south by quite a bit. But really, distance meant nothing to a man as depraved and psychotic as Francisco. Not to mention his connections. The man had a web thicker than a black widow—which was why he was able to keep his hands clean and remain like a ghost.

Why was he suddenly going after young women and being sloppy about it?

Grady rubbed his jaw with his left hand and studied the pretty girl in the picture. So full of life. Now she was dead.

Could have been Isa. Was it supposed to have been Isa?

This woman looked nothing like Isa—there was no way Cisco had mistaken the blonde for Victoria, whom he'd been searching for.

With two fingers, Grady made the newspaper article larger and skimmed through the details. There weren't many—just that the woman was dead, there was some kind of unexplained tie-in with the cartel, and the case was under further investigation. None of that was particularly helpful. He gripped the phone so he could text Mitchel back.

Not my contact. Why is Lopez a suspect?

Can't say too much. You're sure this isn't your contact? Is she safe?

I'm sure.

She's still with you?

She's safe.

Grady looked over his shoulder, back toward town. His heart throbbed hard. *Breathe. Think.* He swallowed. He couldn't think, not through the frenzied fear ripping through his mind, vaulting his pulse, and making his hands shake.

"She's safe," he repeated. "She's with Janie."

That was right. He'd just seen them together this morning, working at the café. And Cisco had moved on. Apparently south, all the way to Lander. Or had that been Francisco Senior's work?

Grady hated the feeling of having no control. No say. Only able to cower—to hide under his bed while a terrorist thrashed his world.

He'd outgrown that terrified little boy. At the age of fourteen, he had taken the situation in hand and made sure the monster who had made their home hell left and never came back. He'd kept his mother safe.

Now . . . now he'd keep Isa safe from the monster who hunted her life. He would.

"I will." He swore it to God right there in the forest. And once Grady made a promise, there was no going back.

Janie stayed at the café for the day. It had been her plan to do so anyway. They didn't have any bookings at the lodge for several more weeks, and while she and Hunter had spent most of their time since their marriage getting the new building ready for guests, most of the work had been done.

Something felt off at the café, with Isa. When she'd said so to Hunter as they'd snuggled in front of a fire several evenings back, he'd kissed her temple and wrapped her in a warm hug. "Go spend some time there," he'd said. "Everything is coming together here."

"Yeah?" She'd leaned back to meet his gentle look in the flickering light of the fire. "You sure? I'd like to spend a week down there, see if I can get a feel for what's going on."

"Of course I'm sure—on the condition that you make your way back up here in the evenings." Hunter leaned in to kiss her nose. "I rather like having you in my bed at night, and I'm selfish enough to say I don't want to sacrifice that."

She had blushed, kissed his mouth, and whispered, "Of course."

Marriage was good. Why the heck had they waited so long?

While that thought provoked a grin, Janie pulled the sheet pan loaded with potato wedges from the oven. She would serve them alongside the spicy crusted chicken breasts and green beans for dinner tonight. It would be a deviation from the typical Tuesday evening stew, but since she was in town anyway, this would give her a chance to try out one of her selected evening meals for the Splendor. The response from her café patrons would help her gauge if she was on the right track with her meal plans.

"Will this become a regular on the menu?" Isa seasoned the roasted green beans with a dusting of salt and onion powder.

"No, it's more involved for what we do down here."

Isa nodded, though relief was evident in her face.

"Has it been okay, you running things on your own?"

Isa brightened. Maybe too much. "Of course. I got this, Janie. Don't worry—I won't break your café."

"It's a lot. And not having Gemma here to help is a big loss. I worked from four a.m. to ten p.m. most days, so I know there's so much that goes into it. This place was my dream, so I put in the work and time, but I know it's different when someone else owns the business."

Isa swallowed. Then she shrugged before she started plating chicken breasts and beans. "It is a lot—but we worked pretty hard at the ranch too, so that kind of commitment isn't new to me."

"But the ranch was yours."

"It's my parents'."

"Okay." Using a lifter, Janie added a pile of roasted potatoes to the plates Isa had already started. "I can start looking for help for you. That's all I'm saying, Isa. The Harmond girl might be interested if—"

"Like I said, I got this." A hint of panic tinged Isa's voice.

Janie set the sheet pan on the counter and dropped the lifter onto the pile of potatoes. "Something just feels off here, Isa. Why didn't you call me when you got sick?"

Isa licked her lips and didn't raise her face to look Janie in the eye. "Grady said he'd cover for me." Now she straightened and pasted on a smile. "You're still a honeymooner, basically. I didn't want to—"

"I need you to be straight with me."

Isa pressed her lips together firmly and covered her stomach as though there was pain in her gut. "I'm sorry. I should have called you, Janie. I just—" She stopped, swallowed, then drew a long breath. "I really need this job. I need this . . . place. Please don't reconsider—I'm grateful to be here, that you've given me a place to stay and work to do."

"I'm not talking about taking any of that away." Why was Isa panicking? "Isa, people get sick. That happens. I'm just saying that maybe I need to find you some help for the café."

Again, Isa shook her head. "I'm good now. And if I get sick again, I'll call you first thing. Promise."

Janie studied the woman. She looked tired. Maybe a little pale? Was it this conversation that had her appearing a little peaked? Seemed like there had been a handful of times throughout the day that Isa seemed to not feel the best. Once she had abruptly and swiftly scooted to the kitchen and up the stairs to her apartment. Like she was sick.

What was Janie supposed to do? Demand the woman tell her she was ill? Like that would work. "You really promise?"

"Cross my heart." Isa smiled one of her sugary sunshine grins, which usually gained her some pretty good tips.

Janie sighed. She wasn't convinced, but there was nothing else to say. And they had meals to serve.

But maybe Grady could shed some light on whatever had happened.

Nine

Grady leaned on the steering wheel, his right arm pressed against the top of it, as he blinked against sleep. The drive to Bozeman had gone by in a blur of high emotion and determination. But now that he had what he'd gone for . . .

He glanced away from the beam of white light his headlights poured out onto the highway and toward the small bag sitting on the passenger seat.

Maybe this was insane.

A small tremor shivered through his core. It was crazy. But it was also the best plan.

Isn't it?

The whole day, from the moment he'd promised God he'd keep Isa safe, he'd spun through different options, each time offering the ideas up to heaven for inspection. This one . . .

This one stuck. So firm and fast, he thought that maybe it hadn't been his idea in the first place.

Another glance at the bag. His gut clenched. What if Isa said no?

Not acceptable. He'd make her see, make her understand.

Because once Grady made a promise, he was going to keep it.

Isa snuggled under the weight of her thick burnt-orange fleece blanket, savoring the softness against the skin of her shoulders. She'd always been one for touch. The silk of her mother's church dresses. The warm velvet of a kitten's neck. The sleek smoothness of freshly polished leather. The thrilling electricity of a caress on her skin . . .

She shut her eyes and banished that last thought, along with the memories that it provoked. Had she not been so desperate to be held, to be wanted, she wouldn't be in the precarious situation she was in. Some cravings led to trouble, and she sure should have known better.

She *had* known better.

Regret snaked through her with a chilling sting. Isa pulled the warmth of her blanket tighter as she hung her head.

"I'm sorry," she whispered. Moisture lined her lashes. "I am so sorry. Please help me."

Softly, gently, a tiny spout of hope emerged. God *had* been helping already. Isa focused her thoughts, and her emotions, on that, rather than letting both run into chaos. Allowing the chaos to rule had been what had gotten her into this mess in the first place. Chaos and rebellion. That stopped now—it had to stop now.

She pressed her palm against her belly.

There was so much at stake now. She had to zero in on that unfurrowing speck of hope.

Whispers of her mother's voice eased the pain of her regret, filling the void of helplessness in her mind. *Dios mío, tú eres todo bondad, ten compasión de mí.*

With practiced ease that was as natural as breathing, Isa translated her mother's recitation to English.

"My God, you are all goodness." She spoke aloud the psalm as a prayer. "Have mercy on me."

Reaching for the Bible José had given her—the one she'd recently been more dedicated to reading—she opened to Psalms. Which one was it? Shutting her eyes, she reached for the memory again. Mama often tagged her memory verses with a location. That was for sure a psalm, but which one?

Isa fingered through the pages, scanning the first lines of poetry. A soft knock at her door interrupted her search. With one finger against a page, she looked up and sucked in a breath.

It was after ten. Who would be at her door this late?

"Isa?"

At the same time, the now-familiar soft, low voice both eased her fear and shot a spike of adrenaline through her veins. Leaning forward to set her Bible onto the coffee table, Isa pushed up off the sofa, set the warmth of her blanket aside, and padded toward the door, her socks muffling the sound of her footsteps.

She unlocked the deadbolt and opened the door a crack. "Are you lost, Grady?"

"No." His gaze met hers with that intensity that made her feel somehow seen and intimidated.

"It's late."

"I need to talk to you."

"Again, Mr. Briggs, it's late. After ten, and I have to be up at four."

"Please, Isa."

The humble quality of that plea softened the immediate resentment she always felt in his presence. She looked him over, catching a glimpse of a small gift bag he held in his left hand. What was this man doing now? Deciding that curiosity would keep her from sleep, she nodded and eased the door open.

Grady followed her into the apartment, shutting the door before he turned to face her again.

"What is it?"

He swallowed. Took another step toward her. "I can't get you out of my mind."

Sucking in a breath, Isa pulled her shoulders straighter. Was that . . . was this some sort of . . . romantic gesture? From the sour-faced fun-hater who thought she was nothing but a worthless flirt? She felt her brows fold inward as she shook her head. "Grady, what are you doing?"

"I'm worried about you."

Oh. Of course that was all this was. "As you can see, I'm fine."

He shook his head while he reached into his back pocket and retrieved his phone. With a few taps of his thumb, he had something pulled up on the screen, and then he passed it to her. "One of my contacts sent this to me today."

Contacts? As in the FBI? Ice washed over her body. She watched Grady's face, finding his scowl had returned and was deepening with every breath. Lowering her attention, she fixed it on his cell and read, "Woman Found Dead in Forest. Cartel Boss Suspected."

Her heart froze in her chest. She squeezed the phone hard before it slipped out of her trembling fingers. "Where?"

"The Wind River range in Wyoming."

That was several hours south of Luna—farther from her home in Bozeman. "Who was she?"

"I don't know. There aren't many details about it at all. The woman didn't look like you."

A slow breath of mild relief escaped from her lungs. But then understanding dawned—if this woman was killed by one of the Lopezes or their lackeys, that meant Isa wasn't the only one they were after. It also meant that they weren't messing around.

"Does it say why they suspect the cartel?"

"No." Grady reached for the phone and eased it out of her shaking hands. "But there must be something compelling for my contact to forward this on to me. He asked if you were safe."

"He knows about me?"

"Only that I have a contact who has information about Francisco, and that you're female. He thought maybe . . ."

"Maybe this woman was your contact." She gulped. "That she was me."

Grady nodded while he pocketed his phone. Then he narrowed the space between them even farther, going so far as to close a soft hold on her shoulder.

His hand was rough and warm and strong against her skin. Isa pushed away the mild thrill of his touch. It was just Grady, the sour-faced fun-hater, and it meant nothing. She had to learn not to make nothings into somethings.

"Isa." Her whispered name from his lips sounded like . . .

She squeezed her eyes shut against the headiness she shouldn't feel. *Oh, girl. Stop.*

"Marry me."

Her heart came to a dead stop, and she shot her gaze up to him. "What?"

"I swear I'll keep you and the baby safe."

Drawing in a breath was impossible. Had she heard him right? "What?"

"I can give you a new name. I'll claim this baby as my own." His hand left her shoulder, and he fiddled with the gift bag. From it he withdrew a small black box. And then he was lowering onto a bended knee. "I'm not proposing a fake marriage, Isa. I can't—if I promise to be your husband, I won't cross my fingers and take it back. That's not who I am. I'm asking you to marry me, before God, for the rest of our lives."

Isa stared at him, her mind wild with thoughts she couldn't make sense of. Everything in his expression said he was entirely serious. And then her gaze lowered to his outstretched hands.

A ring. Grady held out a small diamond ring nestled in that black box.

The world around her whirled in a disordered blend of fear, hurt, and—heaven bless it!—hope? No, not that.

She was horrified.

No, that wasn't right either.

"You think we should—" She didn't dare say it out loud. If she did, the idea would latch on like a grappling hook. How desperate did that make her, that she would want to marry a man who only ever frowned at her? Who looked down on her? Who made her feel . . .

At the moment? Seen and valuable. So much that he would sacrifice the hope of finding the love of his life to make sure she was safe.

Who did that? Why would Grady do that for her?

She had to think straight. Isa eased a step back, shaking her head. "The Lopezes don't know my name. And they already came here looking for me—and left. This isn't—"

"This woman is *dead*." Grady tapped the phone in his shirt pocket. "Isa, they know you're from Bozeman, and they are relentless. How long do you think it will take them to find out who you really are? Do you really think they won't come back looking for you?"

Isa's throat swelled. A tear flicked from her lashes. "You don't want to marry me."

"I told you, I can't get you out of my mind." He took her hand and pulled her closer. "I need to know that you're safe."

She tugged on the hand holding hers, and Grady stood back up. Her lips quivered as she shook her head. "You don't even like me."

The fingers still gripping hers squeezed. "Not true." He shifted to take the ring out of the box and slip it on her left ring finger. "I'm asking you to marry me."

"But . . ." She choked on the breathless word and swiped at the tears seeping from her eyes. This wasn't how this moment should go. For either of them. He was supposed to propose to a woman who stirred his heart, one who he found worthy of his love and devotion. One who made him smile. And she . . .

She would never be that woman.

Lifting her left hand, she stared at that small diamond. He'd bought her a ring? What would drive a man to do such a thing for a woman he could barely stand? She twisted the band, working it off her finger.

Grady closed both hands over hers, stopping her from removing the ring. "Isa."

"You can't marry me." She bit her lip, willing the emotion out of her voice. Then she lifted her face and met his waiting gaze. "You can't do this. I won't let you. Marry someone you love. Marry someone you can make a life with, who you'll be happy with."

"I believe when two people decide to make it work, they can make it work."

"I didn't say marry someone you can make it work with."

"I can give you a new name. I can take care of you and the baby." He pulled her hands to his chest and pressed them there. "I want you safe. I *need* you to be safe."

If he told her he loved her, would that be more breathtaking?

A fresh batch of tears flooded her eyes. "Don't make this so hard."

"Just say yes." A wispy, teasing smile peeked at the corner of his mouth. "That can't be that hard."

Isa drew in quaking breath. With her lips pressed firm to stem the trembling, she gave him the only answer she could.

Ten

Isa had barely slept, so getting up fifteen minutes early wasn't hard. The surprising part—the mildly breathtaking part—was hearing a soft knock on the back door to the alley five minutes after she'd flipped the kitchen lights on.

Her heart fluttered and then raced as she guessed who was behind that light rap. Even so, she cautiously cracked the door open, to find the man rubbing his neck while waiting in the deep shadows of predawn.

"Morning," he rasped, the low, unused quality of his early morning voice sparking an unqualified thrill through her veins.

"Grady," she whispered. "It's not even four."

"I know." He held her stare. Then nodded toward her, as if to say *Let me in*. Only it wasn't bully-ish.

Isa pulled the door open, clinging to the handle because she wasn't exactly sure what to do. The conclusion of the previous day—not even twelve hours past—still pressed heavily on her. Had she made the right choice?

Closing the door and turning to face him, doubt swirled relentlessly, causing her tummy to clench.

It seemed to be the only good choice she had. Even so, her pulse shouldn't throb as if this was some kind of spell-binding scene between lovers. He was just Grady, the fun-hater. She was just Isa, the massive screw-up. He was Grady, the Incredible Sulk. She was Isa, the Reckless Flirt. They would never be lovers at the heart level. They would be lucky to carve out a respectful friendship. Which made his proposal . . .

What? A sacrifice?

He'd only felt compelled to protect her—unreasonably, she might add. That was where this story ended.

Grady had made it to the counter, where he'd glanced at the sheet pan she'd managed to set out before he'd knocked.

"I couldn't sleep." With a slow, hesitant pivot, he turned to face her.

"I didn't get much sleep either."

He took a step toward her. "I wanted to make sure you didn't change your mind."

One step nearer became two, then three. A few more and there he was, in front of her. Near enough she could make out the kick of his heartbeat against the crispness of his uniform shirt. Enough for her to drink in the sweet crispness of forest with the deep, almost sensuous touch of saffron that clung to him. Near enough for her to get lost in the flecks of dark brown in his amber eyes.

A shiver washed over her shoulders as she momentarily imagined that long-held look meant something more tender than a stubborn resolve.

"I haven't," she whispered.

His steady gaze shifted from her eyes toward her mouth. Would he kiss her? Did he even want to?

Why would he want to? This wasn't a romance. His offer had been a concoction of pity and an absurd amount of overprotective instincts.

But why, then, had he taken her hand in his?

The sound of the door latch rattling, immediately followed by the whoosh of it opening, startled Isa from her dreamy stupor. Janie swept through the black entry and into the bright kitchen light, her denim jacket halfway off before she turned from shutting the door to spot Isa and Grady.

Grady. And herself. Standing near each other, face to face. Hands still . . . together.

"Uh—" Janie ceased all motion, one arm still stuck in a half-folded sleeve. "Isa . . ." Her brow folded as she shifted her look to Grady. "Grady?"

Isa's heart hit a hard stop and then immediately set off in a sprint. She swallowed, glancing up at Grady. He was ready for that look, meeting her eyes with a calm steadiness and a silent question. *Ready?*

No. Was he? What were they thinking?

His hand squeezed, and she felt the odd coolness of that ring.

He bought me a ring. The odd wonder of that still reverberated through her heart.

Lips parted, Janie studied them while slowly untangling herself from the denim jacket. "What's going on here?"

"Good morning, Janie." Grady spoke with a quiet calmness.

"Um, good morning?" Janie hung up her jacket, then returned her attention right back to Grady and Isa. "Everything . . . okay?"

"Everything is good." Did his voice just crack? Pretty sure that sounded like a voice crack.

Janie's right brow lifted. "Isa?"

Isa summoned a smile. "Morning, Boss. Didn't expect you this early."

"I see that."

"Grady just got here, like, two minutes before you did."

"Interesting." Janie tipped her head, as if dealing with a child caught being naughty. "Why is Grady here at four o'clock in the morning?"

"Couldn't sleep, and I knew that Isa would be up."

"So naturally you came to see her." Janie walked over to the small coffeepot that held a fresh brew Isa had started first thing. She poured a mug and took a sip.

"Naturally." Grady looked down at Isa. "Any man would want to see his fiancée as soon as possible."

Coffee sprayed from Janie's lips. "I'm sorry." She spluttered while she reached for the nearest dish towel. "What?"

Grady lifted Isa's hand, displaying the ring he'd given her, and then slipped his arm around her waist. "I proposed to Isa last night."

If incredulous had a face in the dictionary, it would be Janie's. "You . . ." She stared at Grady, shook her head, then looked at Isa. "You're engaged?"

"Yes," Isa said breathlessly. Nice touch, there. She looked up to Grady and fixed a sweet grin for good measure.

"You're getting married?"

Grady held Isa's look, playing surprisingly well the part of a man enamored. "That's usually what happens after two people get engaged."

"To *each other*?"

"Janie." Grady used his all-business voice—the one that Isa found demeaning. Nice to know he used it on other people occasionally. "You're being silly."

"When did this happen?"

"I just told you, last night."

"No." She waved at the pair of them. "When did you stop . . . loathing each other?"

They responded simultaneously.

"I never loathed Grady."

"I didn't loathe Isa."

Janie scowled. "There was most certainly some strong dislike."

Isa swallowed.

"Fighting attraction." Grady kept that firm no-nonsense voice on hand. "You know a little bit about that, don't you? How long did it take you to finally realize you were still in love with Hunter?"

Janie's lips snapped shut. Then she crossed her arms. "That was different. Hunter and I had history."

"Are you saying you don't approve?"

Isa's heart shrank at Grady's question. What if it mattered to him if Janie didn't approve?

What if he called it off?

Likely that would be the sane thing to do. She wouldn't be able to blame him. After all, Janie hadn't been wrong. Grady had right near loathed her. And he'd frustrated her. But he'd offered her shelter—and a life for this baby who hadn't asked for the mess she was bringing it into. The thought of him changing his mind—

"Not at all, Grady. Isa." Janie's arms relaxed to her side, and then she cracked a half smile. "I'm sorry, guys." A small chuckle shook her shoulders. "I'm dumbstruck. But if you're happy, I'm happy for you. In fact, I hope you'll let me throw you an engagement party."

Grady's arm around her tightened. They hadn't really discussed how this was all going to play out. She felt his attention land on her for a moment.

"I'm not sure there will be a need for that."

Isa met his eyes again. Hesitancy bled through his expression. He rolled his lips together, and it seemed that he was apologizing for something in that small pause. Then he looked back at Janie. "We're planning a pretty short engagement."

They were? Of course they were. This wasn't a normal engagement—and it wouldn't be a normal marriage. Just . . . not a pretend one either.

A flurry of panic gusted through her middle. How on earth were she and Grady going to figure out how to be together in all the ways that a husband and wife were together? And not just . . . in the bedroom. There was the intimacy of everyday life. Waking up in the same space. Sharing a bathroom. Sifting through the reality of mood changes, illnesses, job demands, and then . . . becoming parents.

They barely knew each other. How was this going to work?

I believe when two people are determined to make it work, they can.

"I see . . ." Janie sounded suspicious. Could she guess this was a facade? "How soon were you planning to tie the knot?"

Isa swallowed against that phrase. It conjured up an image of Grady heading to the stocks and made her feel awful.

Grady didn't answer. Up to this moment, Isa had leaned hard on him to navigate this labyrinth. Now he wanted her to fill in the gap?

She had no idea what to say. Likely he hoped she'd say they wanted to elope on Grady's next weekend off—which she hadn't a clue when that was. But she couldn't. The girlish heart in her wouldn't let her.

"We still have some details to work out." Teeth sinking into her bottom lip, she managed to look at only Grady's chest, because she didn't want to see the disapproval sure to be in his eyes.

His arm slipped from her back. "Right." Then he touched her elbow. "I'll see you after work." He took one step toward the back door, then paused. As if remembering they were supposed to be in love, he turned back, leaned down, and pressed a light kiss to Isa's cheek.

If selling this was his aim, he'd missed the bull's-eye.

Isa wilted inside, not because she was afraid Janie wasn't buying this, though likely the woman wasn't, but because Grady could barely bring himself to peck her face the way the French would say hello to a distant friend.

This marriage might be lonely. But at least he would be there to protect her. And more importantly, at least her child would have a father.

That mattered more than the fleeting thrill of romance. It had to.

Eleven

JANIE SWEPT THE ENTRYWAY at the front, her mind still circling around what she'd walked into that morning. The early crowd and the late-breakfast bunch had been in and gone by then, but though the hours had been full of customers and kitchen work, Janie couldn't steer her mind away from one thought.

Grady and Isa. Engaged!

What was going on with that? If one asked anyone in Luna about the relationship status between those two, the response would range from *they hate each other* to *fire and ice don't mix.*

Engaged? Had she missed something?

Sure, maybe she had been pretty wrapped up in her own story—having just gotten married herself. But to miss Grady falling in love with Isa? She must have had her head sunk in the pond up by the Splendor!

She bent to whisk the dirt into the dustpan, chuckling. Wait until she told Hunter. He wouldn't believe it.

The door at her back swung open, the small bell tinkling. Standing, Janie turned with a grin. "Ella Hammond." Janie's grin grew full. "I haven't seen you all summer. How are you?"

"Um, okay." Ella tucked a lock of hair behind her ear.

Janie's wide grin dimmed at the girl's lack of enthusiasm. "Missing the snow?"

"Yeah, I guess. It'll be nice to get back on the skis this winter."

"I'll bet you keep in shape other ways."

She shrugged. "I run. It's not as fun."

"Do you still shoot?"

"Yeah. Every day."

"You should come up to Elk Lake sometime. Hunter and Hazel have a nice range set up, and not having Nathan up there to practice has been kind of a bummer."

Ella winced. Looked at her feet and twisted her hands together. "Yeah, it's been a bummer not to have him here." She peeked back at Janie. "I was wondering if you knew how I could get in touch with Nate's brother."

"With Bennett?"

"Right. Sorry. I couldn't remember his name."

"Sure. I can call him right now, if you'd like."

She bit her lip. "Do . . . do you think maybe he'd have time to come over? I need to talk to him."

Wow, this seemed ominous. "I can sure ask him." Janie leaned the broom against a table and turned to take the dustpan to the trash. After she dumped it, she grabbed her phone from the shelf beneath the cash register. "Is there something I can help you with, if Bennett isn't available?"

"No." Ella swallowed. "I'm sorry. I just really need to speak with Nate's brother. It's not anything, you know, weird. It's important though."

"Okay." Curiosity spiraled through Janie as she scanned through her contacts. Goodness, but it'd been an interesting day. Bennett Crofton scrolled onto her screen. She tapped it twice, and the call went out.

"Janie?"

"Yeah, it's me. Do you have a few minutes free?"

"I can make some time. Something wrong?"

"No—well, I'm not really sure. Ella Hammond just came into the café wondering if I could get ahold of you for her. She says she needs to talk to you, that it's important."

"Ella? Nathan's friend?"

"That's the girl."

"Has she heard from Nathan?"

"I don't know, Bennett." Janie turned so her back was to the dining room, and lowered her voice. "She seems kind of nervous. I asked her if there was something I could help her with, but she says she really needs to speak with you."

"Okay. I'll be there in just a few minutes."

"Thanks." She pivoted back to face Ella, flashing her a smile and a thumbs-up. "I have a pear turnover and a couple of huckleberry muffins left. Which would you like?"

"Ask Ella what she wants—tell her I'm buying."

Energy coursed through Bennett's body as he jogged the two blocks from his house to Main. From there, he hit the boardwalk that ran along the shops, passing his mom's clinic and the Pantry. Then he veered left and bounded to the front door of Janie's Café. He was winded by the time he passed through the entrance, but not so much from the short jaunt as much as the sense that something was really, really wrong.

He hadn't heard from Nathan in ten days. Just this morning, when Hazel had called to say good morning, she'd said that Nate hadn't answered her text. Worry had laced her voice. Bennett got it if Nathan was ignoring him because the kid was mad at him . . . to be honest, Bennett was mad at himself too. He should have tried hard to keep the kids in Luna with him.

But Nate ignoring Hazel? That was alarming. His younger brother had formed a tight bond with Zel—the kid pretty much adored her.

Running his fingers through his dark hair, Bennett spotted Ella sitting at the corner booth. A pair of muffins sat on the middle of the table in front of her, both untouched. Bennett slowed his gait, straightened his shoulders, and fixed an easy expression on his face. Though he couldn't imagine what else Ella would want to talk to him about, he didn't think freaking her out because he was freaked out was a great approach.

"Hi, Ella." He slid onto the seat across from her. "I see you went for the muffins. Good choice."

The girl attempted a smile. Didn't succeed. "Hi, Mr. Crofton."

Bennett gestured to the food. "You didn't need to wait for me. Help yourself."

She shook her head. "I'm not really hungry." With a visible swallow, she ducked her head and drew a long breath.

"Everything okay?" Clearly it wasn't.

Ella bit her bottom lip.

"Ella, is this about Nathan?"

When her face tipped up, her cheeks were pale, and her wide eyes sheened.

Bennett leaned forward. No use even trying to disguise his angst. "Have you heard from him?"

With a trembling bottom lip, Ella nodded.

A deep sigh rushed from Bennett's chest. "That's good. I'm glad to hear he's talking to someone."

Ella's mouth twisted to the side. "I think . . ." She looked down at her hands. After a pair of heartbeats went by, she peeked back up. "I think you should come with me."

Bennett's heart stalled. "Where are we going?"

With both palms against the table, Ella pushed up from her chair. She picked up both muffins, then met Bennett's gaze. "Please, Mr. Crofton. Will you come?"

Though a zing of caution flashed through him about going to some undisclosed location with a teenage girl, Bennett nodded. "Let me get Janie."

"Don't."

"Ella, I'm a grown man, and you're a vulnerable girl. I can't just go wandering around alone with you. It's not safe for either of us. Whatever this is, Janie cares about Nathan too. And she's trustworthy."

After a moment of hesitation, she nodded. "Okay." Shifting from one foot to the other, Ella grew more pensive by the minute.

Bennett poked his head into the kitchen, finding Janie chopping onions for tonight's dinner. "Janie, can you spare a few minutes?"

She set aside her knife and turned around. "Sure. Isa, you got this, right?"

Isa continued to roll out dough for noodles. "Sure thing, Boss."

Bennett stepped backward and waited by the bar counter near the register. Was that a note of weariness in Isa? Whatever it was, it wasn't Isa's normal cheer, nor had the young woman turned around to flash a smile at Bennett. Maybe Isa needed to see Bennett's mom—it'd been over a week since Isa had been sick and Grady had taken over the café.

Man, weird things going on all around.

Janie swept through the swinging door. "What do you need?"

"Ella wants to take me to show me something." He clamped a meaningful look on Janie. "I thought it'd be best if it wasn't just the two of us."

Janie glanced past Bennett at Ella. "Of course." She untied her apron, draped it on a stool at the counter, and pulled the hairnet off her head.

Side by side Bennett and Janie walked to the door, where Ella waited.

"Lead on, kid," Bennett said.

Ella didn't even try to smile. She pushed through the door and walked down the boardwalk to the east end of Main. There, she pivoted right, which took them toward the highway that ran south of Luna. After five minutes of brisk walking, she paused at the two-lane highway only long enough to make sure cars weren't coming, then jogged across the road.

During the silent trek, curiosity mixed with Bennett's looming concern. Why were they heading toward the creek? Why couldn't Ella just tell him whatever it was that was clearly upsetting her?

They reached the trailhead for Elk Creek Meadow and started on the western fork.

"Ella, how long is this hike going to take?"

"Shh. We're almost there."

Where? Bennett and Janie exchanged a puzzled glance.

Ella took a hard left, cutting into a tight stand of evergreen trees. Bennett paused, and Janie stopped behind him.

"This has been one strange day," Janie said.

Bennett glanced back at her, ready to agree, and also curious what else had happened. But before he could ask, Ella poked her head out from the trees.

"Guys?" she said.

"Where are you taking us?"

She eyed them, drew another long breath, and then emerged from the shelter of boughs, dragging something behind her.

Not something. Someone.

Air emptied from Bennett's lungs at the sight of the kid wearing all black, including a dark stocking cap.

"Ella, you promised." Anger—a familiar tone—punched his voice.

Bennett didn't care. Not one ounce. He reached forward and grabbed the boy's arm, tugging him into a tight hug.

"Nate," he breathed. As adrenaline gave way to reality, Bennett's muscles trembled in the arms that held his little brother. He squeezed his eyes shut. "Thank God."

Twelve

THE LONG, SLEEPLESS NIGHT was catching up with her. Isa paused before she pushed through the swinging door that separated the kitchen and dining room, pressing her face into her shoulder to cover her long yawn.

The ring pressed with an unfamiliar weight against her finger as she held a tray full of soup bowls and bread. She looked at the food ready to serve, and hunger growled in her belly.

Good grief. She'd just eaten a bowlful of homemade chicken noodle soup less than an hour before. At this rate, she'd be showing by tomorrow. Another reason to follow Grady's lead on this marriage thing, and get it done quick.

But . . .

Oh, there were so many buts when it came to that. Isa stopped the stream of arguments before they could break loose. There were tables of people out there waiting for their supper. She had work to do.

Fixing her smile—the one she used to earn the best tips—Isa turned, pressed her shoulder into the door, and leaned to pass through to the dining room. A soft hum of voices filled the front of the café, a now-familiar harmony of conversations scattered throughout the space. Isa set her destination for the table at the front window, where three familiar faces waited for their meals.

When had Nathan come back to Luna?

Isa tucked away her curiosity and braced the weight of her serving tray against the table. "Three bowls of soup, side salads, and a basket of Janie's famous homemade rolls." Isa grinned as she passed out the food. When she handed Nathan's bowl to him, she winked. "It's good to see you again, Nate. Back for a visit?"

The boy looked . . . uncomfortable. "Yeah, sort of."

His retreat made Isa want to try harder to unearth his smile. Nathan wasn't the friendliest of guys, but he hadn't always been a hunk of ice, either.

"You look pretty pleased to be back," she teased.

He winced, and Bennett cleared his throat. "This looks good, Isa. Thanks."

Isa felt his disapproval and knew she should leave. But not having won at least one smile from anyone at the table rubbed against her need for approval.

"Warm soup should go a good ways to fix a long day." Isa hugged the now-empty tray against her.

Hazel lifted her face, meeting Isa with a wary look. Then she caught the gleam of the ring flickering on Isa's hand. Her brows lifted and lips parted.

"I better get going," Isa said before Hazel could ask. "Lots of hungry people in Luna tonight." She smiled the sort of smile that stretched so wide and fake that it hurt, then spun on her heel.

"Nathan, you can't stay mad at Ella. Clearly she cares about you."

Nathan's jaw tightened as he turned his face toward the window. A span of silent tension settled at the table. Bennett curved both hands around the half-empty mug of coffee in front of him, squeezing the ceramic while the adrenaline and frustration pulsed through him.

Beside him, Hazel shifted and cleared her throat. "Nate, if you want to be treated like a grown-up, you've got to handle this like a grown-up. The silent treatment isn't your best option."

Nate shifted his glare from the windowpane to Hazel, who sat stoic, not flinching as she met his javelin of anger.

And the wonder between those two continued. Tension drained from Bennett as he watched his little brother's expression morph from teenager resentment to manly thoughtfulness and then, heartbreakingly, to a young man pummeled.

"We want to help you, buddy." Bennett pushed one hand toward Nathan, letting his palm rest on the table just short of touching the kid.

Nathan shrugged, his chin dropping toward his chest. "I know. But there's nothing you can do."

"That's not true."

"Yeah, it is." His blue eyes flashed with challenge as he looked back to Bennett. "If there was something you could do, why didn't you do it in May?"

The shot pierced Bennett square in the heart. He'd known he should have fought Chip on this. He should have tried harder.

Swallowing, Bennett nodded. "I know you're mad about going back to Chicago. Frankly, I'm not happy about it either."

"But there's nothing we can do, right?" Nathan sounded like a twelve-year-old. Snarky, but underneath the disrespect ran a deep wound. "He's my dad, so . . ."

"Have you talked to him?" Hazel asked.

"Who? My dad?" Nathan's fists both curled into tight fists. "I tried. He doesn't listen. He doesn't even know if I'm there or not because he's so wrapped up in his work, so why would he bother to listen? Case in point, I've been gone for four days. Think he's noticed?"

Hazel shot Bennett a glance that asked if that was true.

Bennett ran a hand through his hair as he sat back hard. Yes, sadly, he could believe it. He'd not had a call or text from Chip saying that something was wrong—that he couldn't find Nathan.

"How did you manage it?" Bennett asked, fighting to mask his festering resentment toward their father.

Nathan shrugged. "Wasn't that hard. Told Mom I was hanging with a friend for the weekend and asked her for a couple of Benjamins so I could buy some new kicks, which she didn't think twice about. Ditched my phone at school, caught a bus, and away we go."

"I knew you were smart and could handle yourself," Hazel said.

Bennett cast a silent warning at her. He wasn't sure she should be encouraging Nathan's independence like this.

Bennett let Hazel's comment go unaddressed. "What about Gemma?"

"She knows where I am." Nathan eased back against the seat. "After all this time, she's turned out to be not so bad. She promised not to tell."

"Why would she do that?"

"It's one thing she and I can agree on. Going back to Chicago sucks. We didn't want to in the first place, and every week there has been crap."

"Why is it crap? I mean, at least for Gemma? She had friends and liked it there."

"Turns out her friends are jerks—they moved on while we were here, and they don't care that she's home. And even if that wasn't true, watching Dad and Mom sucks. It's like being forced to watch a bad soap. Not interested, thanks."

"What do you mean?"

"They're done with each other."

"How do you know that?"

"Dad's clearly got something going with some young intern working for his company. Calls her his *future investment*, but we all know he's not talking about his company. Pretty sick if you ask me—she's like maybe ten years older than me, at the most." Nathan raised his brows and looked at Bennet. "That would make her younger than you, right?"

Bennett worked to douse the fiery anger flaring toward his dad. Man, it hadn't been enough to ditch him and his mom back when Chip had decided that he wasn't a pastor, wasn't a Christian, and didn't want to be his dad? Now he had to go for a rerun?

Done with the wife and kids. Wash, rinse, repeat.

"And Mom . . ." Fresh hurt made him wince. "She spends a lot of time talking to someone in Italy. I looked through her phone log last week. His name is Enzo. They talk or text at least a dozen times a day. He calls her *Vita mia*." Nathan's expression twisted into something painful. "I looked it up—it means *my life*. And Mom"—he swallowed hard—"she calls him her *new hope.*"

And there it was—the daytime drama that shouldn't be Nathan and Gemma's real life. *God, why?* Another reminder of the brokenness that surrounded him. Brokenness that had scarred his life and that had, for a time, defined his own wrecked course.

Bennett bowed his head and lifted a silent prayer. *Not Nathan. Not Gemma. Save them . . .*

"You're going to send me back, aren't you?" Nathan's harsh whisper was part resentment, part resignation.

As his vision blurred, Bennett glanced at Hazel. Her pleading eyes met his, and he knew exactly what she wanted him to say.

No. A hard, unflinching no. And he wanted to. The last thing he wanted was to send Nathan back into the maze of chaos that was their father's selfish life.

But what was the right thing to do?

Again, Bennett squeezed his eyes shut, and while Hazel's hand gripped his beneath the table, he prayed for wisdom.

"Please, Bennett. Let me stay with you."

"I want to, Nate." Bennett leaned forward. "Honest. I didn't want you and Gemma to leave in the first place."

Nathan swallowed and looked toward his lap. When he lifted his face again, the face of a wounded kid had hardened into the scowl of a young man resolved. "I'll just run again if you send me back. Next time you won't find me."

"We're not the enemy," Hazel said.

"Then help me!" The space between them pulsed with desperation. "I hate it there. I hate *him*. For the first time in my life, I was happy here. You know I'm better here—I didn't get into trouble. I was doing well—even had good grades." Nathan focused on Hazel. "Please, Zel, you've got to make Bennett see—"

"I *do* see, Nathan." Bennett felt his own desperation grow alongside his brother's. "I know."

"So?"

Bennett had a lawyer back in Chicago, but the man didn't do family law. Maybe he'd know someone though.

"I can't make any promises. But I'll try."

Nathan slumped, defeated.

"Nate." Bennett reached across the table and gripped his shoulders. "I'll try. We'll talk to Dad. We'll do everything we can to make him understand."

A tear flicked from one eye as Nathan shook his head. "Dad doesn't lose. Ever."

That wasn't true. Their dad had lost everything that mattered. The worst part of that? Chip was so consumed with himself that he didn't even know how much he'd lost.

Resolution clamped down hard on two counts: First, Bennett would fight for his younger siblings until there was nothing left in him to fight with. And second . . .

He would never be like Chip. Not ever again.

Thirteen

As thunder rolled somewhere over the western peaks, Grady fought against the fatigue that tempted him to guzzle some instant energy. Somewhere he'd read that the stuff was not only stupidly addictive but could also kill you. He'd seen the demon of addiction—not that those energy drinks would produce the horrors he'd witnessed—and even with life a little bizarre at the moment, he wasn't ready to die from stupidity.

So the energy-in-a-can was out—which was a given anyway, because he didn't have any with him.

He rounded the last curve on the trail that led him past a trio of evergreen giants and dumped him into the trailhead parking lot. Several more steps, with the rocky dust crunching under his boots, and he made it back to the truck.

Reaching into the cab, he snagged the clipboard from beneath the seat, opened the plastic keep-safe paper protector, and scanned through the list. No incidents to report. Signs of deer, moose, and fresh bear on an aspen four feet off the trail. He made a mental note of that and would bring a trail cam this way tomorrow. Fresh bear activity was always something to track.

When he got to the *trail markers* section, he noted the damage to the initial sign, then slid the sheet back into the protective hard plastic and secured the latch. He shut the vehicle door and reached to open the latch for the metal toolbox fixed in the bed of the truck. A hammer and a fresh nail should right the situation quickly, and then he could call it a day. A good thing, as the next growl of thunder shook through the sky. The late-afternoon rainstorm was moving in.

Sort of matched the internal affairs of his mind and emotions. Electric, with a mixed sense of anticipation and warning.

Grady had always liked a good thunderstorm.

When he'd texted Isa earlier that afternoon to check on her, she'd mentioned chicken noodle soup. Janie's chicken noodle soup was not to be missed. Was Isa's as good? He assumed they used the same recipe.

That musing had him eager to head back to town. As did the idea that he'd see his fiancée.

His fiancée.

How had that status change in their relationship suddenly changed what he thought of Isa? A few weeks ago she was an irritant. A woman who smiled and flirted and frustrated him.

He had yet to fully examine why his response to her had been so strong. Maybe he should take the time to autopsy it. But that felt . . . uncomfortable. Almost as much as the idea of discussing when they should get married. Go figure that—he warmed at the thought of Isa as his fiancée, but it made him itchy to think about discussing when they'd tie the knot.

Was that normal?

Grady snagged the small portable toolbox and started for the damaged trailhead sign. A gust of rain-scented wind rushed down the forested hill and hit him head on. He inhaled the fresh buzz of natural energy and jogged the rest of the distance to his destination. Once there, he repositioned the flat piece that read *Black Gulch Falls* against the post and sank a new nail into place.

Normal? Proposing to a woman who had only last week winked at a stranger and called him *hon* while she'd served him a pear turnover and coffee—both of which had Grady's mind buzzing with the negative variety of energy. *Nothing* about any of this was normal.

But that aside, a good chunk of his reserve regarding the *setting the date* discussion had to do with the way Isa had stiffened this morning when he'd announced that they had wanted a quick engagement. He'd assumed she would understand that was necessary. Apparently she hadn't. And then the rest of his hesitation?

That text exchange he'd had with her earlier in the day.

He blew out a breath and put away the hammer. Then he removed his hat and crammed his fingers through his hair.

Hi. I'm just checking in with you. Everything okay?

Fine

Nothing unusual to report?

No

So everything at the café is good?

Peachy

Okay. What's on the menu for tonight?

Chicken noodle soup

And that had been it. There had been no hint of winking or pet names for him. The whole exchange had been about as warm and enticing as a dark cave in a cliff. He'd thought she would appreciate that he was thinking of her—because as he'd told her last night, he couldn't get her out of his mind. By her clipped answers, she found him an annoyance.

Replacing his hat, he bent to pick up the toolbox and started back for the truck.

That buzz of energy fizzled as another peal of thunder cracked the dark sky. Gone was the anticipation. He was left with only the immutable reality of the coming storm.

So far, the future was looking *peachy*, to put it in Isa's terms. That was awesome. They weren't even married yet.

Isa had saved two multigrain rolls and a large bowl of chicken noodle soup for Grady. Also a hearty slice of caramel apple cheesecake, as she happened to know Grady really liked that dessert—he preferred it to the huckleberry pie that was also available.

The man—her fiancé—strode through the front door of Janie's Café ten minutes to eight. That made him nearly two hours later than usual. By the deep scowl that drew his mouth and brows down, he wasn't in a great mood.

She hoped that had something to do with the soaking-wet hat he pulled off his head and the dripping raincoat he shook off and hung near the door. But she doubted it. Especially when he looked right at her and couldn't muster even half a smile.

Great. She was engaged to the Incredible Sulk, and worse, his dark alter ego was apparently triggered by none other than herself.

Looking away from his mighty frown, Isa turned toward the kitchen to retrieve the food she'd set back for him. In the privacy of the back room, she squeezed her eyes shut and sighed. Fingering the cool band on her left finger, she leaned against the counter and prayed. *God, I thought this was the way—a path of mercy from You. Am I being an idiot all over again?*

Grady wasn't a bad man. In general, she knew him to be a good man. Just one who didn't light up when he saw *her*. Was it wise to marry a *not a bad* man? One who frowned at her more than he smiled?

"You mad at me?"

Grady's low voice startled her. With a jolt, she opened her eyes and covered her churning stomach with one hand.

Standing next to the door, Grady fixed a stern glower on her.

She wanted to wilt. Instead, she pressed her shoulders back and held his hard gaze. "No, but I'm pretty sure you're unhappy with me, which is a mystery since I haven't seen you since before sunrise."

"Why would you think that I'm unhappy with you?"

"Have you seen yourself when you look at me?"

He blinked. Then with what appeared to be an intentional effort, his features eased into something less fierce. He rolled his lips together, then wiped his face with one palm. "I'm sorry. It's been a long day."

Isa bit her bottom lip. If this was a normal relationship, she'd go to him and offer a back rub. Or a hug. Maybe even try to kiss away his frown. Should she try to act like this was a normal relationship in the hopes that pretending would eventually lead to reality?

What would Grady Briggs do if she did?

Even while the idea had some appeal—Isa had always loved a challenge—she shrank from it. Grady's offer of marriage was her best hope of protection and the best chance for her unborn child. If he rejected her efforts at tenderness now, how could she go through with marrying him? She couldn't live in a cold, lifeless marriage.

That sort of fortitude wasn't in her. She needed life . . . and tenderness.

Maybe that could begin with some sort of honest conversation.

"You're later than usual," she said. "I thought maybe you were avoiding me."

Grady took two steps nearer. "I wasn't." He pushed his hand through his hair, and because it was wet, his fingers left it spiked in rows. His shoulders fell on a sigh. "Well, maybe I was. A little. Your texts made me think you were upset about something, and I couldn't figure out what. But that's not why I'm so late. I got a flat tire in between the Black Gulch Falls trailhead and town, and the bolts were a pain to break free. It took a while."

"Oh." Isa met his tentative gaze and held it. Holding her breath, she dared a step forward, nearly closing the space between them. When he didn't look away, she reached to trail her fingers down his arm. The wet fabric was cool under her fingers. "You're soaked."

He hadn't blinked. Or moved. When her touch feathered against his hand, he twitched only enough to brush the tips of her fingers with his.

A thrilling snap of energy fired through her veins. "I saved you some soup. It's still hot."

"Thank you."

Her heart pounded while he stared at her. Why was he so unreadable? All she could deccern from that intense look was that he . . . he was an intense man. Isa didn't know what to do with that. The men she'd been attracted to before were fun and light. Maybe they were just superficial. Charming, like Francisco. That hadn't made him good.

Grady Briggs was mostly a mystery, but she knew for sure he was anything but superficial. And she was certain he was good. For some reason, that buoyed her hope where their odd relationship was concerned.

A hope that grew a little more when he reached up to tuck a strand of hair behind her ear. "You were upset earlier though. I don't think I misread that."

She had been. Ever since he'd announced that they would have a short engagement. She should be grateful for his offer of protection and go along with what he thought was best. But the girlish longings within weren't so easily convinced. Also, was she going to forever be a woman run over because she felt indebted to this man?

She couldn't live like that either.

"Hey." A call from the dining room interrupted the extended silence between Grady and her. "Is someone running this joint, or should I just leave without paying my bill?"

Isa winced and gave Grady an apologetic look.

He managed to lift one corner of his mouth and cocked his head toward the door. "Go on. I'll take this out and eat at the bar."

"You'll hang around?"

He dipped one nod. That was it. No soft words of kind reassurances. But no sharp rebukes either. Maybe Grady was just a guy of few words—one who showed his emotions through his actions. Maybe she would simply need to learn to speak his language.

Mulling over how to do that, Isa left the kitchen and took care of Marvin Giles's check. The gruff old man mumbled something about missing Janie since Isa seemed to be easily distracted, and right then, Isa couldn't blame him.

But she had a lot going on. If Marvin knew . . .

Nope. No one could know.

Grady had found himself a metal baking tray, put his soup and rolls and pie on it, and true to his word, settled on a stool at the bar nearest the register. He ate while Isa worked. At some point, his spoon clattered at the bottom of the bowl.

She removed the empty dish from in front of him. "I hope that was enough. I don't have any left."

He nodded. "It was good. Did you make it?"

She shook her head. "Janie."

Grady nodded.

Once again, Isa wondered what that meant. Grady buttered the second roll, and Isa checked on the two tables with remaining customers.

A little after 8:30, the last of the café's guests paid and left. Technically, Janie's Café was open until nine, but unless something was happening on a Friday night—like a home game or something equally compelling—they rarely had anyone past 8:30. Life in a tiny town.

Isa pulled the bucket of sanitizing water out from the lower shelf, dumped it, and began to refill it with fresh, hot water.

"Can I help?"

She lifted a weak smile at Grady. "No, that's okay. You've had a long day—and by the looks of it, you're still wet. I'm sure you'd rather get home."

"I'm fine."

"Me too. I'll just lock up and get everything ready for tomorrow."

"Are you dismissing me?"

She shut off the water and studied him. Did he want to stay? Did he feel obliged to stay? Could she wrangle more than one pathetic lifted corner of his mouth if he stayed? If she tried, would that further cement her as a reckless flirt in his mind, dismantling any shot of winning his respect?

Isa plunged her hands into the hot water with a soft sigh.

"Isa?"

"No, I'm not dismissing you." She wrung out the rag, then carrying the handle of the bucket, she walked to the nearest table to wipe it down.

Grady was silent on his stool. When she glanced back, she found him with his face lowered toward his folded hands, shoulders drooped. He looked as defeated as she felt.

This was not a good start to any sort of relationship, let alone a lifelong commitment.

"Grady—"

"I think—"

They spoke at the same time. Par for the course on this super-awkward journey.

"I'm sorry," Grady said. "Go ahead."

Isa drew in a breath of courage. “I was just going to say that this feels . . . strained. I wish I knew what you were thinking.”

His intense look eased, though his eyebrows drew together. “It does feel . . . hard. If you want to know what I’m thinking, you can ask.”

“Okay. Grady, what are you thinking?”

That right corner of his mouth poked upward. Not a smile, but so much better than his scowl. “I was thinking that maybe now would be a good time to talk.”

She glanced around the empty dining room. “That seems fair.”

“I was wondering why you were upset today. Why your texts were so . . . clipped.”

She swallowed. Plunged the rag back into the water and moved to the next table. She began wiping down the surface before she attempted to respond. “I think it’s probably dumb, and you’re probably right.”

“I haven’t said anything, so I don’t know how I would be right. I don’t even know what it is.”

“You said we wanted a quick engagement. I got the impression you thought we’d run down to the Elk County courthouse on your next day off and seal the deal. Lickety-split, like we were going to a drive-through car wash or something.”

Grady drew back. Offended? Once again, Isa couldn’t tell. If she was to guess by that puckered forehead, then she’d say yes, he was offended. Or at least, not pleased.

“I guess that had been exactly what I had thought,” he said slowly. “Minus the car wash thing.”

Discomfort joined the sound of the water sloshing in the bucket as she rinsed the rag again. Her heart rate sped up as the heat of anger oozed through her veins. She shouldn’t be mad. It did actually make sense.

But . . . but why wouldn’t he ask her, instead of just assuming. And also . . .

“Isa?”

She kept her back to him, putting great effort into scrubbing a spot off the table that was not going to come out—mostly because it was a knot in the pine that lived beneath the glossy finish.

"Isa, tell me what you had in mind."

His quiet response disarmed her. Grady didn't do that—speak with calm gentleness. At least, not to her. He barked demands and frowned disapproval. After all, this was the man who had told her she could serve his coffee *without* all the flirting.

Isa curled her fist around the rag. That small diamond winked up at her from the folds of the cloth. He'd bothered to buy her a ring and to offer her a real proposal. Maybe he wouldn't think she was a ridiculous girl . . .

"I just wish we could have a wedding." The confession came out in a choked rush. She blinked back a surge of tears, knowing this whole thing was stupid. They weren't a normal couple. This wasn't a marriage of romance or even love. She wasn't an ideal bride—wasn't even really his choice.

Why should she have a wedding?

The sound of his boot scuffing softly against the floor came from behind her. Isa straightened and turned, forcing herself to meet his eyes. He studied her with curious intensity, like he was trying to make sense of a riddle.

"A wedding is important to you?"

It sounded so silly. She shrugged and tried to turn back toward the table.

Grady stopped her with a hand on her shoulder. "We have to learn to talk to each other."

Isa winced. Nodded. "Little girls spend a lot of time dreaming of their weddings," she whispered.

He didn't even blink. "How big of a wedding?"

She bit her bottom lip, noting that his hand still warmed her arm. "Not a big one. Just . . . something a little more than running off to a judge." Her posture collapsed. "But it's stupid. Just a silly thing from—"

"Think we can manage to pull together a small wedding for less than a grand, and in a week's time?"

She raised her gaze back up to meet his. He wasn't teasing. Wasn't demeaning her.

He was serious. Impassive in that seriousness, but still. It was . . . kind.

Could a man be both impassive and intense? That seemed like a contradiction. What was it going to take for her to learn how to read this man?

Setting aside that monumental task, Isa refocused on the current subject. A wedding. A small, inexpensive, quick wedding. With Janie's help, she could pull it off.

Isa nodded. "A small gathering—I would like my family to be there. They would be offended if I got married without them, and I've already done so much to hurt them."

Grady thought on that for several heartbeats. "Should I go ask your dad's permission?"

A warm sheen blurred her vision. "You would do that?"

He flinched, as though her question nicked him. "Yes." He hesitated but then drew her close enough to wrap her in a hug. It was stiff and awkward.

But sweet.

"I'll do what it takes, Isa."

What did he mean? Isa wasn't positive as she pressed her forehead into his chest. Whatever it meant—and whoever this man really was—she knew for sure she'd underestimated him.

And she also knew a desperate hope that he wouldn't regret making her his wife. A hope she *needed* to make a reality.

FOURTEEN

HAZEL PACED THE LENGTH of the dock while the sun slipped behind the western peaks. With her thumb tucked in between her lips, she clamped her teeth onto the nail.

"I haven't seen you bite your nails since you were eight." Hunter hopped from the muddy trail onto the wooden planks and tucked his hands into his jacket pockets as he continued toward her. "And you not even hearing me come around from the ridge? Something's up." Near her spot at the end of the dock, he stopped.

Pulling her thumb from her mouth, she crossed her arms. "You haven't heard?"

"Heard what?" He braced his palms against the arms of an Adirondack chair and lowered into it. Beyond his seat, the shoreline of the lake darkened under the shadows of towering pines and firs, and the soft rattle of bright-green aspen leaves filled the evening air. "Please don't say you broke up with Crofton again. Even you can't be that thick skulled."

Hazel's attention drew back from the setting, and she smirked at Hunter's playful wink. "No. Thanks." She plopped into the chair next to him but didn't slide back. "Nathan is here."

Hunter sat forward, looking back at the cabin.

"Not here, as in the cabin. But in Luna. He ran away from his dad's."

"Whoa." When he turned back to Hazel, he looked impressed more than concerned. "He learned a thing or two about being independent, huh?"

"Now isn't a good time for that."

"Why not?"

"Because he *ran away* from home, Hunt. Bennett is torn up trying to figure out what to do."

A fresh rush of cool air stirred the lake waters, sending ripples of dark liquid to lap against the dock.

"Can't he just call their dad, explain that Nathan wants to be here?" Hunter asked. "I mean, surely after that kind of scare, Chip would be more inclined to listen, right?"

"Chip didn't even know Nathan was gone." Hazel wrapped her arms around her shoulders, leaning against her legs. Her light flannel smelled of forest and lake. She inhaled, trying to calm the whirling anxiety within.

"What? How is that possible?"

"Nathan is clever and, as you've noted, has learned he can stand on his own two feet."

"Thanks to a certain mountain woman."

"Please stop." She lowered her feet back to the dock and straightened her posture. "I really don't want to take responsibility for this."

"He's a good kid, at heart. And he needs to know he can do stuff—that he can handle life. I don't think it's a bad thing."

Hazel folded her hands and squeezed. "Our world is very different from the outside world, I think."

"I don't know about that, sis." Hunter reached over and shook her arm. "There's conflict here, just like there's conflict everywhere. Don't you remember having to leave for a little while after Mom and Dad died?"

Hazel pressed her lips together and nodded.

"But we got it fixed."

"I'm not sure this is the same."

"Kinda think maybe it is. A little bit, at least."

She peeked at her brother as a spark of hope flickered in her heart. "How did Nan and Pops get me back?"

He shrugged. "I think Mama Bulldog had a lot to do with that. And I'm pretty sure she covered us all with a whole lot of prayer."

"Think she'd do what she did then all over again? I mean, for Nathan and for Gemma?"

"I know she would—and I'm sure she already prays for those kids on the regular. Just like I do."

Hazel nodded. Prayer was still a mystery to her. She tried, but a lot of times she was afraid she was doing it wrong. And to be honest, sometimes she wondered if she was simply annoying God with trivial stuff. After all, He had the whole universe to look after. Why would He continue to intervene in her little life when she didn't matter much?

But Nathan and Gemma—they mattered. At least to Bennett and to her. Did God feel that way too? If so, how did He have room for all the feelings for all the people?

It boggled her mind. Sometimes with breathless wonder. Sometimes, if she was being honest, with nagging doubts.

"Hazel?"

"Yeah." She huffed out a breath, trying to clear away all the mixed thoughts.

"Nathan and Gemma matter to God too."

"I was just thinking about that." She wasn't willing to confess the confusion about it all. "Bennett doesn't know what to do. I mean, he's reaching out to his lawyer back in Chicago to see if he can recommend someone in family law—I guess it's different than property law. But he doesn't seem hopeful. Chip and Mindi are the parents, and there isn't really a compelling reason for the kids to leave their care. And Bennett is afraid that if he fights them on this, the kids will just end up in the middle of an ugly battle, and it will make things worse, not better."

Hunter nodded. "I guess that could happen."

"What would God want?" Hazel held her hands out, palms up. "That's what I keep wondering. Or why would God want this whole big mess in the first place? You know? It's sort of like losing Mom and Dad all over again, in a way. I get so mixed up about who God is. Is He good, like MB says? Or is He ambivalent, like I had thought He was? I mean, I believe in Jesus, and I want to be saved by Him, but now I see Nathan in the middle of this mess, and I can't reconcile the bad with a good God who would die to save us."

Hazel squeezed her fingers tight, finding that her hands shook. She reached for courage and met Hunter's waiting gaze. "It scares me, Hunt. This tiny flame of faith I have—it's flickering in the storm. What if it's not enough to endure? I don't want the old me—to go back to being cold and lonely. I don't want to become Chip—so jaded and hard that no one else matters anymore. But it feels so . . . so messy." She finished on a long, wavered sigh.

As a space of rustling leaves and lapping water spanned between them, Hunter reached across and covered her hand. "He's a big God, you know?"

Hazel wasn't sure what that meant.

"These questions—this confusion—I don't think God is offended."

"Am I not supposed to just trust Him and be happy?"

"Hmm." Hunter squeezed her hand and then sat back again. "That seems simplistic."

"Are you insulting me?"

"No. I'm saying that I don't think easy answers are always right answers. Can we trust God? Yeah, I think that the history in the Bible shows us we can trust Him. Do we have questions, and does life get hard and messy? Yeah. I think saying otherwise is selling a blind lie and a hard fall. Like I said, He's a big God. Big enough to make these mountains we love and fear. Big enough to create the heavens we stare at in wonder. I think that means He's big enough to handle our questions."

"So you think it's okay to ask God what on earth He's doing?"

"I think if you're pouring out some honest emotions, and at the end of it all, throwing yourself before Him in humility, even with all those questions, then that's just being honest."

"And that's okay?"

"I think it's what He wants."

"And if I'm honest, will He give me answers?"

Hunter grunted a small chuckle and shook his head. "Don't know about that. Losing Mom and Dad . . . that still doesn't make sense."

"So I can ask, but He might not say why? Or make things go the way I want?"

"I think if you stopped and ask yourself who is God and who are you in that conversation, you'll find your answer."

Heat tickled her neck. "Right." She wasn't God. Was that the key, getting that part straight? *You are God, and I am not.*

"Hazel, at the end of it all, we can go back to falling before Jesus, crying out *I am Yours. Save me*. You know?"

She bit her bottom lip. "That's the answer we know for sure—that He will?"

He nodded. "He has. And He will. Let's anchor into that, okay?" He stood, holding out a hand to her.

Nodding, Hazel took it. "How'd you get so wise so fast?"

"I'm your big brother. I've always been smarter." He laughed as she shoved him with her elbow.

He dropped his arm around her shoulders, and they stepped toward the shore. "For the record, I'm hoping you and Bennett get answers that bring everyone peace. And I really hope that means the kids come back. I miss them."

"Me too." They broke apart as Hazel stepped onto the dirt path in front of him. She paused, her gaze pinned to the cabin. "Although that's going to mean some really big changes. More of them." She glanced over her shoulder at Hunter.

He raised his brows as he examined the little cabin. "That's a tight space for four people."

Exactly. Two tiny bedrooms. A tiny kitchen with a little round table—barely big enough for two, let alone four. A connected living room that held enough space for a short couch and a woodburning stove. Hazel didn't even own a TV—anything she watched was done on the laptop Hunter had given her a few years back.

How were Nathan and Gemma supposed to adjust to that after growing up in the wealthy Northshore of Chicago?

"You willing to move to town? Bennett's house has the space, and it's done."

Her gut clenched. She'd never once thought of moving out of the tiny cabin. Not permanently.

Maybe she was getting ahead of herself. Way ahead of herself.

But this needed some consideration, because even though Bennett hadn't given her a ring yet, she was certain they would be married soon. And she wanted the kids to come back. For them, and for Bennett, and for herself.

Getting what she wanted might require sacrifice. Was she willing to make it?

Isa brewed coffee in the dim light of the oven lamp. She hadn't wanted to turn on all the lights at once first thing in the morning. The foggy haze of a restless night needed a more gentle approach.

Though when Janie got there, she would flip them all on. But hopefully, that would be at least twenty minutes from now.

And hopefully, Grady would show up first.

Would he come predawn again, as he had the day before? They hadn't talked about it last night before he'd left. The only thing that they had settled was that he was willing to have a small wedding. And even more shocking, he wanted to meet her family and ask her dad's permission to marry her. Isa's shock, and her delight, had snuffed out all other questions.

For being a calm, steady, predictable man, Grady sure was full of surprises.

As a soft smile toyed her mouth, a quiet knock sounded from the back door. That little grin grew as she moved to unlock it. When those intense eyes met her from the other side, her heart gave a little jolt. "Good morning."

His lips twitched into an almost smile, but instead of answering, he held up a small bundle of brown fur. "You have a visitor."

She looked at the little ball wriggling in his arms. It peeked at her and whined.

"Oh my gosh!" Isa stepped into the yellow light of the alley. "A puppy?"

The little thing flinched as she set her hand on his soft head.

"Oh, buddy. Don't be scared." Isa ran her palm over its little shivering body. "Are you cold?"

At her question, Grady tucked the small dog in closer. "He might be. Likely hungry too."

"Where did you find him?"

He nodded toward the garbage bin at the end of the alley. "Behind the dumpster. I've heard something back there every morning for the past week. This morning, I checked. This little guy was huddled up all by himself."

"Think his mom is around somewhere?"

Grady shook his head, his focus on the little furball. "There was a dog on the side of the highway a few days back. She had this coloring and looked like a mix of lab and mountain dog, just like this guy."

"Oh no—was she dead?"

He nodded.

"Oh, buddy." Isa reached for the puppy, taking it from Grady's arms. Shivering, it whined again. "You poor thing. I bet you're so hungry." She looked over her shoulder at the kitchen and then back at Grady. "I don't think I can bring him into the kitchen."

"Probably not a good idea."

She puckered her brows as she thought about what to do. Grady stepped nearer, almost like he was going to wrap her in his arms. Disappointment sank slowly when he didn't, though the warmth of his nearness was a solace.

"I can take him back to my place."

"Don't you have to work?"

"Yeah." His hand covered the puppy's head, and the animal stopped shaking.

"Poor little guy. He's not going to make it on his own."

"No, he won't." Grady's fingers grazed her arm as he lowered his hand to his side. "We'll figure something out."

"Here." Isa passed the dog back into Grady's arms. "I'll go get him something warm to eat. Do you mind staying out here with him?"

"Of course not."

Isa watched the man she was going to marry cuddle the helpless creature with such tenderness and concern. Her thumb went to the band on her ring finger, and warmth pooled in her chest.

Grady looked up from the dog and caught her staring. Isa forgot how to breathe while he held her gaze.

Maybe it was this ongoing revelation of softness beneath his hard exterior. Or maybe it was the gentle light of the breaking day peeking over his shoulder. Or maybe it was the undamming of the secret crush she'd had on him from the beginning. Whatever it was, Isa gave in to the compulsion to know the feel of his lips against her own.

She closed the small gap between them, leaning against his body for stability as she stretched up to press her mouth against his.

Grady responded like a statue. His solid form tensed at her touch, and his breath drew in sharp and held.

A chill of disappointment and humiliation sliced through the tenderness that had gathered in her middle. She lowered to flat feet and drew back. "I'm sorry."

"Why?" He caught her elbow before she retreated completely.

She lifted a confused look to him. Why was she sorry? He couldn't figure that out? Maybe this man truly had been carved from solid marble. "You obviously didn't want me to do that."

He blinked. "I didn't expect you to do that."

"Oh."

In the wordless tension that gripped them, the morning song of the mountain birds accompanied the summer dawn, and the puppy wiggled to bury himself deeper into the crook of Grady's arm.

Isa sighed as helpless defeat settled into what had been a warm pool of hope. "I'll be right back." This time she didn't search out his gaze. Instead, she went back into the kitchen and focused on finding something suitable for a puppy to eat.

And worked to rebuild the wall that was to hold back that fatal crush.

Grady breathed out a long, frustrated breath. As his shoulders slumped, his eyes slid shut. Isa had kissed him, and he had been so caught off guard he'd stood just there like Captain Dead Lips.

"Idiot," he muttered.

He wished for an instant replay. No, he wished for a do-over. If he could, he would at least lean into that timid kiss Isa had pressed against his mouth. Given her some kind of indication that he welcomed her move toward something that resembled a real relationship.

After all, he'd told her he wanted a real marriage, nothing fake or temporary. He wasn't an actor and had no ambition for charades. He also wasn't a liar—wasn't going to speak a promise he had no intention of keeping.

Isa's attempt should have been reciprocated. Or at least welcomed.

But nope. Not this slow, hardheaded ranger. He'd left her thinking that he was offended.

"Nice work, right?" He looked at the sleeping pup in his arms. "You gave me the perfect setup, and I completely muffed it."

The dog opened his eyes and looked at him.

"Yeah. I know—I'm an idiot." He scratched the puppy's chin. "Think you can work out a redo?"

A tiny warm tongue licked his dry and chafed fingers. Grady chuckled. "Good thing she already agreed to marry me, huh? Apparently the only way I can get the girl is if she's desperate."

The dog wiggled, clawing his way up Grady's uniform shirt until he could lick his chin.

The door popped open, and Isa stepped out again. Grady's smile dissipated, but that wouldn't have mattered, since Isa only looked at the dog in his arms and not at him.

"I looked up what to feed an abandoned puppy. Google says this—I hope it's right." She placed a bowl of yellowish liquid on the ground.

"What is it?" Grady followed her and set the puppy down. The animal sniffed the bowl, dipped his nose in until it was wet, and tested the food with his tongue. He must have approved, because he began to lap up the food.

"A milk replacement—milk, egg yolks, a little bit of oil and salt." She wrapped her arms around her middle, like she was chilly.

After a moment of consideration—would she push him away?—Grady stepped behind her and laid a hand on her shoulder.

Yeah. That was brave. She'd just kissed him, and he managed a hand on her arm. Look at him go.

Isa lifted her chin to look at him. Strain pulled at the corners of her eyes. After a handful of heartbeats between them, she swallowed and returned her attention to the puppy. "What do we do now?"

At least she hadn't pushed him away. "We'll figure out something." She was talking about the dog, right? Maybe not.

He lifted his other hand and covered her other shoulder with it.

Isa breathed twice, and then she covered his fingers with her own.

Relief mingled with a sense of confusion that swirled through Grady. He didn't know what to do, how to make this work with her. He doubted Isa did either. But in the moment of that shared uneasy touch, they were together.

They would figure this out.

FIFTEEN

JANIE TUCKED HER KEYS into her purse as she strode through the alley. Through an ear pod, she listened to the prayer that was playing through her phone. While it wasn't a substitute for her daily Bible reading, she found listening to this daily offering helped keep her mind and heart focused as she started her days—particularly when she needed to get up early and drive down to help open the café.

Inhaling, she breathed in Luna—the air a mingling of aspens and pine, dust, and crisp, dewy mountain. And as she neared the back door to her café's kitchen, a touch of coffee. A grin pulled at the corner of her mouth. A beautiful sunrise, a prayer in her heart, and a cup of coffee. Not a bad way to start a day. Especially when that coffee was already brewed and ready to go before she even walked through the door.

While she hadn't been thrilled at Hunter's suggestion to take on Isa last spring, things seemed to be working out. Isa did well both in the kitchen and with her customers. And now that she and Grady were getting married—the shock of that news still hadn't entirely settled—it looked like Isa might be all useful and no trouble, not to mention sticking around.

A movement on the opposite side of the alley from the back door had Janie drawing to a dead stop. Her heart jumped and belly dropped as she jerked her attention to the shadows there. At the sight of Grady, she covered her hammering chest with one hand and chuckled. "Grady, you scared me to death."

"Sorry, Janie."

"What are you doing out here?" *Please don't say Isa won't let you in*. They couldn't have a falling out already. Janie had latched on to the unlikely match of Grady and Isa. Maybe it eased her guilt about dumping Grady the way she had. Or maybe she just thought everyone needed a happily ever after. Whatever the reason, though she would never have imagined them together, she really wanted them to work.

Grady gestured toward a spot on the ground near where he squatted. "Puppy duty."

Sure enough, there, huddled almost underneath the man, was a little fur baby lapping up something from a bowl.

"Where did you get that?"

"He's been living behind your dumpster." Grady pointed to the end of the alley. "I've heard him crying the past couple of mornings. Today I checked on him. He's all alone. Pretty sure his mom got hit on the highway a few days back."

"Oh no." Janie pushed out her bottom lip just as the back door opened.

"Oh, hi, Janie." Isa paused before she stepped out of the kitchen. She held an apple box lined with a fluffy towel.

"Good morning, Isa," Janie said. "I see you've had a fun morning."

Isa shrank. "I hope you don't mind—I used some milk and eggs from the fridge. And this"—she held up the box—"which I found in the storage room. I'm sorry. I should have asked. But the towel is mine, I promise."

Janie waved her off. "I'm not worried about it. I was actually concerned you and Grady had a fight and you wouldn't let him in the kitchen." She laughed.

Isa didn't. "Oh."

"No fight." Grady stood to take the box from Isa.

Worry sprouted again. If they hadn't had a fight, then something else was going on. These two were the strangest couple ever.

Janie knew Isa to be a smiling, flirtatious woman. She knew Grady to be a kind, though quiet man. But put together, Isa was solemn and withdrawn, and Grady was clipped and also withdrawn. Shouldn't they be giddy and gooey eyed the day after their engagement?

What on earth was going on with them?

"I was actually hoping to catch you before I had to head to work this morning," Grady said.

Janie squinted at Grady. "Me?"

"Yeah." Grady met Janie's eyes for only a moment before he settled his attention on Isa. Was there wariness in his expression? "Isa and I talked last night, and we decided we'd like a small wedding."

"Oh." So they were still getting married. Maybe that wasn't such a good idea, even if Janie would be sad if it didn't happen. Would they make each other miserable? At the moment, Janie couldn't testify that they made each other happy.

Isa's tight expression eased, and her smile resurfaced—albeit slowly.

Maybe this was all just really fast for them, and overwhelming. That would check out—no one in town even knew they could stand each other, let alone had been dating.

Had they dated at all? Surely they had. No one just decided to get married, right? But when the dating had happened, Janie couldn't figure. So many oddities with these two.

"Would you like some help with a wedding?" Janie asked.

Isa breathed out a sound of relief. "Yes. Would you be willing to help?"

"Oh yeah!" And with that, all of Janie's legitimate reservations took a backseat to her love of romance that ended with a wedding. If she was the one to help with the last part, maybe she'd get to hear some of the sweeter details of this unlikely couple falling in love. "The lodge is all yours, my friend. And I have so many pretty things up there already. With our wedding only just in the rearview mirror, everything is easy to access. I still have my wedding to-do list saved in Excel." She couldn't contain the bubbling up of excitement as she took Isa's hand and squeezed. "Goodness, you can even use my dress, if you'd like to!"

A streak of pink touched Isa's cheeks. "Really?"

"It'll be fun—and good practice for the future." Janie's optimism chugged full steam ahead. "We hope the lodge will be a destination for this sort of thing—it would help the summer months fill up with bookings. Maybe we could even use some photos from your wedding for advertising—if that's okay with you?"

"Great." After settling the puppy into the box, Grady stepped backward. "I'll leave you two to figure it out. Now, to figure out the puppy problem."

"Is he a problem?" Janie peered back down at the little thing. It sniffed the towel, circled twice, and plopped down into a contented ball.

"Well, he can't stay with Isa, obviously." Grady gestured toward the kitchen. "We'd hate to have your café in violation. And I'm gone most of the day. I don't really love the idea of my house getting torn apart, nor do I want this little guy in a kennel all day. I guess he could just camp out here—"

"I can call Hunter, if you want." Janie reached down to touch the warm fur of the puppy's head. She grinned at the softness beneath her fingers. "I'm sure we can take him in, even if it's just for a while."

Grady glanced at Isa, and Janie followed his attention to her. She looked disappointed.

"Oh no." Janie straightened. "You've already fallen in love, haven't you?"

Isa's attention snapped to Janie, her dark eyes wide, as though she'd been caught. "What?"

"He's pretty cute. And sweet. I can't say that I blame you."

Blinking, Isa's wide-eyed expression morphed into a scowl.

"The puppy, Isa," Grady muttered.

"Oh." Isa looked away, hiding her face. "No, I just want him to be safe." She fixed a practical expression on Janie. "Call Hunter, if you think he won't mind. You would be his best chance. I can't give him the life you can."

She brushed her palms together and looked at Grady. There was something distant and resigned that passed between the pair in that silent exchange. Grady reached for Isa's hand, closed the gap between them, and bent to kiss her cheek.

And that was it. He turned to go on his way, and Isa pivoted the opposite direction to return to the kitchen.

Janie's excitement sank. Something was really, really off.

Inhaling the fragrance of onion, garlic, and warm pastry, Isa cut the mushroom and spinach quiche into eight equal portions. Her mouth watered and tummy rumbled with hunger—a relief since she'd felt sick most mornings for the past week.

Behind her, plating cinnamon rolls, Janie chuckled. "Sounds like you need to plate one of those for yourself. I thought you weren't a fan of the savory dishes though."

She hadn't been up until that exact moment. But as she plated individual servings to put into the holding oven, her mouth watered. Pregnancy was weird.

But she couldn't say that to Janie.

"Maybe I'm developing more grown-up tastes."

Janie laughed. "I get that. I used to hate mushrooms. Now I use them every chance I get. Hunter's not too sure about that development in my tastes." She nodded toward the plates Isa was picking up. "Go ahead. Take one for yourself."

Gratitude welled up in Isa toward her boss for the second time that morning. Also, toward Grady. She hadn't expected him to bring up the wedding with Janie, but it had been a nice surprise.

"Hey, Isa?" Janie met her at the warming oven to place her tray of cinnamon rolls on the second shelf. "Can I ask you something?"

And just like that, the warm gratitude cooled to wariness. "Okay . . ."

"What's really going on with you and Grady?"

"We're getting married." Isa shrugged, telling herself to dial down the defensive tone. "We already told you that."

"But there's something not right with that."

Ears ringing and heat flaring up her neck, Isa crossed her arms. "I know that it looks strange, but we're both committed to this. We're determined to make it work."

"See, this is what I mean. You don't sound like a girl in love."

Isa turned away. "Please just trust that we know what we're doing."

"What does that mean?"

"It means we *both* know what we're doing."

Janie held up both hands. "I'm not coming down on you. I'm just worried that maybe you guys are rushing into something you need to stop and think through. Maybe you're both reacting to some disappointments and you need to pull back a little?"

Disappointments? Isa knew what Janie meant—that Grady was rebounding from her choosing Hunter over him and that he was making bad choices. She pivoted to set a firm look on Janie. "I know I'm not you. I'm not what anyone imagined for Grady. But we've thought this through. He knows what he's doing."

"Whoa, whoa, whoa. Pull back there, Isa." Janie took a step forward and laid a gentle touch on Isa's arm. "I'm not bringing this up because I'm worried about Grady."

"Really?" Isa didn't believe that.

Janie's touch fell away, and she leaned back on the counter. "I think maybe we need to clear the air about him. About what you think happened between him and me. I think you overestimate what our relationship was. There were no promises between us. No *I love yous*. We were dating, and pretty casually at that. And not even for very long. That's all."

"You went on a backpacking trip with him for a week, Janie."

"First, I didn't make it the full week. And second, it wasn't anything like what you're assuming."

Silence took over in the kitchen, interrupted only by the whir of the refrigerator and the hum of the convection oven.

"Isa." Janie's quiet voice was calm and entreating. "He wasn't heartbroken. I know he's not acting on the rebound. Like I said, I didn't bring this up because I was worried about him. I'm concerned for *you*."

A steamy blur clouded Isa's vision as she hugged herself.

"Sweetie, what's going on? It's like . . . like you're in trouble. I just want to help. To be your friend."

With the back of her knuckles, Isa brushed against the single tear that rolled down the side of her face. "Thank you. That means a lot."

Janie closed the space again and gripped Isa's shoulders. "Are you okay? Truly?"

Isa nodded. "There are . . . things." She forced herself to meet Janie's concerned stare. "Reasons. I have made some really, really bad mistakes."

"Is Grady one of them?"

Ache folded around her heart and squeezed, forcing another tear from the corner of her eye. But she shook her head. "No. Grady . . . is stepping in when he doesn't have to."

Janie's brows puckered with deeper worry. "Isa, that sounds cryptic."

"Maybe. But he knows the whole story, and he's willing to help me. I would be a fool not to accept what he's offering, and I've been stupid enough for a whole lifetime already. He's a good man, and he's offered me a way out."

"That doesn't ease my mind or heart about this. For either of you. Are you sure—"

"I'm pregnant, Janie." Isa shut her eyes. Would Grady be upset with her for telling Janie? The man was so unreadable . . . But people would know soon enough. Wouldn't it be a relief to know at least someone among his friends knew the truth—and that it wasn't his fault?

Janie drew back, her concern twisting to confusion.

"The baby isn't his." Isa answered Janie's unvoiced questions. "But he's willing to be a father. He's willing to take us both as his own. Maybe it's not the romance I used to dream of, but a girl could do way worse than a good man who would make that kind of sacrifice. Don't you think?"

Janie nodded, silently taking in Isa's revelation, though her expression remained firmly in the *deeply concerned* column. The moment felt precarious. Would Janie rebuke Isa for taking advantage of Grady? Would she tell others Isa's secret? Would she go to Grady and talk him out of it?

"Please, Janie," Isa whispered. "Please keep this between us."

A hand slipped around Isa's, fingers warm and gentle, and squeezed. Then she tugged and wrapped Isa in a firm hug. "I get it," Janie whispered.

"Do you?" Isa choked.

"I do. And I'll do anything you need to help." She leaned back and braced a hand on Isa's shoulder. "Starting with your wedding."

Sixteen

"Dad, you're not listening."

"I hear you just fine, Bennett." Chip's tone carried an icy chill. "I can't believe you didn't call me the minute you found Nathan. He's in a lot of trouble, and he needs to get here, pronto."

"Wait a minute—you can't believe I didn't call? You didn't even know he was gone!" Bennett gripped the phone like he wanted to strangle something. Not too far from the truth. He drew in a hard breath through the nose, desperately fighting for control.

This was a negotiation. A hostile one, yes, but a negotiation just the same. He was good at those—particularly at the hostile kind.

"Here's the deal, Chip," Bennett said. "I will fly back to Chicago with Nathan at the end of the week—"

"No, you'll put him on a plane tomorrow."

"That's not even on the table. First, Nathan isn't going alone. Not moving on that point, so you're better off accepting it. Second, I need a few days to sort things out. Friday is the soonest I can make things work. But I would prefer a full week, if you want to keep pushing."

"Who do you think you are, Bennett Crofton? *I* am the kid's dad. You're just his brother—and only a half brother at that. You have no weight in this."

"Oh, trust me, I have weight." Bennett leaned in hard on the conversation he'd had with the family lawyer he'd talked to an hour before. After the whole tale had been laid out—starting with Chip demanding that Bennett take Nathan and Gemma in last year—Emmaline Sanchez assured Bennett he had some legal ground to stand on. Not much, but some. And if Nathan—and Gemma—wanted a voice in this matter, she was more than willing to give them one.

Short story, Ms. Sanchez said she could make a case. She couldn't promise a win, but she suspected Chip Crofton wouldn't want the court expenses and the possible bad press. There was a good possibility they could work this through out of court.

"What makes you think you can just take my son from me?"

"That wasn't what we were talking about just now. But if you want, we can start that discussion."

"You have no idea what you're getting into."

"No, but the lawyer I just spoke with has a very clear idea. She's highly regarded in family law and is well known in Chicago. Her success record is impressive."

"Lawyer?" Chip's voice boomed into Bennett's ear. "You contacted a lawyer! You couldn't spare a minute to let me know my boy is safe, but you had time to track down and speak with a lawyer?"

Bennett tugged at the collar of his button-down. "Calm down, Dad."

"Don't tell me to calm down. I could call you in for kidnapping!"

"You could. But then the police would do an interview with Nathan and find out that he ran away. And then they'd want to know why, and there you go. Full police record of why Nathan left your care to come here. You'll also risk having the Illinois Department of Children and Family Services showing up at your door. Do you really want to chance having Nathan placed in foster care?"

"You don't know who you're messing with, Bennett."

"That may be true." Bennett spoke with dead calm. Maybe this was the ignition point of a long, drawn-out fuse. Maybe it was unavoidable all along, no matter how much Bennett had hoped and prayed and worked for reconciliation. Maybe confrontation was the only destination he and his father's paths shared.

While a fight wasn't what he'd wanted, Bennett wasn't going to shrink from it—not when Nathan's and Gemma's hearts and futures were on the line. "But on the flip side, you don't know who you're dealing with. And that's your own fault, Dad."

A strained silence stretched between them. Bennett could imagine Chip's red complexion while his father paced in front of that huge cherry desk that ate up the real estate in front of the large lakeview window of his home office.

The irony hit Bennett with painful poignancy. Surrounded by wealth and comfort, Chip Crofton was a man completely empty of character and depth.

So were you, and would still be, if not for grace. Bennett let the humbling whisper penetrate his angry thoughts. It stung, but in a way that brought hope and gratitude.

"Put Nathan on the phone," Chip demanded.

"Nathan is at Janie's Café with Hazel right now. I'll have him call you in thirty minutes, after he and Hazel get back."

"What!" Chip dumped a string of profanity into Bennett's ear. "Put *my son* on the phone *now*!"

Bennett responded with a tight grip on control, repeating that whispered truth to himself again. *If not for grace...* "He's not here."

"Then walk your miserable ass over to the café and get him!"

"I won't, Dad. I'll have Nathan call you in thirty minutes. That's the end of it."

Once again, Chip's silence boiled into the phone.

"Dad."

Nothing.

"Chip." Bennett bowed his head and prayed for the words to be firm and clear but still humble. Could he be unmovable on this for Nathan's sake yet still be respectful to the father who didn't seem to deserve it?

"What?" the man growled.

With measured firmness, Bennett spoke. "I'm going to be transparent with you. When Nathan calls you, I will be with him, and you will be on speaker. The conversation will also be recorded." Bennett paused to let that sink in. "Keep that in mind before you say something you'll regret."

"I'm not a bad guy, Bennett. You—my son, of all people—should know that."

"Really?" Bennett couldn't stop the sarcastic snort. "How exactly would I know that?"

How was he supposed to honor a man who provoked him with his long history of dishonesty, selfishness, and total lack of regard for his children? To Chip, his offspring were objects of manipulation who should be pacified with his occasional notice and chunks of guilt money delivered at strategic intervals. How could the man truly believe that he could buy love, like his kids were some sort of merchandise for his cold heart?

God, I don't think I can do this the way You want me to...

Silence sank from the other side of the phone call. Chip's lack of response was as aggravating as his demands.

"We'll call in thirty minutes." Bennett ended the call with a firm press of his thumb. Now, to gain true composure before Nathan got back.

He couldn't lose his head in all of this. Nathan and Gemma needed him to be on his A game.

My contact says they're 99% sure it was the Lopezes. You're sure your source is safe?

Mitchel's text weighed on Grady's mind. Every time he thought about that news article, he imagined a petite dark-haired woman rather than the blonde who had been in the picture. He imagined it had been Isa, and fear made his blood race and his stomach twist.

It hadn't been though.

But it could be. Isa could be next—he already knew for a fact she was on Francisco's radar, and Francisco was not a man who let things go. Whatever his reason, it appeared the cartel boss was going after his old lovers.

It made Grady sick to put that label on Isa. What had she been thinking?

People made mistakes. And Isa—young and flighty, and with some sort of need for attention—had no idea who Francisco really was.

With the energy that came from adrenaline, anxiety, and frustration, Grady scraped the wheel wells of the Game and Parks truck with a flathead shovel. Mud dropped in volleyball-sized chunks, splattering the tires, the wet gravel of the parking lot, and his boots with thick brown muck.

Rain had fallen in a steady drizzle since midmorning, adding to the wetness that had poured down yesterday, to make a sloshy mess of the back trailheads. While he was grateful for the moisture, especially when he thought of his friend Hannah, who was working the fire tower in the area right now—the mud slowed everything down and made him a touch grumpy.

Or maybe the gray mood had more to do with lack of sleep? Likely his downcast spirit had everything to do with Mitchel's text, which Grady still hadn't answered. And the unsteadiness he felt about his very recent and very quick engagement.

Arching his back and working his shoulders, Grady lifted his face to the sky. "You sure about this?"

The question was both for himself and for God. He'd felt certain a few days back. Sure that this was the mandate God had pressed on his heart. Sure that this was the path the Sovereign of earth and time had planned for him.

And mostly, he was still certain about that part.

So maybe the question was more introspective than prayer. Was he sure he could do this? Become a husband to a woman who hadn't shown any sort of interest in him—which particularly stung since she'd seemed to be interested in *every other* male person above the age of fifteen.

You gonna hold that against her forever?

The challenge was intrusive and was tagged closely with a similar sentiment about Isa's physical relationship with Francisco.

Would he hold that against her? No. He didn't hold it against her now. Though he didn't struggle with the need to be touched, to be held, he knew it wasn't wholly uncommon.

But why had Isa been with *Francisco*? Why was she so hungry for attention? She was a beautiful, vivacious young woman. Why would she seek the licentious intentions of crooked and cruel men?

The queries summoned back old ones that had nothing to do with Isa but were equally as puzzling. And equally disrupting to his peace.

He would never understand his mother's choices.

But he couldn't change them. More, they weren't his to be responsible for. He could make his choices and make the best of them.

So again, was he sure about this?

With both hands braced on the side wall of the truck bed, Grady bent his neck and shut his eyes. In the darkness behind his lids, he remembered a story a Bible school teacher had told him long ago.

It had been about three trees—one became a manger that held baby Jesus, one became a boat where Jesus spoke to the crowds, and the third became the cross where Jesus gave his life to save sinners.

The teacher had several points in that little tale she told using chalk art. But one stood out with profoundness—*God grew that tree, boys and girls. He knew one day it would be used to build a cross where Jesus would suffer and die. But God grew the tree anyway. Because He loves us.*

Did God work in contradictions? Sometimes, yes. He grew a beautiful tree that would become something ugly and horrific. But then, to believers who looked to Jesus to be saved, that horrific cross became a beautiful symbol of hope and redemption.

All because God chose love at all costs.

Choose love.

Grady had told Isa that he believed if two people decided to make it work, they could. They would.

And he could choose love. Beginning that moment, he could choose to love Isa, no matter her past or the things that he couldn't understand. No matter what she chose with regard to him, how she felt about him now or ten years from now.

He would choose love, every day, whatever the cost. And pray that God would make something beautiful out of their choices. The good, the bad, and the ugly. All of them.

Isa fiddled with the strap to her purse, her pulse racing as the ranch house came into view.

"That it?" Grady asked.

"Yes." She couldn't look at him. She couldn't even swallow. "That's home."

They were doing this—this was happening. What would Papi say? José—would he glower and demand she tell them what was going on? And Mami—would she cry?

That would be the worst, to have Mami cry. She'd already done so much of that recently, all because of Isa. Because Isa had cast all caution and warnings to the wind and chased after the desires of the flesh.

Could she ever explain why? Squeezing her eyes shut, Isa lowered her head while her grip on the purse strap tightened. She couldn't even explain it to herself, let alone to her family. And to Grady? He hadn't asked . . . yet. If he did, and she tried, could he understand?

Isa couldn't even imagine why Grady was doing this.

The truck stopped, and Isa opened her eyes. They were in front of the long covered porch, and Grady shut off the engine. He sat back, keys in his hand, and stared at the front door to her family's home. After five pounding beats of her heart, Grady turned to study her.

"You okay?" he asked.

Her lips trembled.

Grady switched the keys from his right hand to his left, then reached to place a tentative hand over hers. "It's going to work out."

"Are you sure?"

"Yeah. I mean, your father is likely to be upset, but I can deal with that. Trust me, Isa—I can be respectful even if he's angry."

She met his gaze. "I mean, are you sure you want to do this? You don't have to. I'm not your responsibility."

"You're my fiancée."

She shook her head. "I don't have to be. I'm saying you don't have to do this—there's still time to change your mind. We can tell my family that you offered me a ride here. That we're . . . friends." She twisted the ring until it slid off her finger. "You can take it back, if you want."

Grady watched her with a furrowed brow until she finished, and then he lowered his look to the ring she held between them. He took the band, then lifted his gaze to meet hers again. "Do you not want to marry me?"

"That isn't what I'm saying." Isa blinked against the hot moisture in her eyes. "I'm saying that you can get out of this right now, if you want."

To her shock, Grady chuckled. "Get out now, or never?"

Isa drew back. How was she supposed to respond to that?

Adding more to her shock, Grady lifted his hand and drifted a knuckle along the curve of her jaw, then he picked up her left hand and replaced the ring. "I pick never."

"You pick never?"

"I'm not getting out now, so I pick never." He lifted her hand and pressed her knuckles to his lips. "I told you," he whispered. "I keep my promises."

"You don't love me," Isa said in a breathy rush.

"We have a whole lifetime to work on it."

"What if we never fall in love?"

"I chose to love you. I'll choose to love you every day for the rest of our lives."

"That is . . . isn't the same." Not the romantic, heartfelt, passionate declaration she'd craved her whole life. Though, by the warm surge of emotion filling her heart, it was somehow still profound.

"Isa."

With a stuttering draw of air, Isa forced herself to look up from that diamond and to Grady's steady gaze again.

And her heart melted.

Those dark eyes, so serious as always, held her with promise. Not with the fiery passion of a lover, but with the rock-solid steadiness of a man who would remain faithful, come what may.

What was Grady's story? What made him this way—so serious and solemn, and yet beneath the cold veneer he'd shown her, he was tender. And he was unwavering. Isa had discovered that sort of quiet resolve was a rare thing in a man. At least it had been in the sort of men she managed to attract.

"Do you want out?" Grady asked.

Isa blinked. Now was her chance—she could still pursue a life full of whirlwind romance and wild passion. A life that felt like a rush in the moment, one that made her feel beautiful and desirable for a night.

A pursuit that had landed her squarely in disaster.

Or she could choose Grady.

"No." She had no idea how they would make a marriage born from her stupidity and his hero complex work. But she knew she didn't want to walk away from him. As she had told Janie, that would make her a fool beyond even her own imagination. "If you're still willing to give me a chance at a fresh start—and this baby a chance at a good life—" Her throat closed over as both shame and gratitude overwhelmed her.

Grady reached across the space of the cab and circled her shoulders with his arm. He drew her close, and she inhaled the warm aroma of saffron and crisp pine that clung to him.

"I'm willing," he murmured against her hair. Then he leaned back enough to cup her face in his hand. "Take me to meet your family. I'll ask your father, and it will work out."

She nodded, still taking in his smell and the kindness of his touch. They were both like fuel for her courage.

"And, Isa?"

"Yeah?"

"We'll have a good life. Okay?"

With all her heart, Isa hoped so. For Grady's sake, and for the sake of this baby, she prayed he was right. Even if she knew that she didn't deserve such a hope.

Seventeen

Hazel breathed out a long, stabilizing breath as she walked on wobbly legs through the Jetway. Bennett's warm hand braced against her back as they passed through the door into the airport terminal, a steadying touch she had needed. She glanced up at him with gratitude, but found his eyes scanning the waiting space, his expression pensive.

A good reminder for her—this trip was not about her. She'd left her dogs in Hunter's care, braved an airplane, resolved herself to visit

Chicago when she had no particular desire to go back to that huge city, and was there with Bennett and Nathan now for *them*.

Because she loved them.

Her heart felt stretched and full—a good feeling, even if it was still new and unnerving.

Slipping her arm around Bennett's waist, she glanced back. Nathan looked at her with the same tense expression Bennett wore. Neither of the Crofton brothers were glad to be back in Chicago.

Bennett paused, adjusting the strap to his backpack as he shifted to glance at Nathan. "Dad said he'd meet us at baggage claim."

"I'll believe it when I see it." Nathan adjusted his dark hat and reapplied the headphones he'd kept on his ears during the flight. With brows furrowed and mouth in a tight frown, Nathan pointed his attention toward the floor, closing off further conversation.

Hazel's heart cracked. This version of Nathan wasn't the kid *she* knew. It was the kid who had first shown up in Luna almost a year before—sullen, chock-full of attitude, difficult, and . . . deeply wounded. She would do anything to get the other version of Nathan Crofton back. The one who grinned with abandon while he raced around a snowy track on a pair of cross-country skis. The one who held himself strong and steady while he took aim at a target.

Hazel would do anything to get that life back for him. Anything, including becoming his and Gemma's legal guardian alongside Bennett after they were married. And moving to town where there was a house big enough for the four of them.

But that wasn't as simple as she and Bennett getting married. People made life so complicated.

A maze of worries and what-ifs spun through her mind as the three of them scurried through the terminal. When they finally reached the escalator to baggage claim, she was clutching Bennett's hand. Halfway down the moving stair ride, a flicker of color drew her attention.

"Oh man, come on," Nathan muttered from behind her.

The color came into focus—a bouquet of red and blue balloons alongside a sign that read *Welcome back, Nate!* Behind the sign stood a couple—a woman with dark hair like Nathan's and an oval-shaped face like Gemma's—and Chip, whom Hazel had met. Holding the balloons was Gemma, her way-too-bright smile the sure tell that she was not at all comfortable with what was happening but didn't want anyone to be upset.

"What is this?" Bennett grumbled beneath his breath.

"A show," Nathan said, a little too loud. "Nothing more than a show to make them feel better."

"Nathan!" The woman—Nathan's mom, Mindi?—squealed and came around from behind the sign. She jogged to Nathan and wrapped her arms around his neck. "I'm so glad you made it back." She leaned back, cupping his face. "And you're safe. For heaven's sake, you gave us such a scare!"

Nathan held himself like a wooden chess piece. "Hi, Mom," he muttered.

"Hi, Mom?" Mindi stared at him. Blinked. Then laughed, looking at Bennett. "That's my Nathan. Full of spark." Shaking her head, she stepped back and then held out a hand. "It's good to see you again, Bennett."

Bennett gripped her hand but stood stiffly as she moved in to hug him.

"This must be your lovely girlfriend." Mindi continued with the smiling charade. "Hazel, right?" She moved to hug Hazel.

Hazel stepped back and held a hand between them.

Pausing in the awkwardness of the moment, Mindi's brows folded. But then she took Hazel's hand and held on. "I'm Mindi, Bennett's stepmom. Gemma talks of nothing but you. Seems our Bennett has found himself one in a million."

Hazel attempted a smile. "It's nice to meet you," she mumbled.

Chip had busied himself rolling up the sign and tucked it under his arm. "Nate." He stepped beside Nathan and gripped the kid's neck. "Glad you finally made it back. We have some things to discuss."

"Not here, Dad," Bennett said.

Chip met Bennett's solemn look with raised brows. "Of course not." Then he broke out a smile. "We celebrate first. Let's get your luggage, and then we're headed to Offshore Rooftop."

"That's on the Navy Pier," Bennett said. "And I'm pretty sure you need reservations."

"Exactly. Our table will be ready at eight."

"Dad, we haven't eaten since nine this morning."

"Then you're sure to enjoy your meal." Chip clapped Bennett on the shoulder and then reached for Nathan with his opposite arm. "A homecoming celebration requires a great dinner, don't you think? Offshore is your favorite, right, Nate?"

Nathan glared at Chip, then ducked under his arm and walked toward the baggage belt that was now spinning with various sizes and shapes of luggage. He waited for his black duffel bag, snatched it up with more muscle than needed, and slung it over his shoulder.

"How about you two?" Mindi asked, ignoring Nathan's obvious irritation. "Do you need help getting your bags?"

Bennett patted his backpack. "We both carried on."

"Oh." Mindi looked at Hazel, taking her in from head to toe. "Were you planning to do some shopping while you're here? I am an expert on the Magnificent Mile, and I'd love to have a girls' day out. We can go tomorrow while the guys are at the game."

Acutely uncomfortable, especially since Mindi made it plain that Hazel's worn boots, Wranglers, and short-sleeve button-down were not impressive, Hazel shifted her attention to Gemma.

"You look perfect," Gemma said, her grin sincere in that moment. Then passing the balloons to her mom, she stepped close, and Hazel wrapped her in a hug. "I'm so glad to see you."

"Me too," Hazel whispered. "You okay?"

The girl nodded against her, though Hazel could feel a ragged exhale release from Gemma's body. Hazel hung on for an extra heartbeat.

"What's this about a game?" Bennett asked.

Chip smiled like he was handing out candy to children at a parade. "Yep. Cubs, tomorrow. I landed some box seat tickets." He shook Nathan's shoulders. "How about that?"

"I hate baseball," Nathan muttered.

"What?" Chip snorted. "No you don't. You love the Cubs. Remember when I took you to that game and you said it was the best day ever?"

Nathan pinned a raised-brow look on his dad. "When I was six?"

Chip rubbed his neck. "Surely not. Hasn't been that long . . ."

Nathan shook his head and started for the exit.

Hazel watched him pass through the double sliding doors. Bennett's fingers wove with hers. "Welcome back to Chicago," he whispered.

She squeezed his hand and shot him a sympathetic expression. No wonder neither brother wanted to come back. Nice dinners and extravagant gifts were a poor substitute for real love.

Had Chip ever known real love at all?

Janie had gone to work, and she hadn't disappointed. Not that Grady had known what to expect or had anything to measure some kind of hope against. But the lodge had been tastefully decorated with hurricane lamps, soft gray-green foliage, and a dotting of daisies in just the right places.

On the covered front deck, where the small number who had gathered for a quick night-before-the-wedding dinner, gauzy white curtains fluttered in the cool mountain breeze, lit in a soft yellow-white haze by twinkling lights woven within the fabric. The long wooden table ran down the middle of the deck, set with crisp white plates and shimmering crystal glasses, and decorated with the greenery, lamps, and daisies that adorned the inside of the lodge.

Yep. Janie had done what she'd promised—given them a simple, elegant wedding to mark the day of their marriage. Now there was only to go through with it. Tomorrow at eleven, the earliest the JP of Elk County had been available.

Grady slipped the back of his knuckles down Isa's arm as she fiddled with the skirt of her summer dress. The vivid coral color of the long, flowing fabric was stunning on her, accentuating her honey-bronze skin, dark-chocolate eyes, and glossy dark hair.

This stunningly beautiful woman was about to become his wife. His heart lurched and breath caught as the thought trounced all his reservations about this giant leap forward.

Isabel Briggs.

Isa Briggs.

Grady and Isa Briggs.

As he rehearsed the fit of names together, he couldn't help the lift of his mouth. They worked together, a harmony of sound.

Isa sucked in a quiet breath at his touch, then glanced at him over her shoulder. Her eyes didn't have the usual merry quality he'd come to expect from her. No teasing glint. No flirtatious fire. In truth, she hadn't seemed happy all evening. Instead, she wore a look of exhaustion and worry—one that she'd tried to mask with a fake smile that certainly must make her face ache by now.

"You okay?" Grady whispered.

She glanced at the deck just outside the open double doors where they stood, then looked back at him. "I need to talk to you."

While dread coiled through his middle, Grady ran a quick inspection over the people settling into chairs at the table. Mr. and Mrs. Romero, who had been surprisingly pleased with Grady after recovering from the initial shock of having him ask for Isa's hand in marriage. José and Rosalina, Isa's older, protective brother and his wife, who were more reserved about this fast engagement and wedding. Hunter and Janie, along with Mama Bulldog and Tara Crofton.

That rounded out the wedding party—such as it was. The only people who knew about Grady and Isa's coming nuptials—besides Bennett and Hazel and Grady's mother, Sue, who would arrive in town sometime tonight so that she could witness her only son's wedding.

Not what Grady had imagined for his wedding, the few times he'd imagined getting married at all. But that was hardly a bother. In his view, one didn't actually need a wedding to get married. This was all for Isa, and he was certain that it wasn't the large spectacle she had imagined for her wedding.

Was that what was wrong? Or was she going to call the whole thing off? Grady found her pensive stare still on him. He nodded, took a light hold of her elbow, and led her to Hunter's office, which was tucked to the side of the large front room.

Once they were both inside, he shut the door and turned to Isa. "Something wrong?"

Seemed an inane question. She looked . . . terrified.

An urge to comfort this woman who was facing so much upheaval had him closing the space between them. His fingers found hers.

Isa swallowed, and her hands trembled.

"Isa, it's going to be okay." Was she worried about the wedding or about things after they were officially husband and wife? "After tomorrow, we'll take . . . *things* slow."

She winced and didn't meet his eyes.

"I swear, Isa. I'll never hurt you."

"I know, Grady." She looked up, honesty in those dark eyes. She nodded as emotion strained her features. "I know that," she repeated, relief in her breathy voice. "I'm not afraid of you."

"Do you not want to do this?" Strange, how everything in him cried out for her to deny this out he was offering. Should he be this emotionally invested in a marriage that was for her protection and not one ounce for love?

Of course he should. He'd promised he'd choose to love her every day, hadn't he? So there was at least an ounce of it in this.

She bit her lip, then slowly shook her head. "No, that's not what I was thinking."

"You're upset."

This time she nodded.

"Tell me."

Deep color infused her face. She drew a breath, exhaled, then squeezed his fingers that he'd woven with hers. "I . . . I don't want our first kiss to be in front of everyone."

Grady blinked. Their first kiss? That was the last thing he'd been worried about. As his heart slugged with warm pleasure, a grin worked its way onto his mouth. "Are you asking me, the sour-faced fun-hater, to kiss you?"

Her lips rolled together, her expression a sweet concoction of vulnerability and hope. "You weren't supposed to hear me say that about you."

Though he should feel the twinge of irritation—and rejection—at having remembered clearly Isa saying those exact things, instead he felt the stirrings of hope. And attraction.

Oh, so much attraction. He was tired of fighting that.

Grady couldn't remember thinking a woman was so alluring than Isa was in that tender moment. He drew her closer and lifted his hand to trace the curve of her jaw with his thumb. "We've kissed before," he whispered, lowering his head toward hers. "In the alley. Remember?"

Eyes wide, she shook her head. "That doesn't count."

Thank goodness. He'd gladly take this chance of kissing redemption. Sliding his palm to her neck he lowered farther, until his lips were mere whisper from hers. "You sure?"

"Yes." Her breath was a mesmerizing thrill against his mouth. How was a man supposed to resist that?

Grady didn't even try. He was a groom, after all.

He brushed her lips with his. Electricity fired through his veins. A heady fog wrapped around him as he took another pass. And another. The sweet haze took him in deeper. Kissing Isa was like taking a long breath after being pressed under water. Simple. Profound. And not enough.

Before he regained steady thinking—remembering that he was *not* an enamored groom and she was *not* a lovestruck bride—Grady had her tucked in close, and they both worked to find an even breath.

Heart thundering, he pressed his head against hers. Isa slid her hand from his neck to his chest and released a shuddered sigh.

"Will that do?" he teased.

Her smile was relief and wonder. And so heart-stirringly lovely. "I think so." Then her eyes fluttered open.

Ah. There was the warmth. The teasing. *The flirting!* Grady drank it in, nearly giddy that this time it was all for him.

"I think you're right." He stepped back and traced the line of her lips with the tips of his fingers. "The alley kiss didn't count at all."

Astonishment filled her expression. And then she laughed.

Grady tucked her close to his side, and they walked to the door. He paused, his hand on the doorknob. "Are you ready to marry me now?"

"Yes." She pressed into him. "I think you'll do."

All of nine people were there.

Isa tucked away the small disappointment as she stepped from one of the first-floor suites in the Splendor—a room Janie and Hunter had named the Spruce Suite. The cream silk she wore had been Janie's wedding dress and was a touch too long. Isa gathered the length in one hand as she surveyed the tiny gathering near the stone fireplace.

Not the wedding of her dreams. She was certain it wasn't what Grady had hoped for either—particularly since his mother hadn't shown up.

Did that bother him? She didn't know him well enough to say for sure. And that was . . . upsetting.

But when the tug of disappointment and worry began to make her heart sink, her groom turned from his quiet conversation with her brother and settled his gaze on her. The twitch of his mouth wasn't exactly a smile, but his expression warmed. As Isa met his look, she was transported back to the evening before—to the moment Grady's lips had first brushed hers.

She hadn't been prepared for the way his kiss stirred her. Enveloped her with warm desire while at the same time wrapping her with a sense of peace. In truth, she hadn't been prepared to kiss him at all. That wasn't why she'd told Grady that they'd needed to talk before they'd joined the others for dinner last night.

Before he'd taken her hand in his after shutting them in the office, she had rehearsed a speech that would have made this day a very different day.

She hadn't wanted him to sacrifice his life this way. And perhaps a little more honest and a whole lot more selfish, she wasn't sure she could commit to a cold, loveless marriage, even if it was the smart move. Even if Grady was good and trustworthy and committed to keeping her safe. Imagining awkward evenings with a man who would scowl at her attempts at making life fun, long nights of yearning for things not possible between them, and mornings of relief when they parted ways for the day made her exhausted and sad.

It all sounded like a life Isa could not endure.

So she was going to call it off. Until Grady had turned to her with that warm, concerned look in his eyes. Until he'd taken her hand in his.

Until she'd asked him to kiss her.

And wonder of all wonders, he did. Oh goodness, did he ever.

This marriage might not be lifeless after all.

Her groom kept a keen watch on her as she rounded the large structural beam in the center of the lodge and stepped toward the small group waiting to witness their vows. Was that wonder in his eyes? Isa hoped it was, and not simply her imagination fed by way too many romance novels. Grady was as handsome as he was good, and as much beyond her as he was solemn, and if he wanted her . . . if he could *love* her . . .

A painful squeeze clamped in her chest. Such a beautiful, dangerous hope.

She didn't deserve him, and a small, pernicious voice whispered that Grady knew that fact just as well as she did. That someday he would resent that he'd been trapped in this marriage with her. But she'd given him three opportunities to walk away. He'd firmly remained on this matrimonial course, eyes wide open. And by that kiss last night, he was committed to making the most of it.

As she neared the fireplace and the man who, in moments, would become her husband, Isa determined to make it worth his sacrifice.

Grady lay on his side, arm beneath his pillow, propping his head up just enough to stare down at the sleeping woman beside him. Cool night air skated over his bare shoulder, and he wondered if it chilled his wife's arms as well.

Isabel Briggs. My wife.

He'd not expected the thrill that made his heart rate spike. There had been much in the past twenty-four hours that he'd not expected.

White moonlight poured through the crack in the bedroom curtains, spilling over his shoulder and illuminating Isa's lovely face with a serene, if not surreal, glow. He'd not expected to wake up like this. Next to her.

While he had been willing to take *things*—as he'd said to her—slow, Isa had come to him with other ideas. He had resigned that his wedding night wouldn't be anything like most men would hope. Isa though . . .

"You took me as your wife," she'd whispered to him last night. "Take me as your lover too."

He'd been utterly stunned. And spellbound. For a fleeting moment, he'd wondered why she would be willing to move so quickly into intimacy and thought to press her about it. But with each deepening kiss, such worrisome questions faded beyond comprehension.

He had taken her as his wife. And now he knew her as his lover. In the soft, intimate light of the moon as he gazed upon her, curled up beside him, he had no regrets.

"I take you as my own. To honor and to cherish. To love and protect." He reached to finger the soft sheen of her dark hair, brushing a lock from her cheek and tucking it behind her ear. The impact of his vows hit deeper, more profoundly as he repeated them softly to his sleeping bride. "I choose you as the one with whom I will spend my life."

Isa drew in a deep breath and released it on a sigh. The mattress moved beneath him as she shifted, burrowing in closer.

He wondered what she saw in her dreams, what she felt in the midst of sleep. He hoped it was him, as he drew her in close, pressing a kiss to her temple.

"Choose me," he whispered, almost inaudibly. The desperation of that plea was so startling and complete it made him ache. "Choose to love me."

Eighteen

Isa wiped down the counter after the afternoon lunch rush, picking up used napkins and a few stray utensils as she went through the cleanup routine. Janie hadn't come down to help today, which was fine, but that meant more prep work waited in the kitchen that Isa needed to get through to be ready for the dinner crowd by five.

As she tossed a fistful of napkins into the garbage, the diamond on her left hand winked at her. She paused, curling her fingers into her palm and rocking her hand so that the stone caught the light.

Sparkles flashed back at her, and half a grin lifted the corner of her mouth.

One week in, and marriage wasn't too bad. She didn't love the drab state of Grady's small rental house, and she hated his dark-green bedding set. But living with the man himself hadn't been so bad. He was neat. He didn't stink. He was polite. He packed his own lunch. And he sure could kiss, when she initiated such things.

Even so, a whisper of longing kept breaking through her recitation of all the good things she could name in their circumstances. She wished for tender good-morning kisses. And would they ever find a place of ease—both in their conversations and in their shared silences—or was it always to be strained and mildly uncomfortable? Would Grady ever come into the kitchen, either here at the café or at the house she was trying to convince herself to call *home*, and walk up behind her to slip his arms around her?

Would he ever whisper the tender words of love she longed to hear?

Isa squeezed her fingers tight and shut her eyes. *Things are good as they are. Be grateful. And make sure he never regrets this.*

Her pep talk made her feel small and defeated. She was grateful. And things were good—they certainly weren't bad.

The bell tinkling over the front door blessedly jarred her out of her mixed-up thoughts. Wiping her hands down her apron, she turned with a ready smile for whomever had come in off Main. That practiced expression faltered at the sight of the man who had walked through the door. Not because she wasn't glad to see him. But because this was the first time her husband had shown up at the café unexpectedly since they'd been married. And because she didn't know how he wanted her to react.

And mostly, because he didn't smile at her.

A familiar twist of disappointment rolled through her. She'd thought perhaps now that she was his wife, he wouldn't always pin her with his frown. With his stern disapproval.

Bottling up a sigh, she reignited her smile. It hurt the tense muscles in her face. "Grady." She ignored the slight pinch in her cheeks, walked to her husband, and tipped up on her toes to kiss his cheek.

Grady exhaled and curled a stiff arm around her waist. Did they look as staged and stilted as Isa felt in that moment?

Disappointment and frustration collided as Isa dropped down to flat feet and pulled away. "I didn't know you were coming in today, or I would have saved you some corn chowder."

"It's okay. I have my PBJ." Grady rubbed his well-groomed beard and glanced around the café.

Yes, she was sure he had his PBJ. He had one every day, along with a bag of baby carrots or an orange, a handful of trail mix, and a frozen Ho Ho.

Ho Hos were apparently Grady's weakness. Good to know he had one.

Isa wiped her hands on her apron, though she didn't need to, and shot a quick glance around the room. Hiram Smith sat in a corner booth reading a worn copy of *A Separate Peace*. Sheriff Jeremy Yates sat at the table beside the front window, a coffee cup near his left hand and paperwork scattered on the surface in front of him. Neither man took notice of them.

Grady pointed to the counter. "Mind if I bring my lunch in and eat it there?"

"Of course not." Unease swirled in Isa's stomach. Was Grady checking up on her? If so, was it because he was worried about her safety, or was he worried that she was there flirting? She would guess the latter—that would explain the frown.

For the record, she didn't flirt nearly as much as Grady believed. She was friendly—which was part of her job. She liked to smile, enjoyed laughing. She liked to find the fun in life. Those things weren't synonymous with flirting. Were they?

At any rate, she'd not been *flirting*. She had made an intentional effort to *not* flirt, keeping her grins extra tame, and any sort of laughing had been reduced to a smothered chuckle. Frankly, the effort had been exhausting and had infected her with a heavy sense of insecurity. But for her marriage—and for Grady's respect—Isa was determined to *not* flirt.

Did he still think so little of her?

You're overthinking this. She brightened her smile—for him. "I can make you a cream soda, if you'd like?" That was one of the few sugary treats, besides the Ho Hos, she'd found that Grady actually indulged in. Oh—and apple pie. But Janie always made those, and his compliments of them gave growth to the vine of jealousy already too big in Isa's heart.

"Thanks." He brushed her fingers as he turned to go out the door, but then he paused. He pivoted back to her and leaned down to brush a kiss against her temple.

If it weren't so awkward, and clearly a second thought, Isa would have claimed the gesture a sweet one. Yep, they were sure settling into this marriage thing well.

Grady left, setting off the bell, only to make the thing jingle again thirty seconds later as he reentered with his brown-bag lunch. Side by side, but there could have been a hundred miles between them, they walked to the counter. Grady saddled up a stool, and Isa walked around to the back side and retrieved a large glass. She poured in the cream, the sweet syrup, and the soda and stirred, then topped off the fizzing liquid with a spray of homemade whip.

Grady had half his apple jelly and peanut butter sandwich gone by the time she set the glass in front of him.

"Mami has a stash of huckleberry jam at home. I could get some the next time I visit."

Grady paused mid-bite, then pulled the sandwich from his mouth. He looked at the bread, then at Isa, and shook his head. "That's okay. Thanks though."

"Oh." Isa pulled her hands back from the countertop and let them fall to her sides. Another failed attempt at fishing out his smile. "Okay then. She always makes a ton, if you change your mind."

At the front window, Jeremy picked up his papers, stacked them neatly, and stood with his coffee cup in hand. He wandered to the counter and plunked the mug onto it. "Thanks for letting me use this as an office space." He laid some cash on the counter next to the mug.

"Anytime," Isa said.

"Mike says it'll be another week before they get the skunk stink out of the jail. So same time tomorrow." He knocked his fist on the counter and turned to go but paused when he saw Grady.

"Well, look at this." Jeremy shifted his papers and clapped Grady on the shoulder. "I didn't realize it was you who came in. Heard the two of you got hitched." He chuckled, giving Grady another friendly smack. "Congratulations!"

Grady turned. "Thanks." Then he accepted Jeremy's handshake.

"Planning a honeymoon later?" Jermey asked.

Heat spread up Isa's chest as Grady's brows folded in confusion. He turned and met her gaze. Was he expecting her to answer? She had no idea what to say.

"We haven't . . ." Grady started, then paused, turning his attention back to Jeremy. "That is to say, we don't have plans for anything soon. I can't take time off right now. Summer is a heavy-traffic season."

"Gotcha." Jeremy nodded, then grinned widely. "Talk about taking people by surprise. No one even knew you were dating. That's the way to do it though, if you ask me. I can't tell you how often people would ask us when we were gonna get married. Got old, you know? And between you and me, the pressure confused things, if you know what I mean. This way, it's just done, and you can get on with life. Am I right?"

"Right." Grady dipped one nod.

"Well, buddy, congrats again. I'm happy for you." Jeremy strode toward the door, meeting Hiram there.

The quieter man merely nodded toward Isa, and she knew that he'd left money on the table for her, as he did every day. Hiram exited the door Jeremy held open, and Jeremy followed.

And then there were two.

"Sorry about that," Grady muttered.

Isa stiffened. It wouldn't have been bad at all if Grady had acted like he was at least half-excited about their marriage. Instead, the man had seemed offended that someone would bring it up. Of course people would comment. They lived in Luna, for heaven's sake. Did he think they'd just slide under the radar of this tiny mountain community?

Grady's eyes widened at her scowl. "Isa?"

"What is wrong with you?"

Dropping back onto his stool, Grady lowered his head and ran a hand along his neck. After a breath, he lifted his chin again. "I got a call about an hour ago." Shoulders slumped, he leaned his elbows against the counter. "I've been assigned a patrol trip in Yellowstone next week—one of the ranger's got married and is taking vacation time. It's a ten-day assignment." He managed a low chuckle. "How's that for irony?"

"Oh." Then there had been something bothering him. It wasn't that he was embarrassed about their marriage or upset with her. Isa crept back toward the counter that separated them and laid her hand against the polished wood near his arm.

He peeked back at her, his eyes full of regret and tinged with worry. "I wish I could tell them no."

Because he would worry about her, or because he would miss her?

Did it matter? Weren't they both evidence of his care for her?

She leaned in, tentatively brushing her fingertips along the fabric of his shirt. "Can I come with you?"

His eyes widened. "You . . . you would want to?"

"Yeah. It could be like . . . like *our* honeymoon."

Color bled onto his cheeks above his beard. He swallowed while holding her gaze. "All said and done, it'll be around fifty miles of hiking, round trip. A couple of the legs are close to fifteen miles for the day."

"I can handle that."

"You can?"

"Sure. No problem." She'd gone on weeklong backpacking trips with her dad and brother on several occasions. They had been amazing trips—and some of her favorite memories happened out there in the wild. "Not my first excursion."

Grady blinked. Sat up a little straighter. "The only patrol cabin is up at Sportsman Lake. Most nights will be in a tent."

Isa chuckled. "I've slept in a tent before, Grady."

For several heartbeats, Grady stared at her in stunned silence.

"What—" He leaned in closer, lowering his voice to a whisper. "What about the baby? That would make it difficult, wouldn't it? I mean, the backcountry is challenging. A lot of it is downright hard."

Her heart warmed at his concern. "I feel fine. No more morning sickness. Now is a good time, I think. And though it might surprise you, I'm actually pretty tough. At least when it comes to hiking. You can check with José, if you want."

Again with the staring, silent response. Isa's heart sank. She leaned back and softened her voice to match his. "Unless you don't want me to go."

Grady blinked, and then his intense look softened on her. "I want you." His answer came in a rush. Then his hand covered hers, and he wrapped her fingers with his. "I want you to go."

She needed guidance.

Isa resolved to seek help, which was why she found herself in Pastor Nolan's tiny office in the church on the west side of Luna.

"I hear that you and Grady Briggs are married now," Pastor said.

Isa looked at her hands and nodded.

"Congratulations."

"Thank you."

A span of silence stretched, making her discomfort double. Finally, she forced herself to lift her chin. She found the man waiting patiently, kindness in his demeanor.

"That's why I'm here."

"Your marriage?"

"Yes. Maybe you were surprised to hear about it?"

"I was, to be honest."

She nibbled on her bottom lip. "The thing is, we . . . we aren't in love. I mean, we are both committed to each other and determined to make things work together. And Grady says he will choose to love me every day. But that's not really the same."

"That sounds . . . unconventional in our day." Pastor chose his words carefully but kept any trace of censure out of his voice.

"Yes." Isa winced. Between the humiliation of this awkward conversation and the disappointment in admitting out loud that her husband didn't love her, she wasn't sure what had possessed her to come here today.

But she really needed help.

"That bothers you."

She swallowed and nodded, fisting her summer skirt in her moist palms.

"Would it help to know that many couples who are, quote, *madly in love* when they get married end up wondering if they'd ever liked each other in the first place later on?"

She chuckled at his attempt to ease her discomfort. "No, not really. But thanks for trying."

He tilted his head, a kind grin on his lips. "How can I help you, Mrs. Briggs?"

Hearing her married name did something strange—something uncomfortable and yet lovely—to her heart. "I want my husband to love me," she admitted in a rush. "Not just *choose* to love me. But to *fall in* love with me."

"Are you in love with him?"

She blinked and looked at her Teva sandals. She shook her head. "No."

"Do you think you could fall in love with him?"

Warm tears rimmed her eyelids as she nodded.

"That's a good start."

The man's gentleness drew her attention up from the floor. "How can I make him fall in love with me?"

"I don't know about a formula, Isa. And I doubt *anyone* can make anyone else do anything. But perhaps I can commend to you what our Lord prescribed to us for all relationships. That is that we treat others the way we would have them treat us." He paused to let that settle.

Could it be that simple? Wait—that wasn't simple. If it was, there would be peace and harmony all over the world.

"Perhaps if you can find the courage, my young friend, you could love Grady the way you would have him love you?"

It was something. A direction. A hope.

"Are you that brave, Isabel Briggs? To love when you have no promise of being loved in return?"

No. Not on her own. "I want to be."

Pastor Nolan smiled with approval. "Yield your heart, then. First to Christ—and ask that He shape you with His love. And then to your husband. Practice love."

Nodding, Isa stood.

Pastor also stood and reached forward a hand. "Isa, falling in love and loving someone are very different. I think you will discover that *loving* is the deeper end of the pool."

Nineteen

Grady sighed, relief emptying from his lungs, as he drove away from the Splendor. Isa's brother had come to Luna and had been up at the lodge fishing with Hunter. A moment of serendipity had Grady and José alone on the rocky beach while Hunter grilled some burgers. Grady had seen the opportunity for what it was—the chance to confirm what Isa had claimed about her backpacking.

José had promised Isa was capable of the trip Grady laid out. Had even chuckled when Grady pressed him for the third time for reassurance.

"I'm surprised you married her without knowing how much she loves the trail." José had given Grady a suspicious glance, but then his expression eased. "She comes alive out there in the mountains and loses this desperate need for . . ." He stopped there.

A compelling demand to know what Isa's big brother saw as her *desperate need* seized in Grady's mind.

But José paused, dipped his head, and shook it. "That's just me being critical." When he tipped his chin up again, it was with a thoughtful look. "Anyway, if you'd taken her out on some hikes before you got married, it would have made sense to me, this out-of-the-blue wedding. I would have thought you were a good match."

Grady hadn't any idea what to say to that. Even now, as he drove back to town to meet Isa for supper, he wasn't sure what to think. Had José meant to compliment them—sort of? Like *Now that I think about it, you and Isa do make sense.* Or was he digging into the quiet concern he'd kept unvoiced but clearly shown. *What is going on with you two?*

Grady had left it alone. Simply thanked José for the assurance that Isa would be good on the trail—and for the offer José had given to bring his sister's gear to Luna when he came for Bible study at the end of the week. Things got more awkward when José suggested—rather firmly—that Grady join them for the study.

"You do read your Bible, right?" José had asked.

"Uh, yeah. I do." That had been the main point Mr. Romero, Isa's father, had made sure of—that Grady knew Jesus as Lord and Savior and would promise to walk in the faith alongside his daughter. *If you promise me that you share that foundation and that you will love her the way Jesus loves His church, then I am willing to give you my blessing.*

Grady gave his word.

But Bible study with Isa's brother? That seemed . . . complicated.

The week before their trip passed in a strange blend of *way too fast* and *goodness, it felt long.*

Because he always kept his word, Grady had met José and Hunter and Pastor Nolan at the café for Bible study a few short days later. And it *had* been uncomfortable.

Not just because Grady wasn't used to such things—he'd never done a men's small group study before in his life. He went to church when he could. Read his Bible on his own. Listened to a syndicated sermon program when he couldn't attend a service. And that was about it.

Being the first believer in his family since he didn't know when, and only coming to faith in Christ through a friend in college, Grady didn't have a whole lot of the church life experience. Certainly hadn't learned it as a kid beyond the weeklong summer Bible school camps he went to.

Not only did he have the ineptness of an amateur when it came to Bible study, there was also having his new brother-in-law there, who seemed acutely suspicious of Grady. And there was also Hunter, who recently married the woman Grady had dated not so long before. It made for solid ninety minutes of discomfort.

Was this how small-town circles went?

Grady opted not to dwell on that awkward question for too long. The men had discussed the section of the Bible they had read, discussed the events of their lives that were relevant to the study—and the events that caused concern (ahem, if Grady hadn't been there, he was fairly certain he and Isa would have been on that topic list), and then prayed.

All in all, it'd been . . . fine. If circumstances had been different, Grady likely would have called it *good*, even. Perhaps would have been hungry to be a consistent part of it. But as it was, he felt on the fringes and under the microscope, and he didn't enjoy either.

Grady hated being the outsider, but that seemed to be his lot in life. He did his best to be friendly and optimistic, but at the end of the day, it was him. Just him. Always. Having a front-and-center reminder that he was on the outside looking in sat in his heart about as comfortably as a burr in his boot.

He was glad to get Isa's gear though. The quality of the pack, and the thoroughness of her supplies, lent him some peace about her going. Even so, he made some *just in case* plans as he charted out the route in the Gallatin Range he'd been assigned. It was a challenge, accounting for the backcountry permits that had been issued that he would need to patrol, yet charting the course that would allow Isa the most opportunities to bow out before they made the hard push through Electric Pass and to Sportsman Lake.

He liked what he'd come up with. And had no trouble getting it approved by the backcountry patrol. As long as he worked in the northwest quadrant of park, they were happy.

When the morning to leave arrived, he woke long before dawn approached. Feet on the cool surface of the floor beside his bed, he looked over his shoulder. His wife's lovely profile peeked through the nest of a pillow, flannel sheets, and dark-green comforter.

Grady's breath caught as his chest squeezed. Pulling in a sharp breath, he turned against the mattress, reached across the dim space, and traced the dark hair that framed her soft face.

He wasn't alone anymore. Nearly two weeks into their marriage, and that reality was starting to break through the iron fence a lifetime of solitude had erected around his heart.

Isa stirred at his touch, and for a breath, Grady felt caught. Her sleepy eyes blinked open, and she shifted to look at him. A long, distinctly awkward silence gripped them, and Grady wondered if she would roll over, giving him her back.

Seemed like a reasonable thing to do. After all, they'd only just gotten married and had barely known each other before that.

But she didn't do that. Instead, her full lips eased into a gentle smile, and she rifled through the burrow of covers until her fingertips brushed his hand. "Good morning," she whispered.

Grady swallowed against emotions he couldn't define. Fear? Hope? Wonder? "Morning." His untried morning voice garbled from his throat.

Her study of him turned curious, and he thought she'd say something teasing. Flirtatious. When she didn't, but only squeezed his fingers and moved to get up, a stab of disappointment sank into his gut.

He cleared his throat. "You don't have to get up yet."

"I'm always up this early." She slipped an oversized Bozeman Hawks sweatshirt over her head and settled it around her small torso.

Had that belonged to a boyfriend from her past? Seemed too large for her to have gotten for herself.

Grady straightened his shoulders and shook away the intrusive question. Like it mattered now. "You could sleep in."

"Not a chance." All sleepiness had evaporated from her. She flashed an excited grin as she straightened the sheet and then the comforter on her side of the bed. "Today we leave for Yellowstone." Her smile widened. She leaned against the mattress with her knee and then braced both hands against his unmade side of the bed. "For our honeymoon." She winked. Then pressed a kiss against his bearded cheek.

Grady had no idea what to do. He could barely think. If he allowed himself to operate on instinct, he would have wrapped her with both arms, pulled her close, and acted like the bridegroom he was supposed to be. That would be what a normal husband would do, right?

He didn't. He kept himself stiff and aloof.

Isa held a brief look on him and then moved away, back to her own side of the bed. Then she fixed the wrinkles she'd put in her made-up side and headed out the door and down the hall toward the bathroom.

Was she upset with him? Disappointed in his lack of response?

Grady remained where he'd been—sitting on the mattress, his bare feet getting cold as they remained planted against the floor. He wanted her to flirt with him. Had no idea what to do when she did. And had absolutely no idea what to expect on this trip.

This *honeymoon*.

That seemed like a surefire recipe for disappointment. For them both.

TWENTY

BENNETT SOUGHT HIS DAD out in Chip's opulent office, located in the back of the house. "Dad, we should talk."

Chip finished typing on his computer, turned from the oversized screen taking center stage on his side desk, and swiveled his chair to face Bennett. Initially, his expression was stern rejection—and Bennett could understand. The man was working. But Bennett found that Nathan had been correct—their dad was always working. And if he wasn't, he was out.

Chip had given his sons the afternoon when they flew in, and the next day—part of the day—when they went to the Cubs game. During that time, there wasn't an opportunity to discuss what needed to be hammered out between them. Bennett had no interest in hemming around, waiting for Chip to decide to address the issues. He had a life back in Luna—one he loved. And he knew Hazel was itching to get back to her quiet lakeside mountain home, not to mention her pack of dogs.

"I suppose." Chip relaxed against the back of his leather chair. "I'm guessing this is about Nathan."

Surprised that his father hadn't dismissed him, Bennett lowered onto one of the large leather wingback chairs that flanked the front of Chip's desk. "Both the kids."

"Son, they're not your responsibility."

Bennett schooled the cringe Chip's use of *son* always provoked. "They matter to me."

"You think they don't matter to me?"

"I didn't say that."

"Implications . . ."

Bennett stifled a sigh. "I know they matter, Dad. But the truth is, they aren't happy here. You work all the time. And Mindi . . ."

Chip held up a hand. "I know. Mindi is leaving. The marriage was over before we even left for Europe. She filed for divorce—it will be finalized in a week. She just didn't want to tell the kids until it was done."

"She wants Gemma to move to Italy with her."

Nodding, Chip seemed to shrug that off. "Seems like a young girl's dream, don't you think?"

"No, I don't." Bennett leaned forward. "It's not Gemma's dream, and having the two of you toss her around like she's a plastic doll is tearing her up. She hates conflict, Dad, and she'll do just about anything to avoid it—including pasting on a smile and doing things that break her heart."

Chip scowled. "You make it sound like we're asking her to do something vile."

"No. But you don't think about *them*—about what is best for Nathan and Gemma." Bennett held a firm stare on his dad. "Why did you insist they come back here when you knew you and Mindi were done?"

"They're my kids."

"They were your kids when you sent them to Luna last fall. That didn't stop you."

"That was a temporary arrangement."

"And what arrangements have you made for life here? For when your ex-wife is gone, taking your daughter with her? What will happen to Nathan?"

Chip shrugged. "He'll stay with me. We'll be fine."

"Right. Dad, you didn't even notice that he'd run away!"

"What makes you think that you're a better parent than I am, Bennett? You barely even knew them until last fall."

Bennett leaned against a knee, pushing his hand into his hair. He prayed for wisdom—and for the Spirit of God to intercede on his heating temper. "Dad, this isn't about me and you. Have you talked to the kids?"

"They're the kids. We're the adults."

"But you only think in terms of yourself. That is the problem, Chip." Bennett kept his voice dead calm. "It has *always* been the problem. For once in your emancipated life, consider the needs of someone else—of your kids."

Chip's boiling glare remained focused on Bennett, but Bennett refused to look away. After several silent moments, Chip stood and paced behind the desk.

"What does your lawyer say?" He stopped, again pinning an angry look on Bennett.

"She says there are grounds to have the kids removed from your custody."

"What grounds?"

"Neglect."

Chip extended both hands, holding his arms wide, as if to say *look around you*. "Neglect? In all of this—"

"Wealth has nothing to do with anything. You left your children for nine months to go to Europe. When you're home, you barely notice them. You have no idea what they're doing, where they are, who they're with. Nathan's troubles prior to coming to Luna are well documented, and they point to neglect."

"What about Gemma?"

Bennett simply held a silent stare on him.

"Mindi wants her in Italy with her."

"Right. For two weeks, so she'll be a part of her mother's wedding to a man she's never met. And then she'll go to school. As in *boarding* school. Do you know how terrified Gemma feels about that?"

Chip's lowered his gaze and slowly sat down in his chair again.

"Dad, *talk* to her. Talk to both of them. I don't want a legal battle between us. I really don't want a fight at all. But I will fight if I have to. I'll fight for them, because I love them."

"You think I don't love them?"

Man, the question that could make or break this. *Do you?* That was how Bennett wanted to respond. But he kept it inside.

"Were you better off without me?" Chip took a different angle.

Another dicey question. Truthfully, as Chip was now, maybe Bennett had been better off without him. "No, I wasn't. I needed a father. One who didn't see me as something to throw money at as a guilt offering." Bennett peered at him, unable to keep the resentment from his voice. "But I had a stable, present mother who was involved in my life every single day. Who showed me what faithful, unselfish love was."

Chips expression hardened back to anger.

"The thing is, Chip, you're doing the same thing to Nathan and Gemma." Bennett stood up and approached the desk. "Just because they're currently under your roof doesn't mean that you're being the father they need. Bluntly put, you're just throwing money at them the same way you did me. If you think that keeping Nathan here is somehow atoning for leaving me, or doing better by him than you did me, then you're wrong."

"Then how should I do it, Bennett?" Chip nearly yelled. "How should I be a father to a kid who doesn't want me, doesn't appreciate what I give him, and has decided he's better off without me?"

Bennett felt his shoulders drop. Rubbing his neck, he sighed and shook his head. After a long moment, he met his father's glare. "I don't know, Dad. All I know is that Nathan changed in Luna. He came to life—and became a pretty good kid. One who was doing well in school, had friends—good friends who didn't get him into trouble. He found something he really loved in the biathlon. He and Hazel really connected. I'm not saying I'm better for him than you, because a kid needs their dad. I know that—trust me. I *know* that."

He returned to the wingback chair and lowered onto it. "But what you've got going on here isn't working. It isn't better for him, and it's not better for Gemma either. She's a beautiful, sweet girl who shouldn't have to carry the weight of keeping the peace for her parents. And she should be heard when she feels terrified about moving to a foreign country, being put into boarding school all alone where she doesn't even know the language. It's not fair, Dad. It's not right."

Chip's stony anger etched away while Bennett spoke, and he was left with a furrowed brow. He shifted to fold his hands on the desk and spent several minutes staring at them. Finally he swallowed audibly, then nodded. "I'll talk to them."

Bennett blinked. He'd gotten through? Chip had . . . had listened? He squeezed his eyes shut. *God, are You working here?*

He cleared his throat. "Thank you." He stood. "Thank you." Emotion made his voice a whisper as he repeated his gratitude. Then he turned to leave the office.

"Bennett."

At the door, Bennett stopped and turned. "Yeah?"

"What happened to you?"

Again, he blinked.

Chip lifted his face to look at him. "Is this all because of Hazel? Because you fell in love with her?"

"What do you mean?"

"You're different. You were . . . like me. Cutthroat. Determined to get what you wanted, no matter the cost. Now, you're soft. Not bad soft, but . . ." Chip blinked and visibly swallowed. "I don't know, just different."

"It wasn't Hazel." Another wave of powerful emotion surged through Bennett. He was different. Praise God, he was a new man. Not perfect, still riddled with error and sin. But he no longer lived only for himself. "But it was Love."

Chip raised an eyebrow. "God?"

Bennett nodded.

"I tried that."

"I wonder, Dad, if you truly did."

"What do you mean?"

"Did you ever surrender to God as your King? As the Lord of your life? Or did you think that God was your ticket to life as you wanted it to be?"

Chip's brows folded inward.

"I'm not accusing you. I just wonder, is all. Soft, make-all-my dreams-come-true Jesus isn't the Jesus of the Bible. Jesus—God is King. I wonder if you ever bowed before Him?"

Chip didn't answer. Instead, he lowered his gaze back to his folded hands. After several beats of silence, Bennett let himself out of the office.

But for the first time since his dad had taken the kids back to Chicago, he prayed for his father's heart. Specifically, for his salvation.

And as he did so, he felt his own heart soften.

The sun warmed the stretch of green fields and rolling mountains as Grady slowed his truck to turn into the Bighorn Pass Trailhead parking lot. Isa's pulse stuttered as she surveyed the expanse of backcountry before her. It would be an epic adventure, this time in Yellowstone's pristine wilderness.

If circumstances were different, it would be an amazing, romantic ten days alone with the man she'd married. As it was, though, the likelihood of that romance seemed about as high as the blue July sky suddenly salting the earth with snow. It could happen . . . but probably not.

Isa knotted her hands together as the vehicle came to a stop and the engine cut off. The drive down had been seasoned with stilted silence interrupted with even more awkward attempts at conversation.

"It was nice of Janie to give you the time off last minute," Grady had remarked at one point.

The temptation to bristle against his comment had lain right beneath her skin. Of course he would compliment Janie. Janie could do no wrong. Janie had his highest opinion. Janie would have made him happy. But true to Grady's savior-complex character, he'd sacrificed his heart to make her happy.

Isa pushed the bitterness and awful sense of inadequacy down deep. "Yep. There's no one like Janie. Good thing she's my boss."

Grady's jaw had tensed, as did his grip on the steering wheel. He kept his eyes on the road and didn't respond.

Maybe she hadn't shoved that bitterness down far enough.

So most of the miles that followed had passed without conversation. That would have been fine, if Isa had felt comfortable with her thoughts. But she couldn't stop assessing the way Grady approached her—almost always with a frown. She couldn't put out of her mind how much it stung to have him kiss her with such passion in the darkness of their shared bedroom but give her chilled distance in the daylight.

And earlier that morning? His stiffness at her touch, her kiss, her intentional flirting . . . made her ache. This marriage felt doomed to be a prison of lonely indifference. She couldn't make him love her, and he couldn't make himself feel things he didn't—even if he had promised that he would *choose* to love her.

“Made it.” Grady’s quiet comment saved Isa from drowning in her hopelessness as they both exited the truck.

Love him the way you would have him love you. Isa replaced her spiraling thoughts with Pastor’s advice. This trip would be the perfect opportunity to begin.

Before her, a green meadow blended into a scrubby patch of sage before it rose up to meet the forested hills that rolled back in layers into the Gallatin Mountains. The breathtaking view was set off in vivid greens, silvers, and purple blues by the bright sun working its way up the clear sky. A pine-seasoned breeze kissed her face as she stretched her back.

With the help of the gorgeous scene before her, Isa summoned a smile. “We did. Now for the fun part.”

Grady met her forced smile with a serious look and then nodded.

Sheesh. What was it going to take?

He rounded to the back of the truck and opened the back of the topper and then the tailgate. He’d taken meticulous time packing both the bags. He’d made lists—one for food, one for equipment, one for clothing—and whittled them down as far as he dared. He’d packed and repacked, weighed each bag, and repacked yet again, ensuring his backpack lugged the bulk of their supplies.

All for this moment. Grady passed her the smaller of the two backpacks.

Isa slung it around, putting first the right strap on her shoulder, then the left. She wiggled it on her back. “This doesn’t feel heavy enough.”

“It’s still two pounds more than I aimed for.” Grady slipped the larger pack over his shoulders.

“How much does yours weigh?”

He adjusted the straps and didn’t answer.

“Grady?”

Clipping the front buckles, he effectively ignored her.

Fine. Isa walked to the front of the truck and retrieved her ball cap from the cab. She smacked the door shut and pulled her ponytail through the back hole of the hat. Once the bill was in proper place, she walked around the front of the truck, meeting Grady there.

"Isa." Grady touched her elbow lightly, turning her to face him. "I'm sorry about this morning. Please don't be irritated with me."

This morning? That was all he was sorry for, all he thought was rubbing her wrong? Did he not know what his constant frowning did? How his stoic demeanor flattened her spirit? She kept trying to breach into whatever soft places might exist in his heart, and he kept resisting with the hard chill of steely indifference.

How was this marriage ever going to work?

Love him the way you would have him love you. That could be harder than she'd thought.

Grady edged a half step closer and slid his hand down her arm until his fingers brushed her. Then he took her hand, lacing their fingers together. "I'm glad you wanted to do this with me."

Her rising anger suddenly drained, and her heart did a small leap of joy. Perhaps he wasn't all cold disinterest and unaffected steel? She lifted her chin and met his gaze, finding those intense eyes searching and . . . hopeful? While she sorted out what she thought she saw, he leaned.

Isa's breath caught when his free hand cupped her face, and he pressed a gentle kiss to her mouth. This was . . . was . . . very unlike Grady.

Her tummy squeezed with electrified joy as her heart pitter-pattered with hope. She returned his sweet kiss before she pulled back enough to seek his gaze.

There was no censure there. No veil. Only an open look, steady on her.

"Shall we begin?"

The corners of her mouth lifted. "I'm ready if you are."

He returned her grin.

He. Returned. Her. Grin!

Then keeping her hand securely laced in his, he led her to the trail. They started their journey into the backcountry, and Isa felt like they were the only two people in the world. Seemed like just the right way a honeymoon should begin after all.

A few hours into their trek, and Grady felt the corners of his mouth lift as the tension drained from his neck and shoulders. What a contradiction—he hefted close to thirty-five pounds on his back. But his burden felt lighter with every step as the trail wound deeper into the Bridger Mountains and farther away from the highway—away from the danger that had loomed over Isa and from the weariness of his life shifting into chaos.

"I can actually see you breathing easier." Isa chuckled as she kept pace behind him.

How about that—even his wife could sense him relaxing, though she only saw his back, and she really didn't know him all that well.

There. Right there—that was what had felt empty and impossible. Grady's thoughts rolled back to earlier that morning, when he had sat like a damaged marionette on the bedside while Isa had flirted with him. Why couldn't he have responded the way a new husband should?

They didn't know each other. Not really. That was why.

But here, it seemed, Isa did have some insight into him. How had that happened?

She tries . . . she wants this marriage to be more than a protective-custody agreement.

So did he. Didn't he? Hadn't he vowed that he would choose to love her?

Did he know *how* to love her?

God, I'm pretty broken, you know? The silent prayer began in his mind but quickly stirred in his heart. Grady poured out things he'd never even really dwelled on before. *I've never had the kind of relationship that . . . that isn't rocky and hard. That isn't a constant lesson in disappointment and frustration. Not long term. Show me how.*

The trail wound into a section of thick conifer forest. As the trees cast a shadow over their path, blocking the warmth of the sun, Grady exhaled a quivering breath. *Help me really love my wife.*

"Wow." Isa's exhaled wonder jarred him from his prayer.

Grady stopped as the trees opened again, revealing a vista worthy of wonder. The trail curved gently to the right, and to the left, the land sloped downward in a dramatic sweep. At the bottom of that lush gap, the Gallatin River flowed, an ancient trail of power and grace. The water shimmered like polished silver, light from the sun dancing over the rippling surface.

"That is stunning." Isa's hand slipped through the hollow of his bent arm while he stood still, both hands gripping the straps of his pack. She leaned her head against his shoulder and sighed. Grady glanced down, his heart warming at the contented delight that filled her expression.

José hadn't been exaggerating—Isa came alive on the trail. They'd been hiking the whole morning, only a break once, and the entire time, she had been excited. Embracing this backcountry beauty with both arms. This woman at his side was bursting wonder and joyful life. And he liked her.

Oh man, did he like her.

Grady turned and bent his head to kiss the top of her ball cap. "I'm glad you're here."

She leaned back and lifted her chin. Sweet, beautiful, rich brown eyes met his gaze, and his heart soared. He leaned down again and found her lips with his own. When she sighed, he pulled her closer, taking that gentle kiss to more intimate depths.

Goodness, but he could get lost in this heady wonder. She was addictive. And that made him terrified.

Pulling back from the kiss, Grady worked to steady his breathing.

Isa fixed the hat he'd knocked askew and then winked at him. "I'm pretty happy to be here with you." She turned back toward the river and nearly skipped down the trail ahead of him.

Grady swallowed, working to reset his mind. He rolled his lips together, savoring the electric sensation that tingled there, and trailed his happy wife as she took the lead. She moved as if the twenty-pound burden on her back was nothing. Her dark ponytail swished against her pack, the sun's golden light weaving glitter into the soft richness.

Grady wound his fingers around the straps of his backpack again, itching to tangle them in that mass instead. What was it about her that he found irresistible?

Maybe he should work to discover that, rather than fighting against the overwhelming attraction. Made sense, since she was his wife.

The trail dipped as it rounded the soft C of the bend, lowering to a thick stand of sandbar willows nestled along the bank of the river. A breeze rustled the thin branches, making the narrow leaves shake.

Grady froze. The breeze wasn't that strong—not to cause that sort of disturbance.

"Isa, stop."

Isa halted.

"Don't move." Grady crept toward her.

The stand of willows shook again, this time accompanied by a distinctive growl that made Grady's pulse fire.

Dear God... He reached Isa before he had a chance to finish that silent plea. Tucking her behind him, he kept a sharp watch on the willows.

There.

He sucked in a sharp breath while adrenaline shot through his veins. With trembling fingers, he reached for the bear spray latched to his left shoulder strap and removed it from the holster.

From the protection of the willows, a dark-brown cub scurried playfully into the shallows of the river.

"Dear God," Grady whispered, repeating his unfinished prayer.

They were in trouble. A whole lot of trouble. There was a mama grizzly and at least one cub in that stand of willows, and he and Isa were only fifteen feet from the riverbank.

His fault. He'd not been paying attention like he knew he should have been. This was prime grounds for grizzlies—they were only a mile from the bear management boundary. He'd been so lost in the wonder that was his wife—the mystery of her and the heady haze that kissing her had thrown him into—that he'd completely ignored the real possibility of bears on this backcountry trail.

Man. He was a forest ranger! What had he been doing?

Keeping Isa snug at his back, he turned at an angle and slowly paced backward, moving them both farther down the trail.

The deep growl rumbled again. Out from the thick mass of branches, a large head of brown fur emerged. The long nose, with its distinctive concave shape, rather than the straight form of the black bear, confirmed Grady's identification. She moved nearer, revealing the muscular hump of her shoulders. This mama grizzly was large—at least three hundred pounds—and was not happy to have intruders in her nursery.

Grady froze again.

"Easy there, mama." Grady unlocked the bear spray with his thumb, keeping the nozzle pointed at the grizzly. "We didn't mean to startle you."

He could feel Isa at his back, moving.

"Stay still," he whispered. Then he thought better of it. "Get your bear spray ready."

"It's ready," she whispered back. "Wow, she's magnificent."

That she was. But that wasn't what Grady was thinking in that moment. More along the lines of, she was upset and could kill them.

Keeping a firm grip on the can of spray, Grady started backing down the trail again. Now they rounded the corner of that gentle curve and headed up the incline toward the next stand of lodgepole pines.

"We're just going to move along, mama," he spoke in a low, controlled tone.

The bear shook her head, snorted, and then with a chilling roar, reared onto her hind legs.

Grady's heart seized, and he pushed Isa away from his back. "Keep moving."

He stood firm, keeping a steady aim with the bear spray. A splash came from the river, drawing the mama bear's attention. Baby grizzly ran upstream, splashing water playfully, ignorant of the standoff. Mama checked Grady again, huffed, and dropped back down to all four paws. Then she turned her massive bulk and lumbered toward the river.

Grady's heart restarted as she walked away. She was more concerned about her cub playing in the river than about the people invading her territory.

"Thank you, God," he mumbled.

Even so, he remained facing the bears as Isa tugged him backward. They moved slowly up the hill, and Grady kept watch as mama and baby crossed the river effortlessly, emerging on the opposite bank completely wet, and wandered into the span of meadow on the other side.

"I think we're going to be fine." There was a thrill to Isa's tone, even if it was soft. Indeed, after a heartbeat, she let a quiet laugh escape, then she grabbed his arm and shook it. "That was incredible!"

Grady found he was as breathless as he had been after their kiss. He turned with wide eyes to find her giddy with delight. "That was . . . stupid. And incredibly dangerous."

"Well, yes. But still, amazing, right?" She smiled as big as the Montana sky. "Have you ever been that close to a bear before?"

He shook his head. He never had *wanted* to be that close to a bear! And his wife . . . He'd let her just wander into that. Not one thought about the possible danger! He blew out a hot, frustrated, relieved breath. "Isa, I'm sorry."

"Sorry? For what? You didn't put the bear there."

"I know better. I know what sort of habitat to be extra cautious about." He pointed back to the willows. "That is exactly the type of place you have to approach with caution. We didn't clap, or whistle, or call out, or anything. We just snuck up on a mama bear and her cub . . ." He gripped his hat. "That was so close! So stupid."

Isa touched his elbow. "Grady, we're okay. Everything is fine."

He shook his head. "How could you be . . . how could you not be scared?"

"You had it." She tilted her head, sincerity filling her eyes. "You protected me."

"We got lucky."

She smiled gently. "Or God intervened."

A rough chuckle released from his chest. "Yes. I think He did."

"See. Everything is okay." She reached for his hand. "But maybe we should keep moving so she can have her cub's playground back."

Who was the forest ranger here? Despite his worry and self-incrimination, Grady felt one corner of his mouth slide upward. *Isa is brave, and she thrives on a good adventure.*

He took that mental note as the first on a list he hoped would grow long on this trip. Because not only was he determined to keep a better watch as they trekked, but he had also decided to study his wife.

So far, he liked what he found.

Twenty-One

After eight miles, they made it to their first campsite. Isa slipped her pack off, stretched her back, and turned a slow circle to take in the full panorama. With a breath of pine and crisp mountain air in her lungs, and the chilling air of late day sliding rapidly toward night, she smiled and made her hands busy.

Tent. Sleeping bags. Bunsen burner. And a quick selection of dehydrated food for dinner. Isa worked beside Grady with an efficiency that would have made it seem they'd done this before. For the record, she had, as had he. Just not together.

Here's to the first time of many more to come . . . The hopeful thought made her grin. She let it settle into the gray-scape of doubt that still existed in her heart, bringing hints of color and light to that space.

Setup was simple and quick, especially since they couldn't start a fire. Only a few specified sites along the backcountry trails allowed an open fire, and they were typically next to a water source. That first night, Grady had been assigned to a place tucked up in trees. There was a narrow opening of the pine boughs, affording a framed view of the slithering Gallatin River below and the layers of hills to the south.

As everything had been so far, the view was spectacular.

"There's a permit for a site not very far from here." Grady finished leveling a wide, flat rock and set the Bunsen burner in the middle of it. "I need to go check it. It should only take ten minutes or so."

Isa nodded. "I can get some water boiling while you're gone."

"You'll be okay alone?"

"Of course."

"You have your bear spray?"

She tapped the holster on her belt. "Right here."

"And a whistle?"

She grinned at his protectiveness and withdrew the whistle that hung on a lanyard and had been tucked beneath her long-sleeve base layer.

"And—"

"Flashlight is on top of my sleeping bag. But I won't need it because you'll be back before the sun sets." She stepped in front of him and gave his chest a gentle push. "I've done this before, Grady."

"I can tell." There was admiration in his voice. "But I haven't."

She snorted. "Right."

He shook his head while he clasped her shoulders, and she understood he was talking about something more than backpacking. "I've never been so scared in my life, Isa. And trust me when I tell you, that's saying something."

The crack in his armor moved into her heart with gentle warmth. Isa touched his jaw. Whatever he kept tucked behind that steel wall must be difficult. "Maybe you can tell me?"

"Maybe." He touched her elbow. "Be back soon."

She nodded, and he turned. Within a minute his back disappeared into the thick evergreen forest. In his absence, Isa took care of her personal needs, washed her face, and used a Whisp to brush her teeth. Then she lit the Bunsen burner and settled a kettle of water over the flame, ensuring both the burner and the kettle were secure and would not tip.

Shadows fell over the campsite, and the chilly evening air descended rapidly. Isa traded out her ball cap for a beanie and zipped up her Omni Heat jacket. The soft gray shadows darkened to charcoal before she heard the scuffle of Grady's footfalls. It had taken closer to thirty minutes than ten, but he came back as promised.

"Everything okay?" She ripped open the package of dehydrated vegetable stew for two.

Grady stopped at the cooking rock and lowered to sit on the dark earth beside her. "Yes. Sorry it took so long. The guy was a talker."

She sent him an easy grin. "Just in time." She poured the boiling water into the two tin cups that Grady had produced from his pack earlier, then added half the pouch contents into each mug.

With metal camp spoons, they stirred their steaming meals.

Grady took her hand, and the simple gesture sent a thrill through her belly. If he noticed, or felt the same, he didn't say anything. Instead, he bowed his head and shut his eyes.

"God, thank You for watching over us. For protecting us from the bear. And for this beauty we get to experience. We ask for Your favor and mercy." There he paused. The breath he drew hitched. When he continued, his voice softened. "And for Your love . . . so that we can learn to love each other."

Emotion surged with such force that Isa had to blink against the warm moisture in her eyes. She looked up at him, finding his gaze held vulnerable uncertainty. "Amen," she whispered.

"Amen."

Their stew had rehydrated by the time Grady released her hand, and they ate in comfortable silence. The first truly comfortable silence that Isa experienced with him. Belly warm and full, she rinsed out her mug, took Grady's and did the same, then thanked him when he produced a mint tea bag and plopped it in her clean mug.

"The guy at the camp came from Mammoth. This is his second night out, and he plans to head to the Bighorn Trailhead we came from."

"Did you warn him about the mama grizzly?"

"Yeah. That's what took so long. I suggested he reconsider his plans and pack out the way he came. He wasn't interested in doing that, and he had a story about a male grizzly encounter that I'm fairly certain is pure fiction." He shrugged, sipping his tea. "But who knows. Maybe a grizzly would lick a fellow in the face only to decide he tasted bad and walk away. Who am I to say that wouldn't happen?"

Isa snorted a soft laugh. "That is quite a tale."

He smiled at her. Goodness, she really liked his smile. The way it crinkled the corners of his eyes and made him seem so much more approachable.

"Then again, so are we," Grady said.

"Yes we are." A blossoming story—one of love and hope and redemption, or so Isa hoped. Inspired by that longing, she set her mug on the flat rock and moved closer to him. "It feels like we're completely alone out here. Nothing in the world could bother us."

Grady shifted so that he could be a back support for her, and when she leaned into the sturdiness of his chest, he wrapped her shoulders with one arm.

She sighed, content in the warmth of his secure hold, happy in this moment beneath the stars.

She smelled of earth and pine, a hint of sweat, and a lingering remnant of the vanilla scent that typically came from her hair. In the space of the small tent—officially a two-person model, though in practical terms, that was false advertisement (not that Grady was complaining)—Isa's scent mingled with the warmth of her very near body to weave a spell of sleeplessness through him. Again, he wasn't complaining.

As he stared at the black space where her breath came and went with a soft, soothing rhythm, Grady shifted to his side. Propping an arm under his head, he resisted the urge to reach for her. She should sleep—they'd hiked eight miles that day, and she'd carried a little over twenty pounds over the trail that gained them nearly a thousand feet of altitude. That earned her some undisturbed rest, even if he was mesmerized.

Grady's mind drifted over the day—one filled with big emotions. He still couldn't believe he'd let her wander into a grizzly bear's nursery without any thought or precautions. Yet she'd proclaimed that he'd protected her. Her simple statement replayed in his mind.

You protected me.

That was why she had married him—for protection. And he'd failed her. But she still believed in him.

She had proven to be the perfect hiking partner. Enthusiastic, full of energy. Willing to talk but keeping her voice quiet so the forest fauna wouldn't be disturbed. Willing to go long stretches with only the sounds of nature between them. Knowing how to set up camp. Willing to eat the dehydrated food and even claiming it was good. Willing to share this one-and-a-half-person-sized tent.

If he had made a wish list of someone with whom he'd want to share the backcountry, Isa would have checked every box. And came with the bonus of being lovely to look at.

A sudden intake of breath from her rocked him. He reached into the darkness for her shoulder. "Isa?" he whispered.

"I'm okay." Her hand shifted, but not to his. He guessed she held her belly.

"Are you?"

"The . . ." She inhaled slowly. "I think I just felt the baby."

He lifted onto his elbow. "Are you in pain?"

"No." She chuckled. "No, nothing like that. The baby moved, and I felt it. It just startled me."

"Oh." He lowered back to his pillow. "Is that the first time?"

"Yes." Wonder filled her voice.

For a heartbeat, Grady suffered from a feeling of exclusion. This was her baby, not his. Her thrill, not his. But he pushed it away. He'd known the truth before he'd proposed. And maybe this time he could choose *not* to be on the fringes. Maybe he could decide to enter into her wonder.

"What does it feel like?" he asked.

"A little bit like bubbles. A rolling tickle, but on the inside."

"Is it weird?"

"A little. It caught me by surprise."

"I thought you were asleep."

"Nearly."

A *hoot hoot hoo* pierced the silence outside of the tent, and both Grady and Isa fell quiet to listen. Sure enough, farther away, a replying *hoot hoot* answered.

"Owls, right?" Isa rolled to her side, her breath tickling his neck as she spoke.

"Right."

"Do you know what kind?"

"I would guess a western horned owl—they're the most common here."

"You know most of the animals and plants here, don't you?"

"Yes." He'd pointed out a red-shafted flicker, a calliope hummingbird, and the fresh tracks belonging to an elk as they'd hiked. "Wildlife biology was my minor—and it's part of my job."

"It suits you." There was a smile in her quiet voice.

Did it? How could she know that about him, when he barely knew anything about her? Not even when her baby was coming.

"I don't even know your favorite color." He moved his hand until his fingers found the curve of her face.

A beat went by before she answered—likely because, from her point of view, his comment had come from nowhere.

"Burnt orange. Like the juneberry leaves or the stems of the willows in the fall. And gray, because it works with everything." Her hand rustled from the sleeping bag and pressed gently on his chest. "Yours is green, right?"

"How did you know that?"

"You're a forest ranger, and you love trees. Also, your bed is smothered with dark green."

Grady chuckled. "It was the cheapest bed-in-a-bag that wasn't girly that I could find at Sam's Club. But you're right—my favorite color is green."

"Hmm. Let's see . . . what else? You like apples, but you're not a fan of huckleberries. But when you live in Montana, you don't say things like that out loud."

He chuckled.

"You prefer beef over chicken," Isa continued. "You don't like rice, but you love pasta. You drink your coffee black, but like a little honey in your tea. You'll take potato soup over chili when given the choice. You're not a big eater of sugar, but you have a weakness for Ho Hos, Janie's pie, and Italian sodas."

His fingers had drifted into the thick mess of her loose hair, and he wondered at the warm softness of it. "Wow, how did you know all that?"

"I serve you at the café on a regular basis, so it's just observation."

"I didn't know you were paying that much attention to me."

An owl called into the night again, and then the forest fell quiet for several breaths before Isa answered, her voice soft. "You're hard to ignore, Grady."

His heart tripped at her implication. "That is . . . seems untrue." He'd been so frustrated with her before because she seemed to ignore him. It had made him crazy. Because he'd been desperate for the beautiful woman behind the counter to notice him.

He wasn't ready to admit that yet though.

Grady shifted his mind back to all Isa knew about him and compared it to what he knew of her. Her list far exceeded his. He had some catching up to do.

"When is the baby due?"

He felt her shoulders move with her deep draw of breath. "February, I think." Her voice carried hesitation and worry, and her fingers slid away from his chest.

"It will be okay," he whispered.

"Will it?" She rolled to her back. "Grady, be honest with me. Do you really think you can love this baby? Claim that it's yours?"

"I do, Isa. Honest." He lifted back onto his elbow and dared to let his hand find her stomach. "I will." What would it be like to feel that little one move beneath his palm?

Perhaps soon he would know, and the anticipation for it caused a small thrill to spiral through him.

She covered his hand and squeezed. "How can you?"

"I grew up wishing for a father. Aching that the only one I knew was . . . was not a good one." Grady swallowed against a surge of emotion. "Kids shouldn't know that kind of pain. I don't want that for this baby."

She sniffed and then laced her fingers with his. "Will you tell me?"

Grady sighed. He'd never talked about it. When people asked about his home or childhood, he said that his father had left and his mom had remarried and he hadn't gotten along with her new husband, and he left it at that. It was a muted truth. A very muted truth.

But Isa had trusted him. She'd married him, even when they didn't share love. She believed that he would take care of her, protect her. That he was good, despite their sharp differences in the past. And she was trying to make their marriage something deep and lasting. Something that he longed for and was at the same time afraid to try for.

"It's okay, Grady."

No, it wasn't. Someday he needed to learn how to trust. Wasn't his wife the best candidate to begin with?

He rolled to his back, releasing her hand, and took a long draw of chilly air. "Mom had me when she was eighteen. Barely out of high school. She was a single mom for a while, and when I was four, she married a guy who . . . who seemed decent enough. He took her out. Made her laugh. Bought me ice cream. But he drank. A lot. As the years went by, he drank more and more, and he was violent when he was drunk. I was terrified of him, and so was my mom. But she's . . . I think they call it codependent. He would sober up and apologize, say that it would never happen again, and that he needed her and that he would die without her."

"So she stayed with him."

Grady's throat swelled as those years of fear and frustration surged through his emotions. "Yeah. For years. Until I threatened him."

"You . . ."

"I was twelve the first time I stood up to him. He was drunk and in a rage, and I came between him and my mom. He broke my nose and cracked a rib."

"Grady—"

"We left—Mom took us to a shelter. But he did what he'd always done, and she did what she'd always done, and we were back with him within two months. The cycle repeated until I was fourteen. I bulked up, took a few self-defense classes, and one night he was brawling, and I lost it on him." Grady curled his fists, discovering that his whole body shook at the memory. He blew out a trembling exhale. "It scared me. I was so out of control."

Isa rolled back onto her side and laid a hand on his chest. "What happened?"

"He was pretty sore when he sobered up. Acted like a whipped puppy. And I told him to leave."

"Did he?"

"Yeah, he did."

"Wow." Her thumb brushed over his thermal shirt. "What about your mom?"

"At first she wanted to take him back, but I told her if she did, I was leaving. She eventually divorced him. For a while, I thought we were going to be okay, she and I. But after I left for college, she met another guy . . ."

"Same kind?"

"Same kind. I interceded on that when I came home my senior year to find her with a black eye. But then Bill came along—that's who she was with the last time I saw her. I guess I gave up. She keeps choosing to be in these bad relationships. I can only do so much, you know?"

"Is that why you weren't surprised when she didn't show up for our wedding?"

He nodded, the movement of his head a quiet rustle against the sleeping bag.

"I'm sorry, Grady."

He covered her hand and squeezed his eyes shut. His pulse pounded—he was certain Isa could feel the hard, fast thud of his heart through the fabric of his shirt. The ache of it all throbbed, though it had been years since he'd last seen his mom.

"Grady?"

"Yeah."

"Is that why you didn't like me? I reminded you of your mom?"

"No." He turned onto his shoulder so fast that his feet tangled in the sleeping bag. "No, Isa. That never once crossed my mind."

Her silence seemed like disbelief.

"The truth is, I'm terrified that I will be just like her. That I'm so determined to rescue—to save someone—that I hurt other people." He touched her face, finding her cheek wet.

She cried for him. No one had ever even known, let alone cried for his pain. Grady had no idea what to do with the enormity of emotion that crashed through him. His core trembled. "I don't ever want you or this baby to know that kind of pain." The words barely escaped through the painful tightness in his throat.

Her hand slipped around his neck, and she pulled him down to her, her arms wrapping a fierce hold around him. "You would never be the cause, Grady. I know you wouldn't." She stroked the hair at the nape of his neck. "You couldn't."

TWENTY-TWO

BENNETT TOOK HAZEL'S HAND and led her to the walking trail that circled the pond. It wasn't what he had planned, but he was putting her on a plane in the morning so she could go back to the peace of Elk Lake. Back to her dogs, and to her brother, and the life she loved.

He needed to stay. He didn't want to, but Chip was cracking open, willing to at least discuss what it would look like to have Nathan live in Luna for the school year. And then there was Gemma—she was scheduled to board a plane next week. He needed to be there when she did so she would know that no matter where she was, she wasn't going to be alone.

Keeping their pace relaxed, Bennett let the quiet beauty of this small sanctuary in the city soothe his tattered edges. The week had been exhausting, and he knew it had worn on Hazel. She'd born it with grace, and he was so grateful to her for it.

In a small, secluded cove, protected by maples and hedged by hydrangeas, Bennett stopped and drew Hazel around to face him.

"It's pretty here," she said.

He fingered the soft whisps of hair that framed her face, having escaped her french braid. "I think so. Not as glorious as your mountain, but pretty. And it has meaning for me."

"Does it?"

Nodding, he tugged her off the trail and into the mowed grass. "I was walking this trail after I came back to Chicago—after my amnesia."

Hazel nodded, pursing her lips as a flash of embarrassment filtered across her expression. She still felt bad that she'd lied to him. Played on his memory loss.

Bennett didn't regret any of it now. He took both her hands in his. "I was about here when I saw a woman who reminded me of you, walking her dog. My heart leapt as, for a brief moment, I convinced myself that you'd come to find me."

She looked down, chuckling.

"That's when I knew I'd fallen for you."

"Must have worried you."

He laughed. "A little." He let her hand go and dug into his pocket. Then he lowered to the grass, planting a knee.

Hazel drew in a quick breath. "Benji . . ."

Grinning up at her, he winked. "I had a different plan, Zel. The scene was perfect in my mind—we'd walk up the trapline and I'd stop you at the creek, where I woke up not knowing who I was. Where you told me that you were my wife and I thought I'd married the most beautiful, unusual creature on earth."

She sputtered another laugh as a tear flicked from her eyelash. "Poor man."

"Lucky man." He lifted her hand and kissed her knuckles. "That had been my plan. But I can't wait. I can't put you on a plane without me without asking you to be my wife. For real. Forever. I love you, Hazel Wallace, and I'm begging you, one more time. Will you marry me?"

"You don't have to beg." Hazel pulled him up to stand. "I can't wait to marry you!"

Isa had two days and over twenty-five miles to process what Grady had shared with her in the blackness of that first night.

The brokenness of his world still wrecked her.

What a contradiction—they were out in the unsurpassed beauty of God's amazing creation, drinking in the clean, fresh air, experiencing the raw astonishment of His power. And yet as they trekked—sometimes hand in hand, sometimes with quiet conversations, and sometimes in companionable silence—the sting of his pain remained lodged under the surface of this amazing experience.

Isa had chosen the path that had brought her to her brokenness. Grady hadn't. From his birth, he'd not had another option. He'd experienced fear and isolation beyond her imagination. Yet against all odds, the man who led the way through this backcountry, who had offered her his name and his protection, was a *good* man.

How, God?

The mystery of it made her tear up with wonder but also feel a stubborn and angry sense of injustice. Grady hadn't had a choice in his childhood. He didn't have a choice about how his mother was then. And even now the woman continued to knife an ache into her son's heart. She couldn't spare a day to witness her only child getting married?

It had bothered Grady, even if it hadn't surprised him. Looking back, Isa recalled the way his eyes had dulled and he'd looked away when she'd asked about his mother's absence the day they got married. *She couldn't make it*, was all he'd said.

Isa tried to unknot the mix of gratitude and anger as they worked through the long day and many miles of hiking through Electric Pass. She was grateful that Grady was the man he was despite how his life had been. And she was angry at the woman—and maybe even God—who had allowed him to experience such horrors.

As the story continued to trouble her heart, she set her mind to the beauty that she'd been allowed to witness. Electric Pass offered vistas of peaks and meadows as they wove in and out of long stands of the fir forest. Where the trees wouldn't grow, there were long stretches of sweet green, followed by vast fields of rock. Rounded peaks, worn by wind and rain, and impressive patches of glacial snow clinging to the northern shadows of those ancient summits.

So much beauty.

Much of it, she realized as a steady, cold wind slapped at her face, brought about by the harsh conditions that defined this backcountry. These glorious hills had yielded to the sculpting hand of adversity.

Life gets hard. What will you do with it?

The question imposed itself against her struggle with Grady's past. She allowed it to settle there, though it was uncomfortable.

She had been a young, impulsive, foolish woman, and now she faced a life she hadn't anticipated. A marriage that looked nothing like her youthful dreams of romance. A baby that was sure to be whispered about because of the timing of its birth. And the disappointment of her family, though Grady had vowed to shield her from that. And worst of all, the ever-present worry that Francisco or his family would find her.

Like the rise in the trail ahead, adversity loomed in front of her.

What will you do with it?

As her husband neared the crest of the curving hill just beyond her, she paused. He walked into the late-afternoon sun, back straight, shoulders bearing the weight of his pack with strength and endurance. As he walked between the two great rises of rock and earth, she felt the strength of his heart seep into her being.

I choose to love you . . .

Grady chose how to live his life. He chose to be a good man, when he might be justified to be a bitter man. He didn't allow the past to choose for him.

Like the sweet sweeping meadows, the silver thread of wandering river, and the soaring views that seemed to go on forever in this wilderness, Grady was a testament to resilient wonder forged in adversity.

And Isa got to witness it.

The miracle of it caught her breath. The wind continued to sweep her face, causing her hair to dance beneath the rim of her beanie. She faced the biting gale head on and inhaled.

She'd made choices in the past—bad ones. Choices that by all measurements, including her own, weren't justifiable. Even so, God had placed Grady in her life and offered a new beginning. Maybe there were hard things still to come.

But what was she going to do with them?

As the wind gentled, her mother's voice whispered through her mind, speaking that verse that was so common on her lips: *Dios mío, tú eres todo bondad, ten compasión de mí.*

She would throw herself onto God's mercy, for it was as vast and strong as these mountains. And she would live in His goodness.

Especially in the time of adversity.

The land leveled as a thick gray blanket of clouds covered the late-afternoon sun. Grady drank in deep breaths, the cold air stinging against his burning lungs. The increase in altitude was definitely affecting him. He turned to watch Isa walking the trail behind him. She had been particularly quiet the past hour, provoking Grady's concern. This section of trail had been the longest of their trip—near fourteen miles. With that climb in altitude, this day's trek was no joke.

Grady felt his spirit sink. He'd asked too much of Isa today.

As she neared him, he held out a hand. "Give me your pack."

"What?" Isa squinted up to him, her nose wrinkling as her breaths puffed rapidly.

"I should have been carrying it since the lunch point."

She stopped beside him and tucked the straw to her CamelBak between her lips. Once she swallowed her drink, she wiped her mouth with the back of her hand and grinned. A tired grin, but one that made those lovely dark-brown eyes shine. "I'm fine. But thank you."

He stood captivated by her sweetness. It was pure—not the flirty *I need attention* kind he'd witnessed at the café. Just . . . sweet.

"Take another drink," he commanded, trying to ignore the way she bewitched him.

She mocked a scowl at his bossiness, then complied. Once her straw was free of her mouth again, Grady reached to unsnap the buckle latching her pack at her chest and then went for the one at her waist.

Isa grabbed his hand. "What are you doing?"

"Taking your pack."

She poked his side, right beneath his rib. He jumped.

"I told you I'm fine," she said.

Not easily deterred, though amused by her attempts to dissuade him, Grady snatched her hand, which was poised to jab him again, and moved for a second try at the buckle at her waist.

"Listen, you rogue." She wiggled her hand clutched in his while moving to poke his ribs with her other hand, all the while giggling. "You need to keep your hands to yourself."

He chuckled at her playfulness. "Since you're my wife, I'm not going to take that seriously."

She ducked under his arm and spun from his slipping grasp. Grady caught her backpack just as she broke free, and tugged her back. She stumbled at the shift in momentum, and he wrapped her shoulders with one arm, steadying her against himself.

"You're being a bully." She laughed, tilting her head up to look at him.

He joined her laughter. "I'm trying to be a nice husband and carry my wife's backpack."

Isa stared at him, and her laughing smile softened. "I like your laugh."

She lowered her gaze, fixing it on the shafts of sunlight that streamed beneath the dark clouds to the west, and leaned against his chest. With a light hold, she gripped the wrist he had pressed against her shoulder. "You are a nice husband," she said softly.

He warmed at the genuine quality of her compliment but noted the rate with which those western dark clouds gathered. There would be rain within an hour. They couldn't stand there like this all evening, even if they didn't need to make camp tonight.

Grady pulled Isa in a little tighter, curving his body around the backpack that bulged between them, and leaned down to peck her cheek. Then he reached to unsnap that buckle at her waist.

Isa jolted upright. "You're a sneaky husband!"

"Let me carry the backpack, Isa." He slipped the right strap from her shoulder.

"How far until we reach the lake?"

"About a mile."

She turned, letting the left strap slip from her shoulder. "I'm really okay, you know."

"I know. But I'll feel better if you let me have this." He held up the pack, then slipped his arms through the straps so that it would fit to his front. Once he had it settled and rigged in a way he hoped would stay, he reached for her hand. "Walk with me?"

She bit her bottom lip, that sweet but sassy look making his heart flip more than once. Then she threaded her fingers with his.

"I'd love to."

Twenty-Three

Sportsman Lake was nestled in between a stretch of sweet green meadow and a stand of rich blue-green fir trees at the base of an impressive rise of granite that was Electric Peak. Towering into the darkening sky at eleven thousand feet, the steep slope was striking. Opposite the peak, in the bowl that created the lake and meadow, a tiny cabin stood as a welcoming beacon to Isa's weary body.

Pausing on the trail before it curved into the trees by which the cabin waited, Isa took in the view with a tired but grateful heart.

This was why Grady had wanted to push this hike into one day rather than two. The promise of a soft mattress, solid walls, a sturdy roof, and a warm fire inside that patrol cabin was worth the extra-challenging day.

"What do you think?" Grady strode up from behind her—still carrying her pack strapped over his chest. He'd insisted she set the pace for the push of the day.

"Gorgeous."

"Not too worn out to appreciate it?"

"Could anyone ever be?"

He snorted. "You would be surprised. I've heard grown men approach this place with a list of complaints and comments like, 'Could have enjoyed it fine in a picture.'"

"That is a travesty."

With a warm chuckle, his hand curled around her shoulder. "You are . . . not what I expected."

Isa shot him a grin and then leaned in against him. "There's that laugh again. I like it, Grady."

His arm tightened around her, squeezing her in a hug, then he stepped away. Before the space between them widened too much, the warm strength of his hand wrapped around hers. Then he led her the rest of the way to the lake and cabin.

After climbing the three short, rough-hewn steps, he stopped on the covered front deck, released her hand, and shed both the backpacks he'd carried. Isa leaned back and took in the structure. It was built of logs, several of which bore the charred black evidence of fire damage.

"It looks a lot newer than I expected. Weren't the patrol cabins put up almost a century ago?"

Grady moved to the door and worked the latch. "Yeah, most were. This one has been rebuilt. The original burned down."

"Ah. We get the best there is?"

He flashed her a grin over his shoulder, then swung the door open. At his silent gesture inviting her in, she picked up her pack and passed into the cabin. Grady followed her, taking her backpack again and leaning both his and hers against the log wall near the door.

"Wow. It's bigger and so much nicer than I expected." Isa wandered into the middle of the gleaming wood floors and stopped where a patch of remaining daylight pooled, let in by a pair of six-paned windows.

She spun a small, slow circle. Near enough to touch was a ladder that stretched up to the vaulted ceiling, leading to the sleeping loft. On the side near the door, an old-fashioned woodburning cookstove sat, cleaned and ready for use. Opposite, beneath the sleeping loft, a much smaller woodburning stove waited, ready to warm the cabin with a fire. All four walls had at least one window, and a simple table had been placed along one.

As a rumble of thunder rolled from just beyond Electric Peak, Grady leaned to look out the front door. "Think we're going to be glad we're in this rather than the tent tonight."

"The benefit of being married to a ranger." Isa walked to the door, stopped next to him, and examined the sky.

"Glad there is at least one."

Isa turned her gaze to him, her heart puddling at the teasing smile she found. "I'm discovering all sorts of wonderful surprises about my husband this trip."

He hitched one brow. "Are you? Is there one you like best?"

She let a mischievous grin slip onto her mouth. "Very recently, I learned that he is ticklish."

With a mocked sternness that looked nothing like his normal severity, Grady shook his head. "That is not something for you to use against me."

Her grin bloomed into a laugh. "Like you can stop me."

Another crack of thunder boomed just as Isa turned. Grady was ready, intercepting her hands before she could test the jumpiness of his core with her fingers.

"Don't start something you can't finish."

"Who says I can't finish it?"

His eyes held her as he pinned her hands against his chest. The intensity of that look ignited a spark in her chest, and her heart vaulted.

From the periphery of her vision, she saw a streak of white light flash against the dark-gray sky. Within three pounding heartbeats, another crack of thunder fell onto the land, this one with enough force to shake the windows.

Grady's gaze flickered from her eyes to her mouth. "It's going to rain."

"Yes," she whispered. Not that she cared about the rain. Not with this man staring in a way that made her deliciously warm. "Careful, Mr. Briggs." She fingered the fabric of his shirt near his heart, savoring the rapid thud that pulsed beneath her palm. "If you keep staring at me like that, I might think you like me."

One side of his mouth hitched into a lopsided smile, and he traced her top lip with his finger. "More discoveries . . ."

Rain tapped against the roof shakes, and then the clouds broke loose. The downpour blurred the view of the lake and trees and the mountain, and Isa was grateful to be safely dry in the cabin.

Mostly though, she was thankful to be there with him. Making new discoveries.

It felt good to wake up in her own bed. And so good to have slept a full night through without the noise of Chicago winding tension through her body.

Hazel stepped out into the fresh, clean morning, welcoming the unobstructed view of mountains and sky.

"Let the mountains and lakes praise the wonders of Your hand," she prayed out loud. "And make my life one of thankfulness too."

She shut her eyes and soaked in the new day.

"Let's go, pups. We have fish to find." With her box in one hand, Hazel crossed the deck and snatched the pole waiting for her against the log side of her cabin.

The dogs, led by Scout, came racing around the cabin from the direction of the corral. Scout reached the steps of the deck and leapt up to the top in a single bound. She slid to a stop in front of Hazel and then bounced into a circle in the air, like she was some sort of canine ballerina.

"Having a good morning, are you?" Hazel chuckled.

The dog panted, tipping her head as if to say, *Absolutely!*

Ice and Cream trotted to the steps and dropped to their backsides to wait. Cream let out an excited yip.

Hazel clomped, in her lightweight Muk boots, down the stairs and onto the trail to the ridge that separated her cabin from her brother's massive lodge. "Okay, gang. We're heading over to Hunter's pond today." She paused and looked back. Still lying in the sun near the deck, Moose lifted his head from his paws. "Not coming, buddy?"

Moose panted twice, then lowered his big head back down and shut his eyes.

A twinge of sadness pinged in Hazel's heart. Moose ventured away from the cabin less and less—and usually the few times he joined her little treks, Bennett was with her. For that man, the dog would exert the extra effort it took him these days.

"Poor old man," Hazel said. Arthritis had hit him hard, and getting old for such a big boy was rough business.

She hoped Bennett would be able to come home soon too. Moose would smile his big doggy grin, lay his chin on Bennett's lap, and soak in the joy of the man's fingers stroking his soft head. And Hazel was happy for the pair of them—a match no one would have imagined. A whole lot like herself and Bennett.

With the three more rambunctious dogs along, Hazel made her way to Hunter's. Her brother was there on the shore, his line already in the water.

"Coming to my side to steal my fish today?" Hunter grinned as he adjusted his ball cap.

"Thought I'd get two chores done at once."

"Fishing is not a chore."

"No, it's not." She stopped four feet down the shore from him and bent to set down her tackle. "But I needed to talk with you."

"Ah, so that's the chore." He winked.

"Always, brother." She selected a lure that had done well for her at the river a few days before and started to tie it to the line.

"It's good to have you home." Hunter chuckled. "What's on your mind?"

Hazel checked the area, then set the reel. With a practiced flick, she sent out a perfect cast. After the small weight on the end of the line plopped into the clear water that reflected the cloudless blue of the summer sky, she looked at her brother. "Bennett proposed."

A grin flashed on her brother's face. "I've been expecting that." Then a serious scowl made his brows crash downward. "You said yes, right?"

"Of course I said yes." She wiggled her hand at him, showing off the ring.

"Good." Hunter chuckled. "So that it? Just wanted to tell your big brother you're engaged, or is there more on your mind?"

Hazel drew in a fortifying breath. "I . . . I wanted to ask you about the wedding."

Hunter's brows slid upward. "You want to talk to *me* about your wedding?"

"I never thought I'd have one. Didn't think I'd ever get married." She set her focus on the ripples of water that continued their journey to the shoreline.

"Okay . . ."

"Is it dumb that I want to have one? I mean, I don't actually think they're important, but . . . well, I'm pretty sure Bennett would like to have a day, a memory to look back on. And maybe . . ."

"Maybe you would too?"

She shrugged while heat circled the tops of her ears.

"Nothing wrong with that, Zel."

She looked back at him. "Thing is, I don't know how to have a wedding."

Hunter smiled. "This seems like a topic for you and Janie. I pretty much just showed up to mine."

"Yeah, except—don't take this wrong, and don't you dare tell Janie—but I don't want her to take it over. Last thing I want is a big crowd, an elaborate dress, and to feel like the fake up there pretending to be someone she's not."

Hunter reeled in his line—no fish on—set his pole on the ground near his tackle box, and strode to Hazel's side. "Zel, I really don't think Janie would do any of that. She knows you as well as I do."

"I know . . ." Hazel sighed, frustrated that she couldn't put into words the crisscross emotions the idea of a wedding stirred in her. "It's just . . ." She blew out a breath.

"It's just that it was often you and me against the world?"

"Yeah." Why was this so emotional?

"And maybe it's picking at a tender wound that you don't have Mom here to help you plan a wedding?"

She winced. That was it. With a nod, she looked up the same moment Hunter pulled her into a hug. For a long moment, he simply held her tight. Then he rubbed her shoulder and stepped back. "I had a hard time with that too. With not having Mom and Dad here. It's okay. Pretty sure that makes you a human being with a heart—and that's a good thing."

Blinking back the watery glaze, Hazel shook her head. "I've kept myself so closed off, you know? I never wanted to feel so much again after they died, and then after Nan and Pop died and you left. Sometimes I don't know how to handle all the things that feel so big."

"That's why you turned Bennett down when he first asked you to marry him?"

"That, and I didn't want to feel trapped." She huffed. "I'm such a mess, Hunter. Why on earth would Bennett want to marry me when he could marry a normal, beautiful, stable woman?"

"I asked him that exact question." He shook her arm.

Hazel rolled her eyes and pushed him away.

"A man loves a good adventure, Zel. And a challenge. You're definitely both of those. And here's a secret I know from life beyond our little sanctuary up here—no one is normal."

She leaned into his side hug. "Thanks. I guess."

"Bennett loves you something fierce. Everyone in Montana can see it."

She laughed. "I know. I don't understand, but I do know it. And I love him something fierce back."

"So marry the man you love. Have a wedding that you'll both enjoy, be married, and live your adventure."

"Back to the wedding . . ."

"Have you thought of talking to Mama Bulldog?"

"It crossed my mind."

"I think you should. She's never let us down, you know."

"No, she hasn't." A jerk on the line had Hazel stepping away from her brother, tugging back to set the hook and working the reel with a steady pace. Five feet offshore, a decent-sized trout breached the surface and flopped back into the water.

"First catch of the day." Hunter pressed a playful slug into her shoulder. "You always were the lucky one."

Eyes on the fish she was pulling in, Hazel grinned.

Yep, that was true. She was a lucky girl. Or perhaps it was blessed.

Twenty-Four

After restoking the fire and refilling the teakettle that sat atop the stove, Grady shouldered his backpack and walked out of the cabin. He pulled the door shut behind him and stepped off the deck and into the gentle dawn. With a long breath, he inhaled the crisp scent of freshly washed forest.

It was a beautiful morning. One of the best, in fact, that he'd known in his life.

With a glance over his shoulder at the small building at his back, he pictured the lovely woman he'd left snuggled beneath the warmth of a sleeping bag. Isa would stay at the cabin today, resting as much as she wanted. Perhaps soaking her feet in the lake. Or maybe she'd string the hammock he'd pulled out of his bag and left on the table, hanging it between the log supports on the deck.

He wished he could stay and just hang out with her, enjoying this alpine solitude together. What new thing would he discover about the lovely woman he'd married? Last night he learned that she thoroughly enjoyed a gentle back rub. Heat ran up his neck and to the tips of his ears as he remembered her generous reward for that kindness.

Perhaps today, if he could stay, he'd find out if she could catch fish with her bare hands. Or maybe she would prefer to use the pristine lake to swim in, even if it was frigid. Man, he didn't want to miss that.

Grady forced his steps into the trees as the trail led him away from the lake. This was actually a working trip, he reminded himself, not a vacation. Even if it did feel very much like the honeymoon Isa had suggested it could be. There were two sites within five miles of the patrol cabin, both of which had permits issued for that day. He needed to check on them, noting any wildlife activity and watching for signs of fire.

But he'd make his way back here before nightfall.

Already looking forward to that, Grady resettled his pack, clicked the waist buckle and then the chest strap, and started on the path that would lead him to another high-country lake. As the sun inched its way higher, the light brightening the waking backcountry around him, Grady began to whistle.

Isa proved to be a surprise, in the most bewitching ways possible. His prayer from the day he'd married her had been that God would show him how to be a good husband and teach him to love his wife. Turned out, that second part might not take as much determination as he had expected.

She sure had a way of crawling beneath the barrier of seriousness and mistrust that he'd kept for most of his life. Or around it, or over it, or whatever. Seemed she was determined to do what it took to get to his heart. And wow, her determination was effective.

You protected me. He felt like a superhero, with the way she'd said that simple statement with such easy trust. Even though he knew that if he'd been more responsible in the first place she wouldn't have been in danger, the effect of her sweet admiration was a great swelling in his chest.

I like your laugh. He sure liked her provoking it. Even if it did involve her tickling him.

You are a nice husband. Man . . . he wanted her to hang on to that impression.

As the lake and the cabin disappeared behind the thick boughs of the fir forest, and the incline of the trail grew steeper, Grady put his heart toward prayer.

Thank You, God. So far, it's more than I dared hope. She's so much more than I thought. I could fall for her. The thought moved from his mind to his heart, bringing a thrill that ran all the way through his body.

"I could fall for my wife," he told the rocks and trees. A chuckle shook his chest. He wished Isa were there to hear him laugh—she would certainly reward him with her grin.

Help me to love her and to be a good husband.

The trail evened out and turned into a scree field of fractured granite. The sun, now fully emerged over the eastern horizon, flooded this unprotected section of trail with brilliant gold, wrapping him with welcomed warmth.

Grady surrendered himself to the pure joy of the day. And to the possibilities that the future might be more beautiful than he'd imagined.

Bennett unloaded the luggage from the luxury sedan's trunk and placed the suitcases on the sidewalk near the outdoor ticketing counter.

"Thank you, Bennett." Mindi was bright with excitement. "It was nice of you to drive us."

He swallowed, the lump in his throat making it difficult. His attention focused on Gemma, and he touched her shoulder. "You okay?"

She nodded, her face pointed toward the ground. He lifted her chin. Tears flooded her eyes, and then suddenly she flung herself against him. As he held her tight, quiet sobs tore through her slim body.

"Gemma?" Mindi's brows folded in concern. "Sweetie, what is wrong?"

"I don't want to move to Italy," she whispered. "Please, Mom. I won't know anyone. I don't speak Italian. I want to go back to Luna with Bennett."

Mindi stared at her, dumbstruck. "But I thought Italy would be such a romantic adventure for you." She blinked as she reached to rub Gemma's back. "Why didn't you tell me?"

"I don't want you to be upset with me."

Glancing at Bennett, Mindi pressed her lips together.

Bennett worked to contain his irritation. How could this woman have *not* seen that Gemma had worked way too hard to be cheerful, *excited*, about moving to Italy with her? How could she have missed that Gemma had been faking it?

Did she not know her daughter at all?

There was such an isolation in selfishness. At that thought, Bennett's ire turned to pity. Mindi didn't know her own children. But to her credit, she did want them to be happy.

Proving that point, Mindi touched Gemma's shoulder to turn the girl to face her. "Honey, I don't want you to be miserable. How about a deal? You come with me now, for the wedding, and in two weeks I put you back on a plane home. I'll make sure all the paperwork is done, and you can live with Bennett for the school year, like your brother?"

Gemma sniffed. "Really?"

"Is that what you want?"

The girl looked up to Bennett, searching for his approval. He nodded. "You are always welcome to stay with me and Hazel."

Another soft cry shuttered through her. "Will you and Hazel wait to get married until I get back?"

He cupped her wet face. "Absolutely."

Swiping away the tears, Gemma sniffed and nodded. Then smiled at her mother. "Okay, Mom. Let's go to Italy."

Mindi smiled—a sad sort, but gentle nonetheless. "Okay, my sweet Gem."

Gemma hugged Bennett one more time and whispered, "Thank you."

As he let her go, watching her drag her carry-on through the glass doors, a grateful, tender ache moved in his chest. God had worked a few miracles over the past week. Both kids would be living with him for the school year.

With him and Hazel. His very soon-to-be wife.

Isa shifted her position, having sat in the same posture for quite a while, but remained planted on the deck. She allowed her back to rest against the log that braced the roof above her, and her bare feet toyed with the dirt and grass scattered in front of the cabin. With her bottom lip tucked beneath her teeth, she studied the scene spread in front of her.

It really was one magnificent view.

To her right, the lake glistened in the late-afternoon sun, with Electric Peak standing like a protective husband close beside. A smattering of trees made dark patches here and there along the steep slope, but mostly the sharp rise was smothered in the dull yellow green of the short alpine vegetation until it reached a definitive line above which only bare earth and rock remained.

To her left, the meadow spanned, it's richer, more vibrant green dotted with the whites and blues of the wildflowers. The grasses and blooms swayed merrily in a gentle mountain breeze—a contrast to the brisk wind that had welcomed them yesterday afternoon.

Ahead of her, the layers of mountains dipped and rolled all the way to the place where the blue sky met the hazy earth. From here, it seemed she could see eternity. Untouched. Unspoiled. And breathtaking.

She lowered her gaze back to the notepad of thick paper that she held in her left hand, and with her right hand she dipped her brush into the muted green paint in her travel set. With a delicate touch, she applied the color to the scene she'd sketched out with pencil, loving the way the watercolor paint bled into the paper.

The various hues of green had been filled in, and she had moved to the blues of the lake, when she heard a rustling near the fir trees. She froze and held her breath while a squeeze of adrenaline heated her chest, the memory of the bear encounter easily resurfacing. But when Grady emerged, his orange pack a bright flash against the dark blue green of the trees, she smiled.

A full hour earlier than she'd expected him to return. She wouldn't complain about that.

She watched him while he rounded the edge of the lake and knew the exact moment that he spied her sitting at the edge of the deck. His head picked up and shoulders straightened, and he paused. Then he swiped the hat off his head, exposing his dark hair to the playful whimsy of the breeze, and left the trail that would wind its way around the lake before working its way back toward the cabin.

Deviating from the trail to take a shortcut was very un-ranger like, if you asked Isa.

Grady didn't stop until he reached the steps that would take him up to the deck, but there he halted. When he failed to speak but only stared at her like he'd not known that she'd be there, discomfort pushed anticipation from Isa's mind. She'd thought he had smiled when he'd spotted her from the lake. But maybe she'd been mistaken?

"Hi." She dared to breech the awkward stall between them.

"Hi." One corner of his mouth twitched.

"You okay?"

That twitch eased upward into a lopsided smile. "I'm good. You?"

"I'm good." She bit her bottom lip. How could they have been so . . . *close* the previous night only to return to this stubborn clumsiness that existed between them?

Treat him the way you want to be treated . . . So far, Pastor's advice hadn't let her down.

Isa set aside her painting and brush and pushed away from the log at her back. The grass tickled her toes, and the dirt felt gritty against her feet as she crossed the short distance between them. Though it felt forced and maybe scripted, she reached to anchor her hand on his neck and then stretched up to peck his cheek.

With an audible exhale, Grady slid a hand to her back and pulled her into a hug.

Still awkward. But warming.

Isa leaned back. "How was the hike?"

"Good." He searched her face, as though looking for something.

"Nothing to report?"

"The lake is smaller than this one. And whoever had the permit had made a fire, which was fine. But they left the ashes warm—didn't douse them with water. I'll have to file that when I get back."

"Oh." She didn't know what else to say.

"I saw wolf tracks."

"Really?"

"Fairly fresh, in the mud. Must have been out sometime after the storm cleared. I don't remember hearing them last night."

"Me either." How could they return to the playful fun and warmth that they'd found before? Tickling had been the catalyst for that . . .

Grady's backpack was still strapped on tight.

Isa lifted her face to him, her mouth molding to a teasing smile. "Are you planning to stay here with me tonight, or were you thinking you were going to pack out of here without me?"

His brow furrowed. "What?"

She tugged on the buckle at his chest. "Trail's end, Ranger. You can take a load off."

"Oh." He unsnapped the buckles, then slid the pack from his shoulders.

Nuts. No luck breaking his smile. In fact, she might have made him upset. Why would he be upset?

Isa sighed, tempted to surrender to frustration. Instead, she set her gaze on his and took the direct route. "Grady, what's wrong?"

Again, his brow furrowed. Maybe that was even a scowl. But it was brief. He shook his head and then lowed his face to brush a kiss across her forehead. "Nothing, Isa. I'm sorry. I think I'm just tired."

"Oh." That didn't seem right. He'd been tired last night, and the evening before, and the evening before that. Backpacking would do that to a person. But he'd been warm in his exhaustion. "Maybe I should have gone with you today."

That seemed to jar him out of whatever stormy place he'd landed in. With a shake of his head, he tugged her back into a hug. "No. You needed to rest—and I planned for you to stay here today."

"Okay. But you're upset."

His one-armed hold became a full two-armed embrace. "No. I'm glad to be back here with you. Glad you're here and you're safe."

That seemed . . . cryptic.

"What's this?" He gently set her back and moved to examine her notebook. After a cursory look, he gingerly picked it up, looked out at the scene she'd been painting, then lowered his attention back to her work. "Wow. My wife paints."

His obvious admiration did much to brush away her worries and annoyance. When his eyes shifted to look at her again, the esteem she found in them made her tummy squeeze.

"This is beautiful, Isa." He grinned. "I don't remember packing a notebook and paints."

"You didn't. I slipped them in when you were loading the truck."

"Now who is sneaky?" He winked.

Ah, now they were back on track. And he winked? At her? The angels must be singing in awe!

Isa shrugged as she glanced over her shoulder at the subject of her art. Then she peeked at him, thrilled to find his warming attention settled firmly on her. "My brother gave me that little travel set for my birthday last year. Small enough for trips like this."

"That was thoughtful of him." Grady picked up the miniature palette of watercolors that could clip onto her notebook. "He seems to care a whole lot about you."

Grady's innocent observation pierced the wounded place in her soul, causing shame to spill out. She looked toward the ground as she curled her toes into the black earth. "He does."

A new lull passed between them. She could use this moment as the catalyst to tell him the things she didn't want to talk about. Certainly Grady had questions, and if she truly wanted an honest and open marriage with him, they needed to talk about the hard things. After all, he'd shared with her the wounds that he'd never told another soul.

That's different.

Yeah, it was. He'd not had a choice, and she'd run headlong into her disaster on her own volition.

But he'd had a choice in marrying her, even when he knew she was both pregnant and in trouble with some really bad people.

Grady chose her, even in the middle of her ugly mess.

Isa lifted her head, turned her face toward the lake. So much striking beauty.

Forged in adversity.

"I'm going to go clean up." Grady closed the small space between them as he moved to climb those three short steps. "I need to wash the mud off these pants. I might go all in and see if I can get the four days of stink off me too." He paused on the deck and bent to reach for his backpack. Before he straightened again, he turned to look at her, a shy look of mischief on his face. "Want to join me?"

Oh wow . . . one little question completely shifted the vibe between them from bumbling to electric. Heat bloomed in her middle and spread like wildfire throughout her whole body. She doubted even the frigid temperatures of that lake would douse it.

Twenty-Five

Isa hums when she shivers. Grady added that quirky discovery to his growing list of things he'd learned about his wife. He tossed a blanket, from the pile folded in the corner of the cabin, around her trembling shoulders, adding the layer to his flannel that she'd snatched and unrepentantly put on.

He didn't mind.

He fished out the only clean and dry base layer he had from his pack and put that on instead. Then he snagged another blanket, wrapped his own quivering body with it, and then pulled her snug against his chest.

Good thing he'd added a log to the dwindling fire Isa had kept going in the stove before they'd ventured into the lake. The pine log snapped as the flames consumed it, the sound as comforting as the heat of the fire.

Grady rubbed Isa's back as she snuggled into him. "I didn't think you'd take me seriously."

"I'm not about to miss a swim in a pristine lake."

He chuckled. "I think you have FOMO."

"You're right."

He wasn't sure it was good or bad. Perhaps both. "Another one to add to the list."

"What list?"

When she pulled back to look up at him, he let her go and moved to grab the steaming teakettle from the stove. "The list of things I'm learning about my wife." He poured hot water into both mugs, then glanced at her over his shoulder. "Tea or just water?"

"Tea."

He nodded, tea bag already poised to go in her mug. He handed it to her, then dropped another bag in his.

"You're making a list?" She held the mug up to her face with both hands wrapped tight around the heat.

Again, he nodded.

"What's on the list?"

He winked. "Maybe I don't want to share my list."

"Is it a list of good things or bad things?"

With brows raised, he shrugged. "That's for me to know."

"And me to find out." She sipped the steaming liquid as a corner of the blanket slipped from her shoulder. "Let me see. Isa talks too much. Isa is foolish. Isa slows you down . . ."

Grady reached to retrieve the blanket and resettled it around her. "Why would I think any of those?"

"Don't you? I wandered into a bear's playground like an idiot."

"That was my fault."

She shook her head. "I struggled with the long hike yesterday."

"If you want to know the truth, I did too. As you said, it was a *long* hike."

"You felt like you needed a day away from me."

There, his frown dipped. "Not even close to the truth." He reached to tuck a loose strand of her dark hair behind her ear. "I left you here because I am worried about you. This is no small trek, and I don't want to ask too much of you."

She pressed her lips tight, keeping her attention fixed on the contents of her mug.

Grady took it from her hands, set it on the stove, and pulled her into a hug. After several heartbeats, she pressed her head against him and sighed.

"Isa comes alive in the backcountry," Grady said. "Isa's laugh is lovely. Isa is brave. Isa is determined and strong. Isa is a talented artist." He paused to tilt her face so she would look at him. "Isa is easy to be with."

She blinked rapidly. "You think those things about me?"

"I do."

"Pastor's advice must be working." There was a hint of self-deprecation in her tone.

She'd gone to the pastor for advice—he assumed about their marriage? Why did that make her feel somehow inferior? "Pastor's advice?"

"He said that I should follow the prescription Jesus gave for all relationships. To treat you as I would want you to treat me."

An explosion of insight lit up in his mind at her confession.

"Does that disappoint you?" She stepped back, tightening the blanket around her with both hands.

"That you asked for advice about our marriage from a man full of godly wisdom?"

She nodded, not looking at him. "I promise I didn't tell him all the things. I just said that . . . that we didn't get married because we were in love. But we wanted a good marriage."

How had the man responded to that? Grady determined that asking about it would be getting in the weeds, and that wouldn't be helpful in the moment. Instead, he nudged her chin up. "Isa is wise."

Tears flooded her eyes. "That is about as far from the truth as we are from the sun."

Seeing her regret spill onto her face knifed pain into his chest. He began to shake his head, but she stopped him with a hand against his jaw.

"You haven't asked me."

"Asked you what?"

"The questions that must be in your heart. Why did I do it? Why did I turn my back on a family who clearly loves me and chase after something so stupid, so harmful?"

Grady rolled his lips together, unsure how to navigate this precarious moment. Yes. He wondered. Yes, the questions bothered him. Especially when he put them next to all the wonderful surprises he'd discovered about her.

But he'd determined not to press her. "I figured you would tell me, if you wanted."

"I don't want to." She pulled her hand away as her posture sagged with defeat. "But I want our marriage to work." She peeked at him. "To be good. For both of us, despite our reasons for getting married. I think that means I have to be open with you."

He nodded, admiring her courage and yet fearing what she was about to tell him. What if he couldn't handle it? He was just a man, as proud and judgmental as any other. Maybe even more. Hadn't he treated Isa with icy disapproval for months because he thought she was a flirt?

That wasn't the real reason . . .

He dismissed that little fact—it was another red herring, and this conversation was too important for distractions.

God help us through this . . . A wave of strength came at the end of that prayer. God had been enormously generous with them thus far. Just this morning Grady had dwelled on that. What he was discovering most about Isa on this trip was that he could truly love her. It wouldn't be that hard.

Perhaps because she was practicing how to love on him. And rather than that being insulting, it was hope giving.

Whatever she had to tell him, there was that hope. They could choose to love. They could practice love.

Swallowing, and curling a grip on the courage that sprouted with the surge of strength, Grady brushed her neck with his fingertips. "I'm listening."

Isa winced, the look provoking another throb of ache in his chest. Then she forced her eyes to meet his. "The raw truth is there was not a good reason."

She pulled in a breath, then released it slowly. "I don't even really understand it myself. All I know is that I was tired of the men in my world looking at me like . . . like I was their cute little sister. Amusing, but not someone they found . . . attractive. I felt like a little girl all the time, and I resented it. I wanted to know what it felt like to have a man look at me like . . ."

"Like a desirable woman?"

She nodded.

If only she knew . . .

"So I flirted. I know—I flirt all the time. But it isn't intentional. Not usually. But I started doing it intentionally. And it worked. Then I met Francisco. He was charming. Full of compliments. Generous to me. I didn't get any scary bad-guy vibes from him." She sighed, her shoulders drooping even more. "I guess I was too ignorant to know the signs of grooming. And too starving for attention to recognize a predator."

Fire rolled through Grady's stomach, and he wanted to shout against the injustice of innocence taken advantage of by evil and selfish men.

"I should have known better. Papi, José, even Bennett had warned me to be more guarded. More careful. It only made me more resentful. That's the real reason." She lifted her face up to him again, her expression tortured. "I was resentful. Ungrateful for the concern and advice of people who loved me. And so I gave myself to a man I didn't know."

Her lips trembled, and tears bulged from her eyes. As the truth of her shame settled hard on her heart, great heart-wrenching sobs tore through her small body.

"I broke my family's heart and ruined my life." She covered her face with her hands and wept.

Instead of disgust and rather than resentment, Grady's heart broke. Split wide open, gushed with that agony of the pain flowing from her. He gathered her close, while tears pricked his own eyes, and held her fast as she cried.

"Not ruined," he whispered against her hair.

She gripped his shirt as a new sob shook her body.

"Not ruined." Conviction poured fresh as Grady repeated that statement. She wasn't ruined. Not because Grady said so, but because God didn't leave broken, repentant hearts in the darkness of shame. Not when they called out to Him for salvation.

The day of his own salvation came to mind, and Grady recalled the chapter that had gripped his heart. It had been Jeremiah 31, where God spoke of His people's rebellion and shame but reassured them of His unending love. The chapter ended with the life-giving promise that only God could deliver: *I will forgive their iniquity, and I will remember their sin no more.*

After reading that chapter, Grady's college roommate had taken him to John 3, to a scene where John the Baptist was again testifying that Jesus was the Savior. In that, there was this statement: *God is true.*

"God doesn't lie. He keeps his promises. He is faithful. So when He says that those who believe in the Son will have eternal life, when He says that He will remember their sin no more, you can sink your life into it," Grady's roommate had proclaimed. "God is true. Anchor yourself to that."

Grady had. And though life hadn't been all perfect sunsets and easy days from that point forward, there had been peace that held him fast in the storms that rolled in. A hope that kept him from drowning in loneliness.

That same hope anchored him as he held his wife. Hope for her heart to heal. Hope for them as they navigated this new relationship. And the best hope: God was true. He would take her shame and cast it away. He would remember her sin no more.

Hazel walked through the front door of the Pantry, searching for Mama Bulldog. She found her restocking canned goods in the short aisle for such things.

"Well, my Hazel." MB stood and brushed her hands down her jeans. "You're back! How was Chicago?"

"Let's just say I'm glad to be home where I can hear myself think."

MB chuckled.

"I have news." Hazel lifted her hand and wiggled her fingers, hoping the diamond sparkled.

With a muted squeal, MB grabbed her into a hug. "It's about time."

"Yes, I think so."

"I hope you're tying the knot soon."

Hazel nodded. "September."

"Oh my, that is soon! Just a few weeks . . ." Mama Bulldog tapped her chin with one finger. "Will you have a wedding, or are you going to the courthouse?"

"The courthouse would be more practical."

MB lifted an eyebrow. "I feel a *but* in that . . ."

Hazel felt like a twelve-year-old girl. "I think maybe I want a wedding."

At that, MB clapped her hands. "All my dreams are coming true!"

"Now I see where Janie gets it." Hazel laughed.

"What can I do?"

"Help me. I have no idea what I'm doing." Hazel held up a staying hand. "But I know I don't want anything too big, too fancy, too . . . not me."

"Of course." MB brightened with a sudden thought and held up a finger. "I have just the thing for you, Hazel love."

"You do?"

She nodded, and Hazel surrendered to the woman's joy.

Twenty-Six

Grady breathed a breath of mixed emotions as he walked toward the Albright building in Mammoth. Isa's hand felt comfortable, her fingers laced with his, provoking the sense of gratitude and joy that had been increasing daily over their ten-day trek. They'd shared more in that span of time than he believed many couples would have shared in a year's worth of meaningless dates, superficial conversations, and self-centered exploits.

But now they were heading back to the everyday reality of life. He needed to check in with the backcountry office in the basement of the visitor's center, and there he'd also find a ride that would take him and Isa back to the trailhead on the other side of the Bridger Mountains, where he'd left the truck. After that . . . home.

That was where the joy tamped down and the anxiety grew. Not because he wasn't looking forward to sleeping in his own bed or taking a long, hot shower. But because there were shadows lurking back home.

Since his solo hike in the middle of this trip, fear had dug in deep, planted right in the middle of the expanding affection he had for his wife. Up near High Lake, in a clearing, he'd gained reception for his cell, a text alert got his attention. What he'd found waiting on the screen had caused panic. The text was from Mitchel.

> Another woman found. There's not a news article, but it's got the FBI's attention. She survived and has confirmed the Lopezes involvement. She was taken out in the woods, beaten, and left to die in the Custer Gallatin National Forest, south of Livingston.

> You've got a good eye on your asset, right?

It had taken every ounce of discipline he had, and an ongoing prayer for Isa's protection, to not turn around that instant and book it back to the cabin. The Lopezes didn't know where Isa was living, didn't know she'd married him, and didn't know she was backpacking in Yellowstone. There was no way they could get to her at the cabin.

But man, Livingston? That was close. Way too close.

What was provoking these hits? Francisco had a reputation for his proficiency with women. He'd never gone after old lovers before.

What had set him off?

The reminder of why Grady had married Isa overshadowed the happiness he'd stumbled into during this trip. The rest of that day, Grady struggled to keep a grip on his fear. The struggle had been so fierce, in fact, that he'd given Isa the impression that he was upset when he'd returned to the cabin.

He *had* been upset. But not with her. He'd been unfathomably relieved to see her sitting on the deck, happily painting and perfectly safe. He'd held himself back from running across the meadow between them, crushing her in his arms, and demanding that she never leave his sight.

The rest of the trip, she was right there beside him. He had the comfort of knowing exactly where she was and that she was okay. And the reassurance of the firearm he was permitted to carry strapped to his waist.

Now though? They were going home. Back to their everyday life, which meant that she would be working and he would be working, and most days that meant they would not be together.

He hated the lack of control.

Reentry into everyday life had proven uneventful the first week. Until the second Friday night after they'd returned.

Isa fidgeted in her chair at the dining room table, which dwarfed Grady's tiny kitchen. The woman who had shown up at her door and now sat across from her had Grady's eyes, but not much else resembled him. She owned a smoker's cough that crackled into the otherwise silent space between them.

"Maybe I'll wait outside."

Isa frowned. "That's not necessary. You're welcome here, of course. Grady should be home any minute."

"I need a cigarette." The woman braced her hands against the table to leverage herself up. Another bout of coughs trailed her as she limped across the house, heading for the door.

Before she reached it, the front door swung open, and Grady came through. He stopped dead when his gaze landed on the woman.

"Mom."

"Hello, son," she wheezed.

He blinked, his attention shifting to Isa. Man, he sure could scowl when he wasn't pleased. He looked back at his mother. "What are you doing here?"

"Not even a hug? Come on, Graders. I haven't seen you in two years."

Two years? That was a long time. She'd known things were difficult, but not seeing his mom in two years?

"I call you at least once a week. And I asked you to come to my wedding."

The woman moved toward Grady and patted his bearded cheek, as though he were seven years old. "That is true. And I always look forward to your calls."

Grady swallowed, glanced at Isa again, then wrapped a hesitant and stiff hug around his mother.

"I'm sorry I missed your wedding," she said. "Bill wasn't up for traveling right then."

"Is Bill here too?"

"No." Grady's mom stepped backward, looking toward her shoes.

Silence pierced the room, adding a chill to the tension.

Isa cleared her throat, and when Grady turned to look at her, she pointed toward the back door. "I've got to go back to the café. It's Friday . . ."

He winced, but then he nodded.

She should probably stay to be a support for her husband. But she wasn't that brave. Anyway, it was Friday, and Janie had already been really, really gracious with her—giving her a full ten days off so she could go backpacking with Grady.

Maybe those were excuses. Even so, she jogged the three blocks from Grady's house to the café, relieved she didn't have to be a part of that little family reunion.

Grady lay on his back and stared into the darkness while his mind whirled.

The day had already held frustrations and worries before he'd come home that evening. He'd received another text from Mitchel—this time with an image of a newspaper article from Bozeman. The picture was not of a dead woman this time, but of Grady and Isa, with the printed words *Joined in marriage*.

You got married? Who is the lucky woman?

Grady hadn't answered Mitchel's text. Instead, he'd fought off the panic of knowing that Isa's family had unintentionally exposed her to the very thing this marriage was supposed to have shielded her from. When he'd walked through that front door, he'd had every intention of showing Isa the newspaper article. But all that was derailed.

His mother had come to visit.

He swallowed against the potent mix of emotions that stirred. The wounded little boy in him wanted to wrap his arms around her finally coming and let happiness do a little jig. The more seasoned and jaded man he'd become knew there was more to her visit than *I wanted to come meet your wife, of course. Anyway, can't a mother pay a surprise visit to her son?*

And the grown man who had served a stint as a criminal investigator? He sniffed a darker issue that had sent his mother in search of him. Didn't take any investigation skills at all to guess why.

The pronounced limp and the fading bruise on her left cheek told him a story he'd known all too well.

Anger simmered as Grady clenched his fists. Bill was a worthless loser. A criminal in Grady's book—any man who would hit a woman deserved felony charges. But his mother continued to go back to him.

What did that make her?

It made Grady feel infuriatingly helpless. He would protect his mother at all costs—but she wouldn't leave the man. It was impossible to help a woman who refused to help herself. And Grady felt awful for thinking such things about his mom—for harboring anger toward her when she was a victim.

What was he supposed to do?

Beside him, Isa stirred against the mattress. As the rustle of sheets whispered into the silence, her hand slid over his. "You okay?"

He squeezed his eyes shut.

In his lack of an answer, she scooted closer. The warmth of her body seeped into his side, and he couldn't resist the comfort of it. Turning, he pulled her close.

Isa didn't press for him to talk. She only threaded her arm around him.

Two are better than one.

Grady reflected on the verse Hunter had read at the beginning of their wedding ceremony. It had drifted through his mind several times when they'd been backpacking—specifically the part about keeping each other warm. That had seemed deliciously relevant as they'd snuggled against the cold nights in that small tent.

But now he focused on recalling the rest of what that verse had said. "If one falls, the other can help him." He wasn't sure why he whispered the words. Even so, he continued. "If two lie down together, they will keep each other warm."

"But how can one stay warm alone?" his wife responded.

Grady tightened his arm around her. "One might be overpowered, but two can defend themselves."

Isa's fingers caressed his back. "A cord of three strands is not easily broken."

A cord of *three* strands.

"God, teach us to love."

Isa's echo of his prayer that he'd spoken that first night of their trek stirred both yearning and peace into Grady's turbulent heart.

"My son has always had a hyperactive instinct to protect," Sue said. "He would rescue anything from crickets to stranded people on the highway, and feel responsible for them for way too long."

Isa wiped down the bar counter, glancing at her mother-in-law as she worked. "He's a good man." When she turned her back to put away the cleaning bucket, she winced. Had Sue intentionally said that as a barb? As a . . . a warning? Or was she covering up her own discomfort at having obviously come to town seeking Grady's help?

Would it be wrong for Isa to confront the woman?

"That's why he entered the reserves right out of high school. That, and it helped pay for school. But he's the tenderhearted sort too, so as soon as his service was done, he left it. He doesn't like to be yelled at."

She could imagine that having a childhood as traumatic as Grady's would contribute to that. Anyway, who honestly enjoyed being yelled at? Isa stacked the clean cups that Janie had brought out from the kitchen, lining them neatly on the exposed shelf along the back wall.

The tiny flutter in her womb caused Isa to pause. She pulled in a quiet breath and marveled at the sensation of life growing within her.

Not a life she'd planned on. And truthfully, when she'd discovered that this little one existed, it had been a life she feared—almost resented. But then Grady happened.

Overprotective, tenderhearted Grady. He was proving to be a wonderful husband—despite all her worrying about his apparent dislike of her. And he would be an amazing dad. Nothing like the father figures he'd had in his life.

That thought soured her patience with the woman who had spent her morning at the café. Isa tried to push aside the resentment that billowed against Sue. "Grady is a quiet and gentle man, and I'm grateful for it." She plastered a smile.

"Oh, he can have a temper, trust you me." Sue's laugh was rough. She leaned against the counter. "I guess you haven't seen that yet, hmm?"

"No." She'd heard about it though. In her opinion, he'd been justified.

"How long have you known my son?"

Yikes. She wasn't prepared for that turn of conversation. Isa turned back to the shelf of glasses. "We met last fall."

"Huh. He didn't mention dating anyone seriously."

"He's a private person. Quiet—like we just talked about."

"I am his mother."

Not the sort Grady would bare his soul to. Isa kept that response tucked away. "Men aren't known for their transparency."

"Your wedding must have been small."

"It was." Why would she say that?

"You didn't have much time to prepare."

Unease swirled in Isa's stomach. "We had just enough to make it special. Janie, my boss, made it wonderful for us." She dialed up a bright smile and turned to face Sue. "Exactly what we wanted."

Sue's brow folded with suspicion, but as she opened her mouth to speak, Janie burst through the door from the kitchen. "Hunter just brought the puppy." She settled her look on Isa. "You want to take her for a walk? She's doing pretty well on a leash."

Janie must have heard the conversation. Bless her for intervening. Isa nodded, reaching to untie her apron. "Fresh air would be nice, and I haven't seen that little fur ball in three weeks."

"She's growing. Hunter thinks she'll be big."

"You got a puppy?" Sue arched an eyebrow.

"No, not really. Grady found her abandoned behind the dumpster."

"A new puppy right after a rushed marriage? And in that tiny box of a house? Sounds like trouble."

"Hunter and I are taking care of her—Grady and Isa said that they couldn't. It was too much all at once." Janie smiled, but her eyes held a flash of warning on the woman, daring her to find another thing to barb Isa about.

The pause in the room sagged with all kinds of uncomfortable weight. A small yip sounded from the back door beyond the kitchen. Exactly the thing.

"Puppy calls." Isa tossed her apron to the back counter and ducked out the door. Once through the kitchen, she burst into the alley.

Hunter said hello and passed her the leash.

Isa had never been so relieved to take a dog on a walk in her life.

"Mom, that's enough." Grady ran forked fingers through his hair, turning from the front door to face the dining room table.

"I'm just saying I know there's more to this story than you and Isa are telling. And I know you, son. You have an impulsive need to rescue things that are in trouble."

He did. Thanks to her. Did she realize how much her own codependence issues had shaped him? Grady worked to keep his thoughts from spiraling. Truth was, Mom had a point—he'd married Isa to protect her. To rescue her?

Was he like his mother?

As often happened, Grady felt the warning of taking responsibilities that weren't his to heart. *God saves, not me.* He rehearsed that phrase he'd adopted since he'd walked away from his mother and Bill several years ago. He could love her the best he could—but she wasn't his to save.

And Isa? He replayed that moment weeks back when the idea had come upon him to marry her. It'd been more than an idea. It had been a conviction. Or had it been that impulsive need?

He held that question up to the Father with open hands. There was no return of conviction of wrongdoing. Indeed, he sensed an affirmation.

"Are you in trouble, Grady?" His mother spoke into his long silence.

"No." He turned back to her. That wasn't true, but he couldn't tell her the full truth. But it seemed that he needed to tell her . . . something. He sighed. "Look, Isa and I—we've both made some mistakes. But—"

"What mistakes?"

Grady paused to consider carefully. Wouldn't be too much longer before everyone knew . . . "Isa is pregnant, Mom."

She held his look with one that was entirely lacking surprise. So. This was what everyone assumed.

It was for the best.

"One mistake doesn't cancel another."

Who was this woman? Did she hear herself? Did she see her own life? Grady capped the resentment building in his mind and worked the tension in his opening and closing fists.

"No, it doesn't. But Isa and I are committed to this marriage, and we're figuring it out." That was the truest thing he'd said all day. "We're going to be fine." No, not that. "We're going to be good, Mom. I promise."

"Everything always seems that way at the beginning."

"Mom, how about you hope for the best for us?"

"Like you do for Bill and me?"

Ouch. That stung, because it was partly true. But also, because the situation wasn't the same. Isa didn't abuse him. She didn't make promises she wasn't even going to try to keep. She didn't fly into blind, drunken rages and cause physical harm.

Not the same at all.

A low growl escaped his lips as Grady worked to control his temper. "When Bill stops drinking and goes to rehab, I'll be glad to believe things are turning around. But until you show up at my door *without* a limp and bruises on your face, I can't believe that you staying with him is the best for either of you."

Mom looked away. For a long moment, she held herself stiff—as if she were going to get up and leave. But then she slumped into the chair. "I left him this time. That's why I'm here."

Grady slid into the chair across from her. "I'm glad you knew you could come here."

"He doesn't want me to see you. That's why we didn't come to the wedding. It makes him . . . jealous, which is weird, I know. But this time I walked out and I told him I was coming to you, and there was nothing he could do or say to stop me."

A pinprick of hope shone into the darkness of doubt. He'd heard this tale before, but . . . He slid his hand, palm up and open, toward her, focusing on that spot of hope rather than the sea of doubt.

She took it, squeezing her grip. "This time will be different." Tears shone in her eyes when she lifted her face. "I promise, Grady. I'm going to be around. I'll make a better effort to get to know your wife. And when that baby comes . . ." A full smile lit her expression. "I'm going to be a grandma!"

Grady nodded. "That sounds good, Mom." Too good to be true. Again, he silenced the doubt and instead turned his thoughts to what needed to be done next. "I'll start asking around about a place for you."

"That would be nice. In the meantime, the little hotel down the road is fine. If . . ."

"I'll take care of it." He had some savings put away. Money he hadn't even talked about with Isa, so certainly she wouldn't mind. This was his mom, after all. Isa was close to her family—they meant the world to her. She would understand.

He felt confident in that, because the woman he'd spent more than a week hiking the backcountry with had shown herself to be full of joy and hope, of strength and kindness. As he dwelled on that, something profound seeped into his awareness.

He loved her.

Twenty-Seven

The last text Mitchel had sent—over a week before—nagged at Grady. Finding a few moments alone with his wife had proven a challenge lately. Isa had taken back full responsibility at the café—quite possibly as an escape from spending time with his mom, Grady guessed. And his job had him out checking trails regularly—often driving more than one hundred miles round trip to patrol some of the more out-of-the-way hikes.

But that day, he had the Black Gulch Falls trail on his schedule, and he needed to reconnect with Isa. Specifically, to talk about the text that wouldn't budge from his mind.

He drove back to town to pick her up from the café at two, after the lunch rush had come and gone and the prep for supper was well under way. Janie stood at the stove when Grady came through the back-alley door. She turned and said hi, then pointed toward the storage room. "Isa's in there."

Finding her on a stepstool, putting up cans of chili beans, Grady jogged across the twelve-by-twelve space, braced his hands on Isa's hips, and tugged her back. "Let me do that."

Isa turned and smiled down at him. "No problem. But I just finished." She brushed her palms, then anchored both hands on his shoulders to hop down.

"Won't be long before I'm going to forbid you from such activities."

"Forbid?" Isa wrinkled her nose. "Think that will be effective?"

"If I ask you nicely not to, would that work?"

She tilted her head, wearing the cutest sassy look that made his heart skip. "I'll think about it."

"I worry about you enough as it is."

With a hand to his chest, she patted his heart. "It's not good for you, you know."

"All the more reason for you to help a guy out."

"Okay. When I can no longer see my toes, I'll stop climbing ladders."

"Not sure that's what I was going for, but I'll take it for now."

She lifted onto her toes and pecked his cheek, sending a pleasant jolt into his chest. Things had . . . cooled between them since his mother had shown up. Grady found he had a strong craving for a long kiss, which made this little day hike even more appealing.

The drive to the Black Gulch Falls trailhead took fifteen minutes. Once there, Grady strapped on his ranger pack, slipping an extra water bottle in for Isa. Then, meeting Isa at the front of the truck, he took her hand, and they were quickly enveloped in the fir and pine forest.

Worry and strain eased from Grady's shoulders as they meandered hand in hand. They talked about everything and nothing, and the beautiful sensation of rightness and romance soothed the anxiety that had been building the past week.

Grady pointed out little things along the way that he thought Isa might enjoy. The rock he'd dubbed *Birdbath Stone* because it had a small divot that collected water and was protected in a wall of granite so that larger birds of prey couldn't get to a small mountain bluebird as it enjoyed a bath. Fresh bear sign deep into the forest—a large gouge cut into a pine by the powerful claws of a bear.

"I'll have to put out some trail cams and close this trail for a week or so," he told her. Bear activity was always something to keep a sharp eye on.

For over two miles, they hiked. Every now and then, when their conversation faded, Grady would consider how he would tell her the things he needed to say.

First, about the announcement her parents had put in the Bozeman paper about their marriage. He'd need to be careful with that, because the truth was, it frustrated him. But that wasn't her fault, and it wasn't her parents' fault either. He didn't want her to pick up on his irritation.

And second . . . that he loved her. Why was that hard to say? It shouldn't be. Hadn't it been what he'd prayed for? What he'd promised her?

Yes, but it felt . . . precarious. What would she say if she didn't feel the same? *Thank you.* That would be . . . humiliating. *That's nice, but I don't feel the same.* Again, awful.

Worst case? Total silence.

But she *acted* like she loved him.

That could be her practicing the advice the pastor had given her. And it was good advice—to treat him the way she wanted to be treated. But maybe it was a false indicator?

Isa, I love you. He rehearsed in his mind. It sounded so . . . so paltry. Insignificant words that really didn't convey what had gripped his heart when it came to her.

Could he do better? He wasn't a poet. Not even a good writer in general. He knew the forest and wildlife. *You make my heart soar like the bald eagles over Black Gulch Falls.* That would be . . . so stupid. He knew how to defend and protect. *I swear, I'll never let anything bad happen to you.* That was . . . a lie. He wasn't God and didn't have that kind of power.

That was it. All he had, which wasn't much. He'd not even had the example of a loving father and mother to pattern from.

Isa, I've fallen in love with you.

Was that better?

"Grady?" Isa's inquisitive voice interrupted his mental wrestling.

Jarred into reality, he found they'd reached the barely visible side trail where he needed to veer off the main branch.

"Is this the spur to the old mine?"

"Yes. Thanks for catching it."

"You okay?"

"Yeah. I was just lost in thought."

"Anything important?"

The understatement of the year. "Actually, yes." His heart sped up, as if a gun had gone off. Reaching into his pocket, he closed his fists and squeezed. He could do this . . . "Isa—" Just three words and then . . . He opened his hand, his fingers brushing against his phone. "I need you to know something." He was a chicken. A total coward.

He pulled the phone from his pocket, scrolled through his texts, and brought up the image of them. "Your parents put an announcement about us in the paper." He turned the phone so she could see.

With folded brows, Isa studied the picture. "I'm sorry, Grady." She looked at him, pleading in her eyes. "Please don't be angry. They didn't know, and this is their way of supporting us. Of showing you their approval."

Her anxiety about his reaction caused guilt to plunge into his gut. He'd shown her the worst of himself this spring, treating her with so much disapproval and coldness. If she knew that he'd been fighting his attraction to her in those days, would she be able to get past her impression of him being a grumpy, calloused man?

Taking the phone back, he slipped it into his pocket and brushed her cheek with his thumb. "I'm not angry."

"You're not?" she whispered.

He leaned down to brush his mouth across hers. "No."

"Oh." She reached to meet his lips again. "Good."

Ah. That long kiss he'd been craving. Grady pulled her in close and savored the thrill of her touch.

Now was the perfect time.

If only he was a little braver. And more confident that her kisses meant exactly what he wanted them to mean.

So instead, he enjoyed what she gave him a little longer, then pulled back to lead her the rest of the way to the mine. There, he noted that repairs were needed to the barrier keeping anyone clever enough to find the mine out of the dangers that were inside. And then they turned back to head home.

Isa remained at his side. Her hand in his, offering a little boost to his fledgling certainty.

He would tell her. Soon.

Bennett strode toward Hazel's cabin, the rightness of being home settling into his bones.

Home.

They needed to make some plans. First—to get married, and he was thrilled and a little surprised to know that Hazel was actually planning a wedding. He'd figured she'd buy a new pair of Wranglers and a crisp white button-down shirt, and they'd drive to the courthouse to speak their vows. And that would have been okay.

But he preferred the idea of a wedding. And he wondered if his bride would wear a dress. The little mountain lioness refused to reveal any details about that part.

Wedding plans weren't what weighed on his mind that morning though. The round plastic tube in his hands had weight as he made it to the deck and climbed his way to Hazel's front door. It was hard to know if they had been on the same page, this undertaking having been done via FaceTime while he was in Chicago.

But he and Hazel had made it this far. They would figure out how to remodel her cabin. And then they would figure out how to go from single and dating to married with a pair of teenagers under their care.

With a whole lot of grace and love—and much daily prayer—the four of them would be okay.

Isa carried the tray of food to the trio of hikers in the corner booth, her smile dialed up to high. In truth, she wanted to take the apron off, toss it at the man in the farthest chair, and tell him to go forage in the woods.

He'd been difficult from the moment she said hello, with his *Where's the wine list* (Janie's Café didn't serve alcohol, as they didn't have a liquor license) and *Why are these seats so abominable?* (they weren't recliners, but who expected that in a café?) and *Why is this taking so long? We hiked three miles today and are staving!* (Three miles? Whoa. How did they ever manage?)

Rather than giving into sarcasm, or worse, the urge to tell them to find somewhere else to eat (good luck with that in Luna), Isa clamped on to overzealous sunshine.

"Okay, boys. I've got your shepherd's pie with a side of fried brussels sprouts. And I've added Janie's fried apples—I promise you don't want to miss that."

"Finally. Better not be charging me extra for the fried apples that I didn't order."

"Of course." Isa kept her posture straight and her smile steady. She even found a wink. "My treat."

The man grinned slowly. "That's more like it, sugar."

Great. She'd given the wrong impression when all she'd wanted was for this guy to stop being a grizzly bear.

With her grin frozen in place, Isa turned to take the empty tray back to the kitchen. When she caught a glimpse of Grady sitting at the counter, a sigh of relief rushed from her chest. Seeing him caused the painful fake happy face to fade and a soft, real grin to take its place. She tucked the tray under her arm and made her way around the counter until she stopped across from him.

"Hi."

Grady lifted his face, revealing a scowl. Wordlessly, he raised one eyebrow.

Wow. She'd forgotten how hard his cold disapproval could hit her. Swallowing, she eased back from the counter. "Bad day?"

"I've had better."

"Want to tell me about it?"

"No." His tone bit. Then he looked at his hands. "Not now," he said a little softer.

"Okay. Can I get you some supper? Shepherd's pie tonight."

"Yeah."

"Fried apples?"

"Sure."

"Coffee?"

"Just water."

"Okay." She waited, hoping that he'd peek at her with the warmth she'd come to expect from him.

"Hey, sugar!" The call came from the back corner booth. "These apples are good. Bring me another round."

With an enormous amount of effort, Isa smiled and nodded. "You got it."

Grady peeked at the men over his shoulders, and then pinned her with a dark look she understood perfectly.

He thought she was flirting. And he was *not* impressed.

The battle in his mind was relentless. How could one day be this bad?

Mitchel. His mom. And now Isa.

God, I need help . . .

His narrow grip on his emotions was slipping. Any moment, and he'd lose it.

Listening to Isa flirt with the men in the corner, and with every other male in the room for that matter, just about killed him. Especially since, after she'd brought him his supper, she'd been avoiding him. Perhaps that had something to do with his dark mood. Likely. But that didn't help things much for Grady.

He was mad. Had been since this morning, when his mom had announced that she had decided she needed to go back and check on Bill.

"Mom, you said—"

"Now, son, you'll learn now that you're married. You say things when you're upset that you don't mean."

"He hurt you, Mom."

"He apologized and promised it will never happen again."

"You haven't heard that before?"

"Grady, people make mistakes. You're a good person—you know that we have to do our best to help the people we care about when they mess up."

"Mom, this has *got* to stop."

"Are you going to make me chose between you and him?"

Grady blew out an aggravated breath. "You always get to make your own choices, and you know you can always come here. But I'm not going to go back to a situation of habitual abuse. I'm not willing to stand by and watch it happen."

"It would go a long way for you to come and make amends with Bill."

At that, Grady had pinned his mother with a hard stare. It was like his mother intentionally shut her eyes to the truth. Once again, he couldn't help her.

He had shaken his head and left the house.

Two hours later, he'd had a phone call from Mitchel.

"Something is going down," Mitchel said. "I think you need to be there."

"I'm not actually an agent, Mitchel. Why would I need to be there?"

"Shoot straight with me, Grady. Who is the woman you married?"

"My wife."

"What is her name?"

"You read it in the article. Her name is Isabel."

"Is that her real name?"

"Where are you going with this?"

"I have a hunch that you married your asset. Am I right?"

Grady's heart froze. How had Mitchel figured that out? From the picture? Grady had given no indication of what his *asset* looked like.

"Look, it doesn't matter that much, other than if you care about whoever your informant is, you should probably be there. We have intelligence that has Francisco and Junior in West Yellowstone. Together."

"Intelligence? Last I talked to the Denver office, they didn't care where the Lopezes were. It wasn't a priority."

"It's become a priority. A couple of dead young women will do that."

A couple? To Grady's knowledge, one of the victims had survived. "I still don't know why I need to be there. I'm not actually an agent. And you're supposed to be retired."

"Look, you're an undercover asset. This is what comes with that. I need you in West Yellowstone tomorrow morning. This was my case before I retired. I'm seeing it through. Got it?"

The end of that call left him confused, scared, and more irritated than he'd been at the start of the conversation—which had already been on the spectrum of annoyed.

What he needed was a trail run.

But he hadn't had time for a trail run. He'd needed to clear a downed pine that lay across the lower Elk Creek trail. Before he had finished that job, rain sputtered from the sky. By the time he'd hiked back to the trailhead, the clouds had let loose, and he reached his truck completely soaked.

And that was how he'd ended his workday. Cold, soaked, and angry. And hungry. Which had him driving to the café, only to find his wife hard at work. Flirting.

This day could not get worse.

"Maybe you need to go home and take a hot shower." Isa tried to keep the bite out of her voice.

By Grady's darkening frown, and the way he crossed his arms over his chest, she'd failed.

She didn't want to fight with him. She was too tired to fight with him. The men who'd stayed for *three* hours, and then left her a *two-dollar* tip, had completely worn her out. Added to that, Grady had been mad from their first hello, and worrying about that had exhausted her.

She'd worked so hard this first month of their marriage. She'd done everything she could to follow Pastor's advice—to treat Grady as she would want him to treat her. To *love* him the way she hoped he would love her. And it had seemed that her husband had warmed to her. There had been moments she *felt* his heart open to her.

That made this all the more devastating. Couldn't he see that she was just trying to survive her job? He'd had a bad day—she got that. But did he bother to stop and think that maybe her day hadn't been awesome either?

"What I need is for my *wife* to not humiliate me in public."

"What?" Isa stumbled back, feeling his words as a slap. "Humiliate you? You sat there like an angry bear. Have you seen yourself when you scowl? You might as well have *leave me alone* written in Sharpie on your forehead, and you basically have a hedge of thistles around your aura."

"My *aura*?" He clearly didn't find her amusing in the least.

"So. I left you alone."

"You certainly did. And busied yourself with plenty of other *people*."

"I'm a waitress, Grady. It's part of my job to be friendly. Which takes a whole lot of extra effort when customers are difficult."

"Friendly and flirting aren't the same thing."

"I don't think you would know."

"That's true. Because you flirt with everyone but me!"

She didn't flirt with him? Did nothing about the past month sink in with him? She had given him everything. *Everything!*

His angry outburst was the final blow. Isa hugged her middle with her trembling arms and blinked against the tears. When they would not be held back, she covered her face with both hands. "I can't do this, Grady."

What more could she do? He said he wanted this marriage to work—she did too. But right then, all the hopeful feelings of a good future together had shattered to pieces.

"Isa." Grady's voice cracked on her name. Remorse filled his much softer tone. When he touched her arms, his fingers were gentle. "Don't say that."

She shook her head. Defeat had swallowed her, and she was too tired to struggle back to the surface. "I can't be the woman you want. I laugh too loud and smile too much, and I don't seem to know the difference between friendly and flirting. You spend more time angry with me than happy."

She finally lifted her chin to meet his gaze. "I'm sorry, Grady. I just can't do it." She pushed away his hands and ran toward the door that would take her up the stairs and to her apartment.

She hadn't stayed there since they got married. But she couldn't imagine going back to Grady's house.

Grady leaned against the stainless-steel sink, gripping the edges while his head sank low between his shoulders.

He'd really messed up.

With a turn of his head, he glimpsed the dark dining room beyond the window in the door that separated the front of the café from the kitchen. In his mind, he could see the evening as it had unfolded. Only this time, he saw things for what they were.

Isa trying too hard. As he'd witnessed earlier in the year. But now . . . now he understood it. That exerted smile. The fake laugh. It hadn't been her flirting.

It's part of my job to be friendly.

That was it. The whole truth of it—and by now he should have known better. He'd seen her real smile. He'd been the recipient of her genuine affection.

And he'd just broken it. Broken his wife. All this time, he'd been so afraid that he'd become just like his mom. Tonight, he'd acted more like . . .

Oh God, no. Please not that.

He *never* wanted to be that.

"Help," he whispered as his head sagged low again. He squeezed his eyes shut and braced against the stinging pain. "Help me love my wife."

It turned out, falling in love with his wife hadn't been the hardest part of this marriage. Loving her well . . . that was different. Because the hardest part of being married was facing the reality of his own failures. He could be a harsh and cold man. He could be judgmental and easily provoked. And he could say things that broke his wife's spirit, damaging her heart. He was a sinful, prideful man in need of mercy.

He'd wanted to protect Isa. Tonight, instead, he'd hurt her.

Horrified by the thought that he could ever behave like the men who had hurt his mom, and ashamed that he'd allowed his dark emotions to lash out at Isa, Grady pushed away from the sink and forced himself up the stairs.

He found Isa in her room. She stood beside her dresser, a tissue in her hand doing little to soak up the pools of tears smearing her face.

Grady's heart broke more. "Isa."

She looked at him with defeat, and another tear rolled down her cheek.

Grady closed the gap between them, cautiously lifting his hands to cradle her face in his palms. When she didn't pull away, he leaned down to touch his forehead to hers.

"Forgive me." Emotion choked his voice. "Please."

"Grady, you don't like me," she cried. "How are we ever going to make this work?"

"Sweetheart, that's not true. It so far from the truth." He eased back so she could have a full view of his face. So she could see the raw emotion in his face. "Isa, I love you."

She winced. "Don't say that if you don't—"

"I love you."

A tear seeped from her eye, and he smeared it away with his thumb.

"I love you," he repeated.

A fresh sob shook her shoulders, and she leaned into his chest. He wrapped both arms around her and lay his head atop hers as a tear trickled down the side of his face.

"I was jealous. From the beginning, I have been jealous of you. I wanted your attention, your smile, all for myself. Every time I thought you shunned me and flirted with someone else, I bristled.

Because I was jealous. That's not an excuse—it was wrong of me to be cold and harsh. I behaved badly. I'm sorry, Isa. Please forgive me."

Her nod was a gentle movement against his shirt. "I forgive you," she whispered. After a moment, she drew in a shuddered breath and then leaned back. "You . . . you liked me?"

"So much." He fingered the hair that had fallen over her face and tucked it back. "You are beautiful, Isa. And so full of life and joy. You are the woman I want."

A tender smile eased the pain wrinkling her face. She slipped her arms around him and leaned against him again. "I want you too, Grady."

Grady shut his eyes and thanked God for mercy. And for his wife, who was the love of his life.

Twenty-Eight

Hunter carried his mug of coffee to the front deck, though the world outside was still in quiet darkness. Janie had already gone for the morning, having told Isa she'd handle the early shift at the café. Watching the sun peek over the hills that rolled to the east had become one of his favorite things. In the slow predawn moments, he was able to bow his heart before the Creator and worship the majesty of the King.

Dressed in a pair of jeans and a Yellowstone hoodie, Hunter stretched what lingered of sleep from his bones. Inhaling the fragrant steaming liquid in his mug, he settled on the wooden rocker near the door. With the book of prayers that John had gifted him for his birthday, and his Bible on his lap, he lowered his head.

Behold, Lord, An empty vessel that needs to be filled.
My Lord, fill it.

Hunter began with Martin Luther's prayer as he had memorized it, let it dwell in his heart, shape his soul, and push him nearer—he prayed—to the God of his salvation.

I am weak in faith; Strengthen thou me.

I am cold in love; Warm me and make me fervent

That my love may go out to my neighbor.

He stopped there, his memory summoned to what he'd witnessed last night at the café. Grady and Isa had been at odds. Hunter's guess? It had been a bad day for Grady, and Isa was doing what Isa did—trying too hard to make everyone happy, even when they were difficult. Grady had misunderstood. Unless Hunter completely missed his guess, after the café had closed and Hunter and Janie had gone home for the night, Grady and Isa had fought.

Compassion moved in his chest. Relationships could be *hard*. Even the best of them took work. Sometimes a whole lot of work—and often that work needed to be done on oneself. Because love had a way of shining light in places in his own heart that a man would prefer not to see. The pride. The selfishness. The capacity to say harsh things without thinking them through.

I am a sinner . . .

Luther's confession was Hunter's as well. And he hoped, for Grady and Isa, Grady's too.

With his elbows against his knees, Hunter leaned into a bow. "Lord, You know each of our hearts. You know we are fragile things, prone to selfishness. Prone to breaking. I don't know what is going on between Grady and Isa, but I do know that You love them. And I know that You have put them both here for Janie and me to love as well. Give us wisdom to know when to speak and when to be silent. Give us love to encourage them. And give them, Lord, Your hope, that what has happened will be used by You for good."

Hunter continued to pray, his heart opened to the Son as the break of day crept over the horizon. As he yielded to the will of God, he felt sure of one thing: He would call Grady. And whatever God gave him to say or do, Hunter would obey.

Grady glanced at his phone, buzzing on the seat next to him. Hunter's name flashed on the screen.

Six was pretty early for a random call, even if Grady had been on the road for an hour by then. He suspected Hunter was calling to confront him about his grizzly behavior the evening before. Rather than resenting that suspicion—as he might have just a few short weeks ago—Grady opened himself to the vulnerability of it.

If he was to become a better man—one who would love Isa the way she needed to be loved—he needed accountability. He needed a friend—even better, a brother in Christ. Who knew but that Hunter's calling was God's answer to Grady's prayer last night for help?

Resolved to be open and honest, and humble rather than defensive, Grady answered the phone. "Morning, Hunter."

"Good morning, buddy."

Buddy? Hmm. A good start?

"You're on my mind this morning. I hope it's not too early."

"No, not too early. I've been driving since five."

"Wow. That's an early start. Where are you headed today?"

"West Yellowstone."

"That's not in the park, is it?"

"Nope, not where I'm going, at least." Grady paused, considering Hunter's call and that prayer for help. He didn't feel good about this trip. Something seemed off with Mitchel wanting him there. He'd called and texted Malcom before he'd left Luna that morning, but the Denver agent didn't answer. Five in the morning was pretty early though. Even so, Grady had that sensation in his gut—the one he was familiar with from childhood. The one that warned him when danger was lurking nearby.

"Listen," Grady started cautiously. "I'm glad you called. I know you probably called to confront me about my behavior last night—and I appreciate it. Isa and I . . . we had a fight. But in the end, it turned out okay."

"Yeah?"

Better than okay. He finally told his wife he was in love with her. And even though she didn't say the words, he felt secure that she loved him too. Everything she did, and had been doing since they'd married, said so.

"Yeah."

"I'm glad to hear it, buddy. Marriage can be a wild ride."

"I'm learning that. And I'm glad that you . . . you called me out. I mean, if that's what this is."

"Not really calling you out, Grady. God knows I'm a failure more often than I'm willing to admit. I just wanted you to know that Janie and I, we're here for you both. I know that your marriage wasn't . . . well, normal. But you have my admiration. Most men wouldn't do what you did. And I know you have the best of intentions."

Wow. Coming from a guy who had resented him for dating Janie briefly, to this?

"That means a whole lot, Hunter."

"Whatever it means, just know that I'm sincere in it. Whatever I can do, or we can do, to support you guys, you've got it."

Grady let that sink in. Could he trust Hunter with more? Seemed like this early morning conversation might be ordained.

"Hunter, this might be way more than you bargained for."

"I'm not bargaining for anything less than a friendship, Grady. What do you need?"

"I don't love this trip to West Yellowstone. To be honest, it has my suspicions on high alert." Grady spent the next few minutes explaining his relationship with the FBI and why he'd known Isa needed help—and that she was in a whole lot more danger than becoming a single mother. "Isa would be mortified to know that you know all of this," he ended.

"She won't know." Hunter gave his word like a solemn oath. "You're worried about her while you're gone?"

"Yes, exactly. Something about this doesn't feel right. I'm not sure—I didn't suspect anything of Mitchel before. But there were things he knew that he had no way of knowing. And he's kept unusually close tabs on me. I don't like it."

"I'll head down to town and keep an eye on things."

"Thank you."

"Call me if there's more. If I can do anything else."

Grady hung up and lifted a grateful prayer. God had sent him a friend—and help. Not just anyone either. Hunter Wallace had grown up in the backcountry around Luna. He was an expert hunter and ex-military. Grady couldn't think of anyone he could trust more when it came to Isa's safety.

Isa woke up alone in her bed, but the pillow beside her still held the impression of Grady's head, and when she pulled it close, the smell of pine and saffron filled her senses. She sighed, a small smile on her lips.

He loved her.

Grady Briggs loved her.

As she savored the joy bursting in her heart, the phone on the bedside table chimed. Hoping her husband was texting her, she scrambled to check.

Nope, not Grady. His mom though.

I am going back to Idaho. Grady isn't answering his phone, but I would like to say goodbye in person before I leave. Is that okay?

Isa sagged against the headboard. Last night Grady had shared with her all that had been bothering him before he came to the café, and his mother had been on the list. Isa felt frustrated and hurt for him—his relationship with his mom seemed impossibly complicated. Having her change her mind and go back yet again to a toxic, abusive relationship was understandably difficult for him to handle.

She sighed. The least she could do was make a better effort with Sue. For Grady's sake. Resolved, she sent a quick text telling Sue that she'd be down at the hotel with a bear claw and a hot cup of coffee for her in about thirty minutes. Then she tossed the gray comforter off her body and put her feet to the floor.

She paused in the middle of the room as a gurgle tickled her womb. With her palm, she covered the place where her baby grew. Soon Grady would be able to feel the movements of this new life within. He'd told her he was excited for that.

What a grace gift that was. Her husband not only loved her, but he already loved the child he didn't have to claim as his own.

Moved by so much profound love, she tilted her face upward. "Lord, help me today. Give me a soft heart that I may treat Sue as I would want a daughter-in-law to treat me someday."

True to her word, within twenty minutes she was walking from the café toward Luna's Creek View Hotel, coffee and bear claw in hand.

Grady pulled into the deserted parking area and shifted into Park. The two-and-half-hour drive hadn't helped calm his anxiety about this. He'd spent the time intermittently praying and then combing through the texts and calls he'd traded with Mitchel. He'd tried Malcom once more too, but still no response.

He hadn't told Mitchel anything about Isa. Her age or build or what she looked like. There was nothing in anything that he'd shared that would have led the man to believe that he'd married the woman who had given him information about Cisco.

Nothing.

Why had Mitchel immediately concluded that his wife was his asset?

A black sedan pulled up beside his Game and Parks vehicle. Windows tinted, government plates. Had to be Mitchel.

Confirming Grady's assumption, Mitchel stepped out from the driver's side, adjusted his dark sunglasses, then his suit pants, and strode to Grady's truck. "Think it'd be best to take yours in from here." Mitchel patted the truck's hood and then made his way around to the passenger side. He climbed in and settled, giving the door a hard smack shut.

Good morning to you too. Grady simply stared at the man. He hadn't known him all that well, to be honest. Had cooperated on a few cases with him when Grady had been an investigator and their jurisdictions had overlapped. Mitchel had given the impression that he was good at what he did. Efficient. Effective. Both of which required him to be impersonal.

Why had he selected Grady for a paid asset? That sort of thing was usually strong-armed onto criminals who opted for cooperation rather than a dire sentence—a plea bargain. Grady had a clean record, and he had been a good investigator, even when the job had wrecked him.

The only thing that made sense was that Grady had left criminal investigation behind in favor of the Game and Parks. He had the right skills, the right background, and the right job with the right location.

The location being the most important. That did make sense—except for the Denver office not seeming to have any interest in the Lopez case at all.

Why was Mitchel so invested in it?

"Burning daylight, Briggs." Mitchel tapped the dashboard. "Let's go."

"Where?"

"Calamity, over in the Caribou-Targhee National Forest."

Hand to the gear shift, Grady paused to look at him. "Bear Creek Road is closed in Calamity."

Mitchel nodded. "That would make sense—why the Lopez boys would pick that as their meetup. Closed and deserted sounds like the perfect location."

"Meetup?"

"They've been at odds for a while now. The son has gone rogue. The father has basically cut him off. My intel has them meeting to come to terms."

Grady's brow furrowed. If father and son had been at odds, why had Cisco come looking for Isa?

"Let's go, Grady." This time Mitchel pounded on the dash with the side of his fist. "We don't have time to lose if we want to catch them both."

"Did Denver send anyone up?" Grady shifted into gear and pulled out of the lot. "Malcom didn't answer me this morning."

"Yeah. Of course. They'll meet us, last I heard."

"Who?"

"Whichever agent Malcom thought he could spare."

Grady drove, his mind spinning and adrenaline firing through his veins. When he reached the turnoff for Bear Creek Road, he eased onto the narrow dirt drive. "You sure?"

"Yeah. Just go as far as you can."

He'd driven through washouts before—he was sure the four-wheel-drive the Game and Parks issued him could handle whatever had shut down the access road. But he wasn't sure that was a good idea.

Log barriers ahead had him easing to a stop. "This is as far as we go."

"Maybe for the truck." Mitchel popped his door open and jumped out of the vehicle. He reached for his firearm, strapped around his chest, confirmed it was loaded, and then glanced back to Grady. "Be ready."

"What are we walking into here?"

"Not sure. Just make sure you're alert. How long since you last fired a round or two?"

He went up to Hunter and Hazel's range at Elk Lake on a regular basis, appreciating the invitation Hunter had extended last spring. But Grady didn't answer. Simply checked his gun and tucked it back into the holster.

Mitchel jogged along the side of the road, ducking under the log barrier. Grady followed, his mind and body shifting into a zone of pursuit. He'd not done this in a few years, but clearly his training waited just below the surface. He felt dialed in, concentrating on sounds and anything out of place as he scanned the forest.

A flash of black amid the blue green of the pine and fir trees snagged his attention. "There." He reached for the firearm and gestured with it.

A black SUV had been parked off the road, mostly hidden in the forest.

Mitchel nodded, took the lead again and crept toward the vehicle. Nothing stirred as they inched nearer. Only the breeze whispering through the trees. But other than that, no chirping from the canopy above. No scampering or churling of squirrels offended at the intrusion of their home.

It was way too quiet.

Mitchel reached the SUV and carefully slid around the side to peek around it. Grady did the same, moving in the opposite direction.

His steady, albeit elevated, pulse stalled at the scene on the other side of the vehicle. One body. A large man with silver hair was slumped, facing the vehicle, against the driver's door.

Francisco. Shot in the back.

Checking that Mitchel had him covered, Grady cautiously moved to the notorious cartel boss and turned him. Blood covered Francisco's tailored suit, turning his white button-down to crimson. His ashen face and stone-still form all but proved the man was dead. A quick check of his nonexistent pulse did the rest.

"Dead?"

"Yes." Grady confirmed. "Where's the shooter?"

Mitchel stepped away from the SUV, oddly lowering his weapon. "Cisco!"

"What are you doing?"

Mitchel ignored him and walked farther into the forest. Grady followed, his weapon ready. Twenty feet more, and the forest opened to a meadow—one that would have been pristine but instead bore the marks of a vehicle cutting through the green grass and wildflowers.

Mitchel jogged to the tracks and stopped. "He was here."

Obviously. Grady followed the scar the vehicle had left in the meadow, stopping abruptly when another flash of black caught his gaze. This time, not a vehicle.

He pointed to the body lying in the grass.

"I see it." Michel jogged forward, and when he stopped, his hand forked into his hair.

Grady followed close behind, and what he found jarred him.

Cisco Lopez lay face down. Shot execution style.

What on earth had gone down here?

"Is Isa coming in soon?" Hunter worked to keep his tone casual while he helped Janie plate a couple of bear claws.

"She already did and headed out. I guess Grady's mom decided not to stay." Janie picked up the tray and walked toward the table of tourists. "Don't worry. I can handle it." She winked with a grin.

Hunter drew in a steady breath. No need to panic. Isa had just gone to visit Sue. "How long ago?"

Janie glanced back at him and shrugged. "I don't know. Maybe an hour?"

He nodded, then sneaked a peek at his phone. No new texts. He wasn't sure what he should expect, but he hoped Grady would let him know if something—anything, good or bad—had happened. Grady wasn't an excitable man. Wasn't a guy given to overreaction. That made his request for Hunter to keep an eye on Isa something to take seriously.

"I'm going to take a walk," he called to Janie. "If you're sure you've got this here?"

"Sure." She shot him a wrinkled-brow look. "You okay?"

"Yep. Just have a stiff leg this morning, and I'd like to see if I can shake it out." He bit back the bad taste of dishonesty. He didn't like lying to his wife.

"Have a nice stroll." Janie stopped beside him on her way back to the kitchen and planted a sweet peck on his cheek.

He stopped her before she could leave his side. "I love you, Janie. You know that, right?"

She laughed. "I do, Hunter." She smoothed his brow and gave him another kiss. "But it's always good to hear."

Grady slowed down to stop at the lot where Mitchel had left his vehicle. The man had been unnervingly quiet while they'd traveled back to their meetup spot, only speaking when he'd called in the suspected double murder.

"I suspected Senior killed Junior, but that doesn't account for who shot Francisco," he stated over the phone.

No it didn't. But clearly Mitchel was working with the benefit of a backstory Grady wasn't fully briefed on.

The vibration of his own phone had Grady reaching to his pocket while he pulled up next to the other car.

Call me. That was all Hunter wrote.

Fiery panic shot through Grady's veins. Shouldn't he feel more at ease, knowing both the Lopez men were dead?

Rather than taking solace in that, Grady's anxiety flared to record levels. He hit Hunter's contact and then the Call button. "What's going on?"

"I can't find her."

"What?" Grady stopped on the brake, sending a cloud of dust to surround his truck.

"Janie said Isa left this morning—sometime about eight thirty. She was going to walk down to the hotel where your mom was staying to say goodbye. Sue says she never showed up." Hunter's voice pitched hard. "Grady, I can't find her. There's no trace of her anywhere."

Grady squeezed the steering wheel in a death grip. He glanced at his watch: 9:50. That had Isa MIA for more than an hour. "Did you talk to Yates?"

"Heading there now. I wanted to talk to you first. You haven't heard from her, have you?"

"No. Get Yates. Tell him everything I told you. I'm heading that way now."

"Got it." By the scuffling sounds in the background, Hunter was running. "Grady, Luna's small. Someone will have seen something."

Right. Or Luna was tiny and, according to the common Montana culture, people minded their own business.

Grady's stomach roiled as he ended the call.

He'd failed. He had married her to keep her safe, and now, because of *him*, she was out there. Somewhere. In the midst of his panic, and the fast-sinking knowledge of his failure, he reached for the weapon of prayer.

God, You see her right now. Please, please protect her.

Mitchel cut into Grady's terrified silence. "What's going on?"

"My wife . . . she didn't show up where she was supposed to be. No one has seen her." Grady turned a glare on Mitchel. "What is going on?"

"Why would you think your wife is in danger?"

"You tell me."

Mitchel shot him a suspicious look. "Level with me, Briggs. Who is this woman you married?"

Grady stared straight out the windshield, his jaw clamping so hard the muscles jumped.

"She's the one who told you where Francisco was, isn't she?"

He swallowed. The moment felt akin to when Isa and he had wandered into the area where the grizzly had been. So incredibly dangerous—and one wrong move could be the end of them both.

"I can't help you protect her if you're not honest with me."

He hadn't been forthright with Mitchel. Maybe he should have been.

"She met Francisco in the spring. She had no idea who he was. By the time she figured out he was dangerous, things had gone too far."

"She was one of his women."

Grady doubled his fist and barely contained the impulse to plow it into Mitchel's face. He turned a cold, hard look and held it on the other man and spoke in a low, icy tone. "Don't ever call her that again."

Mitchel's brow lifted. "You fell in love with her. And married her."

Not in that order. Grady kept his answer zipped in and only held his silent challenge on Mitchel.

Mitchel nodded. "As I suspected. You'd better get back up there." He unbuckled and stepped out of the truck. "I'll be right behind you."

TWENTY-NINE

PAIN STREAKED LIKE FIERY lightning up Isa's leg and burned at the side of her head, just above her ear.

She struggled against the rough ropes keeping her hands bound tight behind her back while she fought to gain an upright position in the backseat of the SUV that had run her off the road and pinned her leg against a tree.

It was broken. Isa was certain her leg was broken, just above the knee. But she had much bigger problems.

Winning the struggle to get upright, she took in the back of her captor and pieced together the memory of her face, which she'd glimpsed before the world had gone black.

She. Yes, her abductor was a woman. Pretty, mid-fifties, maybe older. Hard to tell, because she clearly kept her hair dyed a shiny black and saw a cosmetic specialist on a regular basis. A twenty-year-old didn't have skin that smooth and bright.

That was all Isa could remember, because not long after the woman had exited the car that held Isa stuck against a tree, the woman had taken a rock to the side of Isa's head.

At that memory, a tickle ran down the side of Isa's face. Using her shoulder, she brushed against it and discovered that warm liquid seeped into her shirt sleeve. With a quick check of her arm, she found a dark-red stain on her light-blue shirt.

Her stomach lurched as a fresh explosion of pain streaked through her body. She breathed out carefully, working to control the terror that threatened to overtake her.

"Well, you're awake." The woman spoke from the front.

Isa met her cold glare in the rearview mirror. The deadly chill in the woman's eyes made her shiver.

"Good. You can walk."

The vehicle jerked to a stop, and Isa flung forward, her face planting against the seat in front of her.

The woman shut off the car, jumped out, and stormed around to the door nearest Isa. With a hard fling, the door flew open, and Isa was yanked out by one arm.

The pain that jolted up her leg as she planted her feet on the ground made her woozy.

The woman shoved her upright as she wavered. "I said you can walk," she seethed.

Isa swallowed against the heave of nausea. *Help, God!* "Who are you?"

A loathsome, malicious chuckle that seemed to come straight from the pit of hell curled from the woman's lips. "The other woman. No, wait. I am the *only* rightful woman. Did you think you could take my place?"

Before Isa could make sense of her words, she was shoved forward. "Now move."

She complied, working to block out the massive amount of pain that charged through her body. She focused on her surroundings. A small dirt lot. A trail with a posted sign.

She knew this trail—had just hiked it with Grady last week.

Grady!

He was out of town—hadn't been sure when he'd get home. It could be midnight or later before he got home to discover that she was missing. But Sue . . .

Would the woman even think twice about Isa not showing up at the hotel? And how long would Janie wonder about Isa not showing up at the café to take the afternoon and evening shift? Surely Janie would be worried.

Isa peeked at the sky, squinting against the sharpness of the bright sun. It was ten-ish maybe. Not quite noon, anyway. That meant it could be a few hours before Janie would be concerned.

In a few hours, Isa could be—

She cut off that thought. *Only helpful things*, she demanded of her mind. "This trail is closed," she said.

"Perfect. It will be deserted."

Again Isa focused on her surroundings. They turned onto the trail after the sign. Isa stumbled, intentionally letting herself fall.

"Get up."

She rolled to her back and gripped the branch of a shrub between her hands. Just as she closed her fist around the pencil-sized twig, the woman jerked her by the arm, pulling her to her feet. The leaves ripped off the branch, filling her fists. Isa turned to face her abductor. "I can't walk. My leg is broken." She released the handful of leaves that were in her fist, praying they littered the dark earth of the path in a conspicuous way.

"You will walk. And if you don't get moving, you'll be doing it with a bullet in the other leg." The woman shoved her forward with the end of a handgun.

Isa complied, shutting out the agony ripping through her body. *Survive.* That became her mantra, alongside a continual plea to heaven for help.

Please, God. Send Grady. Or Janie and Hunter. Someone. Please let them see the leaves on the trail.

"You're going too slow." The woman marched around her, then grabbed the front of her shirt to drag her along.

While the faster pace made the burning ache in her leg worse, it gave her the chance to wiggle against the ropes binding her hands. She tucked a thumb in painfully tight and managed to squeeze one hand through the rough hemp of the rope.

With a quiet sigh and a silent *thank you*, she pulled her hand free just as the trail neared the exposed rock wall Grady had named Birdbath Rock. Isa wiggled the ring on her left finger free, then stumbled toward the granite wall. She deposited her ring on the font edge of that little formation. *Please let the birds leave it there.*

"Stupid girl." The woman regripped Isa's shirt and jerked her forward. When she found the rope had been loosened, she cursed.

Isa masked her emotions behind a face of stone. "Sorry."

"Walk." She took the loose end of the rope and yanked, using it to haul Isa forward.

Her shoulders throbbed at the sudden change in position. But Isa swallowed back the cry that bulged in her chest. Up ahead, the tree bearing the fresh scar of a bear's claw was just off the trail. Hoping the blood still trickled from her head, Isa stumbled toward it, catching her forced fall with her shoulder and pressing her head to the exposed flesh of the tree.

"You are pathetic!" The woman screeched. "I should just shoot you here."

Why didn't she? What was this psychotic woman's end game?

"Get. Moving." Another yank on the rope sent a burning sting along Isa's wrist and arm.

Isa righted herself and forced her throbbing legs forward. When they came to the nearly indistinguishable path that would take them to the closed mine, the woman veered left.

So the mine was to be her tomb.

Isa's heart sank. Even if Grady read her trail markings, by the time he got to her, she would be dead.

A tear seeped from her eye. Just when they'd discovered that choosing to love could be glorious. Just when their marriage felt real and right and wonderful.

But at least they had that. They had those ten amazing days in Yellowstone together.

Oh Grady . . . She ached as she thought on the man she loved. *I didn't tell you . . .*

A sob shook through her body.

God, please tell him—help him to know that I really loved him. And that he was a good husband. He would have been an amazing father. There, she gasped as another cry clenched in her chest.

She and Grady had found a hopeful future together. They had found love—and she was grateful for that.

Please, God, help him to remember the good and to be grateful for it. And please give him a good life.

Grady met Sherrif Yates on the highway. He'd gone faster than what had been safe, especially after Luna's sheriff had called him saying that he'd found evidence of an accident off the highway, half a mile away from the hotel.

Yates didn't waste time with a greeting. He led Grady and Mitchel, who had kept a close tail on Grady, toward the damaged tree.

"You can see the tire marks." He pointed to the ground that did indeed bear the marks of tread off the narrow shoulder and into the grass that led into the forest. At the end of the tracks was a damaged pine tree.

The men spread out, inspecting the ground.

"Here." Mitchel stopped and bent to pick up a stone. He held it out for Grady and Yates to inspect.

Smeared blood stained the side of the rock.

Grady's stomach churned. "Who is after my wife?" he demanded of Mitchel.

"Not sure, but my guess is she was hauled off that way." He pointed west.

Yates nodded, walking alongside the imprint left behind by the vehicle. "If you followed the tire marks, the car backed up, pivoted, and headed toward Black Gulch."

Grady pinned a look on the sheriff. Yates gestured with his head. "Let's go."

Grady had climbed into the sheriff's SUV, leaving his truck parked off the highway. Mitchel entered the government vehicle he'd been driving.

"This Mitchel—he's FBI?" Jeremy sped west, keeping his attention fixed on the road.

"Yes. He recruited me as an undercover asset."

"And he called this in?"

Grady nodded. "We should have back up in another hour or so." Not that that helped them now. Another hour could be too late. It could already be too late.

God, please protect her. Don't let it be too late . . .

"Grady, I called the FBI." Yates turned a meaningful look toward him. "They didn't know anything about this."

His gut clenched like he'd been sucker punched. "You called the Denver office?"

"Yes."

A sour, sinking anger filled the pit of his stomach. Grady checked his phone. The text he'd sent to Malcom hadn't been read yet either. The man had been ignoring him, likely still under the conviction that Grady had no business being involved in the Lopez case.

Grady clenched his fist just as the Black Gulch Falls trailhead came into view. "There." He pointed to a small luxury SUV parked haphazardly in the small lot.

Yates nodded. "That would match the tire trail. Could be a tourist though." He took out his cell and tapped the screen.

Grady shook his head. "I closed this trail the other day because I found fresh bear sign."

"I'll run the plates. In the meantime, I'm calling Hunter," Yates said. "He'll be able to get here much sooner than anyone else."

Yates parked the car, and Grady reached for the door handle. Yates stalled him with a firm hand on his arm, ending his call to Hunter, and then looked at Grady. "I've got your back."

Don't trust Mitchel. Yeah, he already didn't. Grady nodded, and both men exited the vehicle. They jogged to the start of the trail, and Mitchell met them there.

"This could just be a hiker," Mitch said. "We'd best split up—you two drive farther up the road and check the next trailhead. I'll take this one."

Clearly the FBI man was ignoring the posted sign at the trailhead that read *Trail Closed*. But Grady didn't argue with him. What would be the point? The man wasn't being straight with him.

A clump of leaves littering the exposed dirt of the path demanded his attention. That wasn't normal—the leaves were all clumped together and wrinkled, like they'd been in a person's fist.

Grady turned back to Mitchel, shaking his head. "I'm going this way."

"We don't have time for you to question my authority. Keep heading west."

"Not happening." Grady pivoted, giving the man his back, and ran into the forest.

"Briggs!"

He ignored Mitchel's call. Instead, he focused on a quick pace, careful not to stumble on the protruding rocks and the uneven terrain. Several minutes in, with his heart a jackhammer, Birdbath Rock came into view. He pressed his pace faster but stopped short when the light hit something shiny on the edge of that protected lip. He veered, noting the pounding footfalls of the other two men behind him.

The glint of light vanished in his shadow, but the metal remained a clear contrast to the granite. He reached and picked it up.

"What is it?" Mitchel asked.

"Isa's ring." Grady connected with Yates's steady look.

The sheriff drew his firearm and nodded. "Lead on."

Grady stepped back onto the path, Mitch behind him, and Jeremy Yates at the back. Pushing his stride back into a run, Grady suppressed the urge to call out for his wife. Wherever she was, he couldn't be certain that her attacker would spare her life if they knew people were nearby looking for her.

Several more minutes of trail running, and he spied a stain of red in the white scar on the pine tree the bear had slashed.

Smart, Isa.

Except, that meant she was bleeding.

God, please protect my wife!

Grady kept running, barely feeling the burn of his lungs as he pushed his pace harder. He slowed as he approached the place where the main trail curved right, toward Black Gulch Canyon, and the mine path, hidden in the brush, would take them left.

"What do you think, Grady?" Yates asked.

"Best keep pushing on the main trail." Mitchell pointed toward the canyon.

Yates didn't even acknowledge the man but kept his attention steady on Grady. "Your call."

"Look, you're just a sheriff, and technically you shouldn't even be a part of this."

Again, Yates ignored him.

Grady scanned the area carefully, searching for any hint Isa might have left for him. There was nothing. He squeezed his eyes shut. *God?*

In the pause, he waited.

No voice. Not a clear *Do this. Go this way.*

Rubbing the coarse beard along his jaw, Grady opened his eyes and took another visual pass. He stopped, attention caught on a fir twenty feet up the hill of the less traveled way. A branch was snapped in half, the partially severed part hanging from what remained attached.

It could be from an animal. A deer. A moose. A bear. Any one of them could have snapped that as they bounded through the area.

Or Isa could have stumbled into it.

Grady hesitated only a moment more and then started up the incline toward the mine. "We go this way."

"I don't think—"

"Then go the other way," Yates said.

Grady didn't know if Mitchel followed him or not. He knew only one thing: He needed to find his wife.

His pulse thudded in his ears, and he registered the sounds of the running footfalls behind him. But nothing else. Not until the trail leveled and opened to a view of the mine.

The barrier had been ripped down. And a woman's voice echoed from within. But it didn't belong to Isa.

What he heard sent ice through his veins.

"My son is dead because of you."

A dull whack sounded.

"You'll pay. You took him. You took them both. You thought you could have what is mine."

Another whack.

"But you can't. I shot my husband. I can kill you too. It won't bother me one bit."

Isa slumped against the cold stone wall of the mine shaft. The metallic taste of blood filled her mouth, and her face throbbed where the side of a wood plank had made contact. Thankfully, most of the blow had landed on the rock behind her, but the contact that the vile woman had made still hurt.

Her vision blurred into a wavy haze of tears. She'd brought this on herself. How could she have been so stubbornly foolish? If she'd been the good girl her parents had raised . . . if she'd been grateful for the protection of their rules and advice . . . if she'd just listened to José and Bennett . . .

So many ifs. Regrets. But as she sank into the comfort of a black void, she recalled Grady's strong arms around her after she'd told him the full story. His gentle acceptance and forgiveness of her sin. And his whispered reassurance that *no sin is too much for God's grace and mercy to forgive.*

And there, her mother's voice also drifted through her mind. *Dios mío, tú eres todo bondad, ten compasión de mí.*

"Forgive me," she whispered. "Have mercy on me."

The cackle of Satan echoed from the cold walls. "Never." Or maybe that was this embittered, rage-filled woman.

Even so, a sweet, gentle warmth enveloped her, and a presence so real and comforting fell upon her.

Daughter . . .

Isa exhaled as a mix of joy and relief filled her, easing the pain that pulsed through her whole body. **He** still called her daughter.

He still loved her.

He was still with her, right there in the worst hell she'd ever known.

He was all goodness, even now.

Light flashed through her closed eyes. Was she dying?

"Grady . . ." she whispered. *Tell Grady I love him.*

"Freeze!"

That sounded like Grady.

The light grazed her waning consciousness again, and Isa forced herself to blink open her eyes.

"No!" her attacker screamed.

"Drop it." That voice wasn't Grady's, but following the demand was a scuffle.

"No!" the woman screeched again. "You promised! You promised my son would live!"

Her rant didn't make sense. But then again, Isa's head had taken several blows, and she couldn't understand what was happening. Was Grady there?

As if she'd asked out loud, he appeared, kneeling beside her, gently lifting her in his arms.

"Grady . . ."

"I have you," he choked.

She leaned her head against his shoulder, and his heat seeped into her shivering body.

"I have you, Isa."

And then she was tucked in close and lifted.

She wanted to wrap her arms around him, but they felt too heavy. Her eyes, also, were too heavy to keep open. So she let them slip shut as the sound of his rapid heartbeat soothed the ringing in her ears.

"You found me."

"You left me a good trail. Smart woman."

"I needed to tell you . . ."

"It's okay. We'll have plenty of time to say all the things."

She shook her head. At least, she thought she did.

Voices sounded around her as the darkness eased toward light. Something about Hunter, and Tara, and calling for an ambulance.

It all jumbled in her mind. All she could focus on in the blurry mess of her scrambled thoughts was that she didn't tell him.

I love you, Grady.

The kind relief of dark oblivion took her into its embrace.

THIRTY

GRADY LEANED FORWARD IN the cushioned chair, which he'd scooted as close to the hospital bed as he could. His elbows braced against the mattress near Isa's hip, he held her hand in both of his.

She looked like she'd gone a few rounds with a heavyweight champion.

A tear trickled down the side of his nose. He lifted a hand to smear it away with the heel of his palm.

He focused on the steady beep that declared her strong heartbeat, and then on the swish-swish of the monitor that had been placed on her abdomen.

She was going to be okay. They both were—his wife and baby. Tara had come in a few minutes before to give him an update. Isa had a broken femur, a dislocated shoulder, and a concussion—not to mention the cuts and bruises that darkened her lovely face with ugly black, blues, and yellows. They'd stitched the gash that had been just above her ear.

"They'll keep her for a couple of days, just to make sure. But right now it looks like she and the baby will be just fine."

Grady couldn't help the small sob that had rattled from his chest.

Tara had been understanding as she gripped his arm. "Her doctor is the overseeing physician for my clinic. I have a good relationship with him, and I promise you I'll be honest with you if there's anything concerning."

"Thank you." Grady nodded.

After she looked at him for a purposeful moment, Tara tugged on his arm and moved to hug him. He leaned into her kindness. "Thank you," he whispered again.

"We're here for you. All of us."

He moved back, as did she, and then she turned to leave the room.

"Oh." Tara paused at the door. "And Grady?"

"Yeah?"

"Congratulations." She lifted a gentle smile. "You're going to be a wonderful dad, and I hope you and Isa will allow me to play adopted grandma."

Something soft and beautiful stirred in his heart. Something unfamiliar but longed for. It felt like . . . like belonging. Like family.

He nodded. "I would like that."

That had been several minutes ago. Isa had remained asleep during the exchange. He hoped the mild sedation that ran through her IV kept her pain at a minimum.

He squeezed her hand and bent to kiss the back of it. Relief mingled with the hesitant knowledge that Isa's body would heal and the baby was okay. But her recovery from the trauma might not be as easy.

"I'll be right here with you," he promised.

A knock at the door had him sitting straight. Without his permission, the door eased open, and Jeremy Yates poked his head in.

"Sorry, Grady. They're getting ready to transport Mitchel, and Agent Fairbury is asking for your statement. Can you give him a few minutes?" Yates nodded toward Isa. "I can sit with her, if you want."

Grady shook his head. "Is Tara still out there? Or Janie?"

"Yes. I can send them both in."

He nodded, and in less than a minute, Janie and Tara both filed into the room and took seats on either side of Isa's bed.

Grady followed Yates down the hall of Big Sky's community hospital and into a conference room. Inside, two federal agents stood guard at the door, and another agent sat at the large table swallowing the middle of the room. Barely glancing up from his paperwork scattered over the table, he spoke. "Did you get Briggs?"

"I'm here," Grady answered.

Fairbury—who had come in place of Malcom, who was apparently on vacation—paused his writing, set his pen down, and stood. "Grady, right?"

"Yes."

He held his hand out. "Cole Fairbury. I'm sorry we're meeting under these circumstances." He gestured toward the chair nearby.

"It seems like it's going to be okay." Grady lowered into the seat.

Fairbury nodded. "Needless to say, Mitchel is in deep. And I'm sorry Malcom didn't take you seriously. I need you to tell me everything, from the time Mitchel recruited you as an asset to today."

Grady rubbed the back of his head, feeling a headache coming on, then nodded. He told Fairbury the whole story—from when he decided he didn't want to be a criminal investigator, to when he found out Isa was in danger, and then the events of that day.

"I was leery this morning," Grady concluded. "Some things seemed off—like Mitchel knowing that the woman I married was also the woman the Lopezes were after. And his reaction when he found Cisco had been executed."

Fairbury nodded. "Didn't take much for Anitra Lopez to start singing like a canary. Seems Mitchel decided a cartel sugar mama was a better retirement plan than the federal government's pension. Francisco and his son had a falling out years ago—and as you might guess, falling from favor from your crime-boss daddy is dangerous. Cisco's idea of getting back at his dad was to go after the old man's lovers, which, as you might imagine, only infuriated Francisco more. When things went violent and her son died at Francisco's hand, Anitra shot her husband and went after your wife."

"Had Mitchel told her where to find Isa?"

Fairbury shook his head. "She discovered it on her own—she had been the one to tell Mitchel your wife was Victoria. She saw the wedding announcement in one of the papers. Anitra had bargained for her son's life—Mitchel was supposed to take out Francisco, either by incarceration or . . . well, you know. Any means necessary—ensuring that her son lived. In exchange, she would use her abundant wealth to see him set up nicely in some paradise that doesn't have extradition laws. Since Mitchel didn't hold up his end of the deal, Anitra had no issue selling him out."

The twisted ugliness of it all turned Grady's stomach. Exactly the reason he'd left this sort of thing behind. He didn't want a life with a front-row view of human depravity. He wanted a life filled with nature and beauty and joy and love.

And he wanted that life with Isa.

Fairbury clicked the End button on his recording device and leaned back. "I think that's all we'll need from you. We'll keep an eye on you and your wife for a while, to make sure there aren't any hidden snakes under rocks. Barring that sort of surprise, you should be able to go on with your life. Sans the FBI."

"That would be ideal." Grady stood.

"I'm sorry about your wife."

He swallowed hard. "Thank you. The doctors say she should make a full recovery."

Fairbury nodded. "I'm glad."

He wished Grady well again, and that was the end of it.

Hopefully the end of Grady's association with criminal investigations. Forever.

Thirty-One

Hazel stood in the middle of her room, by the western window, savoring the warm sunlight that wrapped her shoulders.

Today marked the start of all things new. For her, for Bennett, for the kids. Even for this cabin. In less than a half hour, she'd leave this home that she'd cherished, that she'd been selfish about, that she'd learned how to love in, and she would become Mrs. Hazel Crofton.

She chuckled as the idea tickled her middle. That first day, nearly two years before, when she'd spied Bennett through the glass of Janie's Café, bloomed in her mind. Wearing all hunter orange and sporting a pellet gun, he'd honestly looked ridiculous. But now she found that amusing, not infuriating.

Oh, how far they'd come!

Who would have imagined the rich city boy from Chicago and the mountain lioness from Elk Lake would fall in love?

Well, she was pretty sure Mama Bulldog had. The clever, insightful woman.

And God.

Oh, the great God of heaven! He had used every moment to write not just a romance that would change both Hazel's and Bennett's lives but would weave a greater, more astonishing story of redemption. First for Bennett and then for Hazel.

And now, *please, Lord*, for Gemma and for Nathan?

Hazel took a slow turn around the bedroom that had long ago been her grandparents'. In the past decade or so, it had been hers. Once the remodel was done, it would serve as a family room—a space they would share—her, Bennett, Gemma, and Nathan. And whoever else that God would bring into their hearts.

The prospect of such wild changes made her pulse quicken. Honestly, it was all still a touch overwhelming. But not terrifying. Change was still not her best friend. But it wasn't the enemy either. And with Bennett by her side—his steady, see-it-through personality and his tough, faithful love—she felt braver. And oh so blessed.

As she neared the door, she caught a glimpse of the woman in the full-length mirror that Janie had tacked to her wall. Her breath caught at the view of the creamy satin and lace hugging her body. Not what she'd initially thought she'd wear. Ever.

But it had been her mother's—Mama Bulldog had saved it. The fit-and-flare gown had been shortened, because Hazel was worried she'd trip on the dock and go head-first into the lake. But the design remained as her mother had worn it—a simple but elegant square neckline with thick straps, and an underlaying lace had been cut and sewn into a ruched turtleneck, with long, puffed sleeves that tapered down to long, ruched cuffs.

A swell of emotion filled Hazel's chest. Her mother. Her father. Reflecting on them provoked an ache, but rather than fighting it off with resentment or stoicism, Hazel let it settle. This was the experience of life—joy and sorrow mingling into the same moment. There was richness in that, wasn't there? A telling that she could love, and there was so much hope that was found in it. She had loved her parents and her grandparents, and she had grieved their losses.

But now, rather than shutting herself away, fearful of the pain, she opened her heart to it and let it sink in. For where there was pain, there was hope, because now she knew to cry out to the Healer of her soul. How glorious was that? That the One who called the stars into being, who carved the stone into mountains and told the streams where to run, who told the eagle where to soar and where to land . . . that very same God knew her name and her heartaches.

And He loved her.

Hazel blinked against the warm emotion in her eyes as the door beside her opened. Mama B slipped in, her eyes also sheening, and took Hazel's hand.

"Your mom would be over the moon to see you in her dress."

"Thank you for keeping it for me."

MB squeezed her hand. She drew in a long breath and then exhaled slowly. "How are you feeling, Zel?"

"Excited." Hazel turned a determined grin to her. "And a little teary."

"You miss them."

She nodded. "Is that weird, since they died when I was so young?"

"No. It's good. Because you loved them, and you've stopped closing yourself off to all the feelings that brings."

A single tear bulged from her eye and slipped down her cheek. MB brushed it with the coarse pad of her thumb, then leaned in to kiss her cheek. "I'm honored to stand in for her, you know? Thank you for allowing me that privilege."

That nearly undid Hazel, reducing her to a full rush of tears. Instead, she sniffed and nodded. "Thank you for being my mom when you didn't have to be. You had so much going on already, being a single mom and a business owner. You didn't have to take me and Hunter in."

"I have no regrets about that." MB drew her into a hug. Then she ironed her posture and pulled back. "Now. We have a perfect evening outside. The fall colors are shining. The sky is setting off a glorious evening display. The lake is placid, like glass. And your groom is quite handsome."

Hazel warmed at the lovely description, barely able to believe this wedding was hers. She'd not wanted a wedding, or so she'd thought. But this would be a memory she would cherish forever.

"Are you ready for your brother?"

"Yes," she whispered.

Mama B nodded, kissed her cheek one more time, then slipped from the room. After the soft slap of the front door sounded, she heard the heavier footfalls that must belong to her brother. And then he was there, leaning around the doorframe, dressed in the same dark suit he'd bought for his own wedding just a few short months ago. He drew back a little at the sight of her, looked her over from head to toe, and whistled. "Hazel, my little sister, don't take this to be anything weird. But you're a knockout. No wonder you had zero issues convincing Bennett that he'd married you when he couldn't remember a thing."

Heat filtered into her cheeks. She ducked her gaze and laughed. Hunter's rich, low chuckle joined her, then he pushed off the doorframe and held out a hand. "Ready to go marry him for real?"

"I am."

"You're not going to freak out and run off?"

She lifted a sassy smirk at him. "Would I ever do such a thing?"

"Only every other day."

"Welcome to the new Hazel Wallace. Calm. Rational. And not a badger."

He laughed. "That can't be Hazel Wallace." He winked. "But maybe Hazel Crofton . . ."

She slipped her hand through the crook of his elbow and landed a solid blow to his toned abs at the same time.

He doubled over with a cough. "There's the sister I know and love."

"Maybe I'm calm, rational, and still a little bit of a badger. Take me to the dock, Hunter, and no more insults. There's a handsome man there waiting to promise me forever. If he changes his mind, you'll be stuck with me."

"Let's not risk that." Hunter winked and led her through the cabin and out the front door. On the deck, they paused.

The scene was just as Mama Bulldog had described. Rich yellows and oranges lit the hills with autumn splendor. The glassy lake reflected those hues as well as the apricots and pinks that painted the evening sky. A small gathering of friends waited on the bank of Elk Lake, the group splitting to create an aisle that would allow her access to the dock.

And there he was.

Bennett Crofton, the man she would love for the rest of her life.

"Ready?" Hunter whispered.

"Yes."

Off the deck, down the trail, and onto the dock. Hazel thought she might be floating as her brother escorted her to her groom. Either way, the moment Bennett clasped her hands with both his, she knew she was the luckiest badger woman ever to roam these wild mountains.

Because Bennett loved her. For better or worse, he loved her.

Isa loved the feeling of Grady's hand holding hers. And she smiled at the tickle in her womb as she covered the place where her baby grew.

"Is he being an active little fellow?" Grady asked.

Isa nodded. Her husband had it in his head this baby was a boy. She didn't care either way, but she thrilled at Grady's growing anticipation for the birth.

"It's so good to see you up and healthy." Janie smiled as she and Hunter crossed from the dock where Hunter had stood as one of Bennett's groomsmen and Janie as Hazel's matron of honor. The couple looked as joyful and as in love as they ever did.

Weddings must bring out the romance in every couple.

Grady released Isa's hand and slipped his arm around her. "It is, isn't it?"

Hunter nodded. "I hear you've got a new assignment," he said to Grady.

"Temporary. But it should be a good one. Up in Glacier for the rest of the year." Grady looked down at Isa with so much unveiled love in his eyes. "It comes with a little cabin, just right for two."

As a blush heated her face, she kissed his cheek. "Now who is being a flirt?"

The small group laughed.

"You'll be back though?" Janie asked.

"Yes. Hopefully before the baby is born." Isa touched her belly again. Her small baby bump was noticeable now, and they'd told everyone after Isa had been released from the hospital. To her relief and amazement, no one seemed to judge her or Grady. They all received the news with joy and encouragement.

Grace was so much bigger than Isa had ever imagined.

"Isa has family nearby, and that's important," Grady said.

Hunter arched an eyebrow, then reached to grip Grady's shoulder. "You have family here too, brother. And we expect to see you at Bible study when you get back."

Her husband's arm tightened around her, and gratitude was a deep current in Isa's heart. Hunter couldn't know how much that would mean to her husband.

Janie squeezed Isa's hand. "I hope you'll stay in Luna, and not just because you're a wonderful employee." She ducked, a shy, joyful look crossing her pretty face. "But because we'll have a little playmate for your little one this summer."

It took a moment for the news to sink in. Isa gasped, then gripped Janie's arm. "You're pregnant?"

Janie grinned and nodded. Hunter beamed.

And there were hugs all around.

Isa glanced around at the gathering. Mama B and Tara Crofton, laughing together as though they'd been best friends since birth. Nathan and Gemma, both looking delighted, though Nathan tried hard to keep a cool demeanor. Isa's brother, José, along with his wife and their littles. John Brighton and his wife, as well as Pastor and Mrs. Nolan. A small wedding was what Hazel wanted. What she got was a perfect little gathering of friends, all there to celebrate Bennett and Hazel's marriage.

Suddenly it became clear to Isa:

They were all a patchwork family. A beautiful weaving of love and redemption. And she and Grady were part of that.

Such a wonder!

They would come back. Because this was home. This was family, and she couldn't wait to raise their little one on these redemption shores.

THE END

(for now . . .)

I HOPE YOU'VE ENJOYED this return to Luna, Montana in this fourth book in Redemption Shores! Would you please leave an honest review to let other readers know what you think? Thank you!

Honest question . . . were you surprised to see Isa and Grady as the central characters of this story? Maybe you thought, "Oh man, I don't really like them."

I get it. In real life, there have been more times than I care to admit when I've not had a great first impression of a person, and consequently decided that I didn't like them, only to discover that I had misjudged or didn't have the full picture of that person's precious life. It happens, right? And it's humbling to discover that *I* have been the snobby, ungraceful, and unkind person. This story was a call to myself to bow under that humility.

How about Hazel and Bennett? Three cheers for the happy couple! Were you surprised they had a wedding? Did you enjoy the new, softer development in Hazel? I have loved writing their storyline, and I hope you have enjoyed seeing their tale unfold.

I'll bet you've still wondering what's going to happen to Gemma and Nathan. I have plans for them . . . There are more stories to be told in Luna.

Keep watching for the release of those books.

While you're waiting, allow me to invite you to meet the Murphy Brothers—seven men forging their way through life and love, gripping faith, and learning to walk with God through all things. Theirs are stories of romance, but also of redemption. This nine book series is complete and ready for you to binge-read! Start book one today. :)

Printed in Great Britain
by Amazon

62570386R00160